SNAP SHOT

Meg Chittenden

BERKLEY SENSATION, NEW YORK

THE BERKLEY PUBLISHING GROUP
Published by the Penguin Group
Penguin Group (USA) Inc.
375 Hudson Street, New York, New York 10014, USA
Penguin Group (Canada), 10 Alcorn Avenue, Toronto, Ontario M4V 3B2, Canada
(a division of Pearson Penguin Canada Inc.)
Penguin Books Ltd., 80 Strand, London WC2R 0RL, England
Penguin Group Ireland, 25 St. Stephen's Green, Dublin 2, Ireland (a division of Penguin Books Ltd.)
Penguin Group (Australia), 250 Camberwell Road, Camberwell, Victoria 3124, Australia
(a division of Pearson Australia Group Pty. Ltd.)
Penguin Books India Pvt. Ltd., 11 Community Centre, Panchsheel Park, New Delhi—110 017, India
Penguin Group (NZ), Cnr. Airborne and Rosedale Roads, Albany, Auckland 1310, New Zealand
(a division of Pearson New Zealand Ltd.)
Penguin Books (South Africa) (Pty.) Ltd., 24 Sturdee Avenue, Rosebank, Johannesburg 2196, South
Africa

Penguin Books Ltd., Registered Offices: 80 Strand, London WC2R 0RL, England

SNAP SHOT

A Berkley Sensation Book / published by arrangement with the author

PRINTING HISTORY
Berkley Sensation edition / September 2004

Copyright © 2003 by Meg Chittenden.
Cover photo of man by Kerrick James/Getty Images. Cover photo of trolley by John A. Rizzo/Getty Im-
ages. Cover background photo by Thinkstock/Getty Images.
Cover design by Marc Cohen.

ISBN: 0-425-19803-0

BERKLEY® SENSATION
Berkley Sensation Books are published by The Berkley Publishing Group,
a division of Penguin Group (USA) Inc.,
375 Hudson Street, New York, New York 10014.
BERKLEY SENSATION and the "B" design
are trademarks belonging to Penguin Group (USA) Inc.

PRINTED IN THE UNITED STATES OF AMERICA

10   9   8   7   6   5   4   3   2   1

This book is dedicated to my son, Stephen J. Chittenden, DC, and my daughter, Sharon L. Ilstrup, because they are both amazingly wonderful, kind, compassionate, honest, and honorable people who make me proud to be their mother.

And because I love them.

Acknowledgments

Many thanks are due to the following people for answering questions that came up in relation to various aspects of this novel. Any factual errors are mine, not theirs. Or else I un-blushingly altered the facts to fit the story.

Jason Greenspane, Police Officer, Port Townsend, Washington

Rich McEachin, Chief of Police, Ocean Shores, Washington

Robin Burcell, Sacramento County criminal investigator and author of *Cold Case*

Mary Buckham, author of *The Makeover Mission*

Joe Scarpato, reviewer, mystery buff, and punster extraordinaire

Chapter 1

"DIANA? CAN YOU hear me? The doc says he got the bullet out."

Diana squinted at the wavering white blob that was floating above her. Bradley Jeffers, her partner in G&J Investigations. She was the *G*—Diana Gordon. The black splotch in the middle of the white blob was Brad's Pancho Villa mustache. Apparently her brain was functioning. It had been AWOL for a while. "Tha'ss nice," she managed.

"Lucky for you, babe, the bullet barely nicked your left lung, but it did some nerve and muscle damage. The doc says he did some himself getting the bullet out. Had to go in from behind and resect a rib."

"Don't call me babe," she muttered.

"Whatever you say, babe." He laughed. "Must be feeling better. Sounding like the old Diana we all know and fear." He paused. "The good news is your head wound is negligible. As they say in those police show reruns you're forever watching, the bullet barely creased your scalp. Doc

Wilson had to cut some hair to clean the wound out, but it'll grow back."

Diana's eyes shot open. Pushing up with her elbows, she flopped back when a scalding pain slashed a groove down her back. "He cut my hair? Who gave him permission to do that? Did you tell him he could do that? You know how long it took me to grow that damn ponytail? You know how slowly hair grows? A half inch a month if the ends don't break off, which mine do. Three years it took me to grow that ponytail—and you let him cut it off while I was unconscious—helpless. I'll sue his damn butt off! Yours, too!"

Brad was laughing. Laughing! Hey, the blob had turned into a face! And the rest of him had shown up. "Diana, your ponytail is as unraveled as you are, but intact. The doc just clipped a little clump of hair close to the scalp wound. It won't even show. And there's nothing to worry about with that scalp wound, he says—it just looks worse than it is. He's coming in to talk to you soon as he gets through with his rounds. When a bullet grazes the scalp, way he tells it, a furrow of scraped tissue that looks like shark teeth tears along the edges of the gash. But it will heal fairly quickly. You also have an interesting scar down your back from the surgery—your bikini days may be over."

"Teach me to turn my back on a crook. What the hell happened?" She frowned. Bad move. Colored lights zig-zagged in front of her eyes. "Last I saw, Stockman was about to hop on a cable car."

Evidently, the images had burned themselves into her memory. The tall, burly black man, getting into his car outside his apartment complex, struggling with his crutches, easing them over the back of the seat into the seat behind.

Diana and Brad had followed him to Chinatown, where

he'd parked the car, climbed out, and glanced all around, then locked the car and walked away. Without the crutches.

Diana had felt jubilant yet disappointed. She'd *liked* Stockman, had hoped he was genuine, even while she was pretty sure he wasn't.

But there he was, walking the walk, then running as the cable car passed him, hopping on it at the stop, turning on the step at the last minute, in time to see her photographing him, she guessed. She'd turned away as the cable car clattered onward, and then, suddenly, pain beyond imagining had exploded inside her. Her mind had retained one last image—something had glinted in Stockman's right hand.

"I don't want you worrying about what happens when you get out of here," Brad said. "Yvonne used to be a nurse, remember? She's all set to take care of you at our house as soon as you are released."

She felt Brad's big hand close over her clenched fist. That felt good—safe. She allowed herself to drift back to wherever she had come from.

"WHEN THE HELL are they going to let me out of here?" she grumbled a few days later. Brad had visited every day, and she'd asked him the same question each time.

Brad answered as patiently as he had before. "It's going to take time for you to heal."

He paused as though waiting for a comment. She couldn't think of a whole lot to say. "Somebody broke into your apartment last night," he said into the silence.

"Stockman's out on bail already? It had to be him, trying to find the pictures. I got several of him running for that cable car. Where's my camera?"

"I have it. You dropped it. I burned a CD for the police, Printed out copies for Hedrick Insurance."

She gave a satisfied grunt.

"I'm sorry I didn't see it coming, babe. Stockman started to get on that cable car, I saw he had something in his hand, but I didn't realize it was a gun. I looked to see if you were still getting pictures, you were turning away. You were crowing about catching him running when he was supposed to be unable to walk. I was looking at you, not him. You went down about the same time I realized I'd heard shots."

"What an idiot," she said, adding when he drew in a breath, "Not you—Stockman. 'Stead of the fraud charge, he's going to be up for attempted murder. This is going to ruin his musical career. He'll have to play his guitar gratis to the prison inmates. The police *did* get him?"

"They picked him up that very day, real easy."

"Good."

There was a heavy silence, then Brad said, "He didn't have a gun on him, babe. It wasn't found in the immediate area. Or in his car or apartment. No record of him ever owning one. And apparently nobody saw him shooting you. At least nobody's come forward. And there's no gun showing in the photos. No residue on his hands. Of course he'd had time to scrub up before the cops arrived. They had to let him go."

"Shit."

"You made the newspapers. Not as big as you might have done—another one of those trucks carrying immigrants stalled in the Arizona desert, abandoned. Everybody dead. Kids, too. Mexican strike force cracking down, but so far they haven't come up with any leads to whichever smuggling organization was involved."

Diana closed her eyes. She hated those stories. People wanting desperately to make a new and better life for themselves and their families, taken advantage of by lowlifes, callously left to die. Made her own situation seem puny. At least *she* was alive.

They were both silent again for a while, then Brad said, "Doc says you'll need some physical therapy for your back. He's going to refer you to a therapist in Oakland, once you get healed."

"Not Oakland," she said firmly.

Brad's dark eyebrows rose. "What's wrong with Oakland? You were shot in San Francisco, not Oakland."

She had to think about it. Her response had surprised her as much as him. It took a minute to recognize the reaction as the flight-or-fight syndrome. She wasn't in much condition to fight, so flight must be uppermost.

Flight. She was *afraid.* She should be angry. Anger was good, clean, sharp, hot. Fear was shadowy, dark, cold, shameful.

"Mene, mene, tekel, upharsin," she intoned, trying to make a joke of her fear.

"Say again?"

"The handwriting on the wall. My parents used to quote stuff like that at me all the time. Bible. Book of Daniel? Means something about being weighed in the balance, but that's not what . . . *shit!"* The pain had returned.

Brad indicated the IV setup. "You're supposed to press this button if you need a shot of morphine. The nurse said not to worry, you can't overdose, do it when you need it."

She did as directed. "What I mean is, I have seen the handwriting on the wall." Her tongue seemed too large for her mouth. "I need a drink."

"Scotch and soda? Vodka martini?" He was smiling, but there was tension around his eyes. In spite of the jokes, he'd been worried about her. Good.

"Sissy drinks, gimme some straight rye," she said.

A nurse who had previously been invisible produced a glass with a bent straw. Diana sipped gratefully. Apple juice. Nectar of the gods.

"I'm leaving," she explained to Brad's face.

The nurse materialized next to Brad. "You'll have to stay in the hospital until Doctor says you are ready to leave," she said firmly before disappearing again.

Brad nodded. "You're not going to be in shape to go chasing after crooks for a while, babe."

"Don't call me babe." Her eyelids were closing. She forced them open. "That's the whole point. I don't *want* to chase after any more crooks. I didn't mean I was leaving the *hospital*. I'm leaving San Francisco. Soon as I can get around. Quitting. Retiring. You don't even have to buy me out. The business is all yours. Get another partner. Work solo. I don't care. Tell Yvonne and the kids good-bye for me. Give my regards to the Golden Gate. I don't wanna play PI anymore. People killing people, stealing stuff, wanting me to follow their wives or husbands around to see if they're getting it on with someone else, people like Sam Stockman pretending he can't walk since he fell off that stage, cheating an insurance company just because it's there, trying to kill me and getting away with it. I've been beat up too many times—last time those thugs were no more than sixteen, remember? You might also remember I broke my left arm jumping over a hedge last year, getting away from that aggressive Doberman with the hundred and fifty teeth. Fell in a ditch in January. Now this. How much damage can one person survive? If I was a cat, I'd have used up all my chances. I'm thirty-four years old. Not as eager to confront dirtbags as I was at twenty-four. Wanna nice peaceful rest of my life."

"You don't mean it babe—Di—soon as you're out and about you'll—"

She started to shake her head against the pillow, gave that up in a hurry. "You can't talk me out of it, Brad. You'll find someone else to take my place. Someone who doesn't know any better. Me, I've made up my mind. I'm going away. Somewhere with water. Been marinated in salt air all my life. Can't live without it. But somewhere else . . . somewhere quiet . . . small, peaceful . . . I remember a place like that . . . Port something. I went there with Larry once. My last husband. Port Findlay. Somewhere near the Canadian border. Somewhere . . ."

Distantly, she could hear Judy Garland singing "Somewhere over the rainbow . . ."

Chapter 2

SOMETIMES, CONNOR CALLAHAN talked to his dead wife's photograph on his dresser. Other times, like now, he'd catch her up on what was going on in his life while sitting on an ancient stone bench next to her grave.

Quite often, she talked back to him.

Oh, he wasn't into all that *I see dead people* stuff with sixth sense and channeling and visits from the dearly departed. He was well aware that it was his own imagination feeding him Liz's comments. He'd often known what she was going to say when she was alive. That kind of telepathy develops during fourteen years of marital contentment.

The cemetery was high on a bluff overlooking Port Findlay Bay, one of the waterways between Puget Sound and the Strait of Juan de Fuca, which separated the northwest coast of Washington State from Canada's Vancouver Island.

Connor found it restful to visit the old churchyard, only a mile uphill from his chiropractic clinic, not far from his house. It was the kind of atmospheric graveyard you have the urge to explore if you happen to drive by. The type that ought by rights to be haunted. Madrona trees with peeling bark. Lilac in full bloom, filling the air with fragrance. Marble or granite tombstones etched with Indian names, German, Portuguese, British. Plots covered with broken-up shells or red rock, or shrubs.

The place in no way resembled the kind of open cemetery that looks like a farmer's pasture except for flat nameplates the caretaker can drive over with his ride-on mower.

The section Liz was in was more modern than the ancient section, but at least it had a proper marble headstone with her name, Elizabeth Kilmartin Callahan, and her dates. She had died two years ago at thirty-eight, which still seemed grossly unfair to Connor.

It was only natural that he'd read the *Port Findlay Chronicle* to her when he was featured in it: " 'Local chiropractor, Connor Callahan, and Diana Gordon, owner of Photomania, to cochair the annual Port Findlay Arts Alliance photography show, May tenth and eleventh,' " the story proclaimed, before plunging into some less-than-exciting details. " 'Dr. Callahan was born in Chicago forty years ago of Irish immigrant parents, and raised in Peoria, where his parents still live.' "

Forty! How could he possibly be forty? Sure, he'd been reminded lately of a song his grandmother used to sing about "silver threads among the gold," but he could still remember when he'd thought thirty was ancient.

Lowering the paper, he scowled at Liz's headstone. "What's this obsession newspapers have with a person's age?" he grumbled. "What's my age got to do with running the damn photo show?"

Just read the story, Connor, Liz said in his head. *Never mind the commentary.*

" 'After graduating from the University of Illinois, Dr. Callahan married Elizabeth (Liz) Kilmartin, his college sweetheart, traveled west to attend a four-year chiropractic college in Oregon, then opened a clinic in Seattle. Three years ago, he and Liz moved out of the city and made their home here in Port Findlay.' "

That was a while after Liz was diagnosed with breast cancer, right after she finished chemotherapy and radiation. That part wasn't mentioned, to his relief, nor was the part the young reporter probably wasn't old enough to know: the heartache, the sheer relentless agony, of watching someone you love die way before she should—and being powerless to prevent it.

As the print blurred, he twisted to gaze at one of his favorite views. He could see a good chunk of Port Findlay from up here, the high red tower of the courthouse dominating the other turn-of-the-century brick and stone buildings. The bay was calm today, a mirror for the puffy clouds and sunny blue sky above.

One of Connor's elderly patients, a Japanese-American professor who had died a few months after Liz, had questioned why the cemetery had been built on top of the hill. "We Christians believe the soul mounts to heaven and the body returns to dust, so who is here to see the view?" he'd asked.

Old Sakae was buried up here, too, now. Maybe he'd figured out the answer.

Port Findlay wasn't a large town, but it was a pretty one, a hill town whose east-west streets were named after flowers and north-south avenues after trees.

It was a relatively low-crime town, with good clean air and water—a fairly exclusive enclave of artists, former military people, doctors, stockbrokers, lawyers, bankers, and businesspeople, along with an inordinate number of retirees, altogether numbering around nine thousand if you didn't count the tourists who flocked there throughout the year.

Connor turned back to regard his wife's grave. "I don't think much of the picture Vic Newcombe took," he said. "Why do so many newspaper photographers squat to take people's photographs? Do they get bonus pay for giving people double chins and baggy eyes?"

You're so vain. Liz had always teased him.

Diana Gordon had refused to let Victor take her photograph. Connor had thought that was odd at the time, a photographer not wanting to be photographed, but he thought he understood now. Too bad the newspaper hadn't asked Diana to take his photograph. Her byline was on several others. He was willing to bet she'd have done a better job of him, and she was tall enough to get a more flattering angle. What he'd seen of her work impressed him. What he'd seen of *her* impressed him. Attracted him. Scared him.

There were few details about her in the newspaper report. The story included her age, which was thirty-four, and a few current facts: she was a local professional photographer who was always in demand at weddings and other events; she specialized in family portraits and vintage photographs, for which she created interesting settings.

He was disappointed that nothing was said about her past. He was curious about that. She'd come up to Port Findlay from the Bay Area about a year ago, but he had no idea what she had done there. It seemed odd that the newspaper would give his whole family history but nothing of hers.

Standing up, he dropped the newspaper on the ground, then knelt on it to plant the freesias he'd brought along. He was gambling there wouldn't be any more frosty nights. Liz had loved the smell of freesias.

"Things are going well at the clinic," he told her. "We didn't have rain for a while, and then we had that cloud-burst last weekend. Cars skidding all over the place, with accompanying whiplash for the drivers. Kept us busy."

"Us" being himself; Jomo Smith, another chiropractor; Elliot Ramsey, a physical therapist; and Tammy Griffith, their big, redheaded, incredibly efficient office manager.

"It's probably pretty weird for me to hang around talking to you now that you're dead," he commented. "I know it's irrational, verging on crazy, but I'm lonely, Liz. Talking to you comforts me."

Everyone has to handle grief in their own way.

He'd heard Liz say that when she was alive.

"Remember the patient I had a few years ago whose lover had gone back to his wife? Norma Sorenson. She wrote to him daily. By the time she came to see me, ten years later, she'd written him three thousand six hundred and fifty-two letters, counting leap years. Didn't mail them though. Packed 'em all in an old green cabin trunk at the foot of the bed they'd made love in."

Norma had quit writing the letters a couple of months after Connor got her going on an exercise routine and a more nutritious diet. Said she was cured. He supposed she'd probably been hoping desperately for an excuse to stop writing those useless letters. If he put himself back on his old exercise progam and started eating right again, would that cure him of talking to his dead wife? Did he *want* to stop talking to Liz? No. Talking to Liz stopped him from thinking too deeply about the hole in his life.

"So anyway, the photography show opens this week-end," he said, to clear the sudden constriction in his throat. "The committee took in the entries a couple of days ago. More than five hundred photos. We almost ran out of space on the display stands—the pictures are packed real close.

Rosemary went wild with the press releases. All the West Coast newspapers, others, too, she said. Some entries came from California, some as far away as Chicago! One person entered a great picture of a pelican diving. You'd love it. It looks like a rocket, coming straight down out of a cloudless sky. Symbolic. Some beach in California, the description said."

In her last weeks, Liz had enjoyed sitting out on the upper deck of their house, which was above the uptown area and had a bird's-eye view of the bay. She'd spent hours reading, glancing up often to watch Canada geese flying by in formation, a hawk gliding on a thermal, a bald eagle regarding the neighborhood from the top of a tall conifer.

"Rosemary Barrett pressured Diana Gordon into helping me," Connor continued, as he gave the soil a final pat. "Rosemary's still president of the Arts Alliance. We're thinking of electing her Empress of Everything. Al Rutherford is vice-president. Rosemary's choice, he's an absolute sycophant." He frowned. "I really hate that woman. Rosemary."

Hate's a strong word.

"It's a strong feeling. Besides, you never liked her yourself."

Hmmm. So tell me how you feel about Diana.

He caught himself smiling. Liz always had seen right through him.

"Diana appeared in Port Findlay a year after you . . . a year ago. I may have mentioned her to you a couple of times."

More than a couple, Liz would have said.

He laughed and immediately wondered what anyone would think if they came upon him laughing as he crouched alongside his wife's grave. Pretty obvious what they'd think.

"Diana's a hell of a . . ." He stopped himself. "She's an *interesting* woman. Brash, tough, says exactly what she thinks and to hell with the consequences. Big Al Rutherford for example. You'll remember he always insists on being called Big Al. Diana said if his name was Dick she'd do it, but not otherwise."

He laughed. "She's not a beauty like you. Or as restful. Colorful would best describe her, I guess. Exotic even."

Uh-huh, Liz said inside his head.

"She's a few years younger than me. I call her Flash. Irritates the hell out of her—and she's got a mouth on her to let me know it—but it's a natural—a photographer, last name Gordon. Remember the Flash Gordon movie? Great messy campy movie. I was in high school when I saw it!"

He was silent for a while. The salty breeze blew through his hair, reminding him he was overdue for a haircut. "Only way I know Flash—Diana—is from the Arts Alliance. She's tall, mostly because of her long legs, wears her black hair in a ponytail. Her eyes are really dark, almost black. She puts me in mind of Diana the huntress. Remember the note cards you bought in that art gallery in Seattle? Not that this Diana hunts anything, as far as I know. But I can imagine her with a bow and arrow, tracking someone down and letting fly. She gets a few verbal arrows off fairly often. She's a professional photographer, did I tell you that? Opened a studio in that two-story building on the waterfront where The Bushwhacker used to be. Calls it Photomania. You used to get your hair done at The Bushwhacker."

When I had hair, Liz said.

Humor had helped them handle her illness.

He was talking too much about Diana Gordon, he realized. Time to get back on topic. "Tomorrow the judges will decide on the best in each category. Then tomorrow evening we'll have a judges' reception for the people who entered and the members of the Arts Alliance. Taylor's deli will cater."

He stood up, retrieved the newspaper, and dusted off his khakis, grunting at a cramp behind his knees. He should get back to jogging. Working out at the gym. He should get back to a lot of things. Funny, he hadn't even realized until today that he'd stopped jogging and cycling—the way he and Liz used to. He could get out his bike, instead of driving all the time. He could surely ride downhill from his house on Carnation Street to the clinic on Azalea once in a while, even if that did mean riding back up again. If he cycled to downtown's Rose Street for lunch, that would give him close to another mile.

Just this morning, he'd caught sight of himself in the mirrored doors that fronted Liz's clothes closet. How long had it been since he'd wielded an iron? Comfortably rumpled was the best he could say for himself. A comfortably rumpled, lonely, forty-year-old doctor of chiropractic, in need of a haircut, talking to his dead wife about a woman who so far had barely noticed he was alive. Pathetic.

Chapter 3

"I CAN'T IMAGINE what's happened to Diana," Connor muttered. "She's supposed to have the keys—said she'd be here at ten o'clock to let us in."

Ashley Robinson frowned. Joshua Patton shrugged.

Connor and the two photography show judges were sheltering from the rain under Quinn Center's porte cochere, waiting for Diana Gordon to come unlock the double doors.

"I should have known there'd be a glitch," Connor added to keep the judges entertained. "Year before last, one of our volunteers put several photos in the wrong categories. One of them was a picture of a teenage girl in a leopard cat suit; it won first place in the Animals division. Last year we had a false fire alarm, first day of the show. Had to evacuate the premises—photographers pacing back and forth worrying about their entries going up in flames."

Neither of them appeared to be amused.

Arts Alliance president Rosemary Barrett had commissioned the two judges. Ashley Robinson, a bone-slender young woman with short blond hair, wore a perky and transparent raincoat, open to show that her stretchy white shirt stopped short of her navel, leaving a gap of a couple of inches between it and her thigh-high black leather skirt. She had on a lot of neon-purple mascara, and lipstick the exact color of cabernet sauvignon.

Joshua Patton had pale blue eyes and brown hair cropped in a buzz cut. He was slightly overweight and either in need of a shave or fashionably stubbled, dressed in a blue anorak style jacket, blue jeans, and brown suede moccasins that looked more like slippers than shoes.

At age twenty Patton had been shooting pictures on Oregon's Mount Saint Helens when the volcano erupted with a force equivalent to several thousand atomic bombs. May 18, 1980—Patton's lucky day, according to his bio.

Considering the fifty-seven people who had died as a result of the eruption, not to mention countless animals and birds, and the 234 square miles of verdant forest that had instantly become gray, windswept desert, Connor thought that comment beyond tactless.

After taking spectacular photographs of the destruction, Patton had managed to get off the mountain with his camera and film intact, though minus soles to his tenny-runners, and with severely burned feet. His career had zoomed in the wake of several prizes, including the Pulitzer, which was mentioned in his bio no less than six times. A first-rate publisher had subsequently put out a book of the photographs Patton had taken that day.

Patton lived in Port Angeles, an hour or so drive from Port Findlay, but he'd informed Connor right away that he rarely ventured into Port Findlay—it was too touristy. He preferred to spend his time in the nearby Olympic Mountains, or else he took his boat across the Strait of Juan de

Fuca to the western side of Vancouver Island in British
Columbia.

Belying her resemblance to a teenybopper, young Ashley Robinson was a writer and photographer of some
renown. She illustrated her books on the many aspects of
urban Seattle life with strongly dramatic photographs in
black and white. Rosemary Barrett had been thrilled to get
her, too.

Connor perked up as Diana Gordon came striding into
the community center grounds. She must have walked
from the two-story building that housed her apartment and
studio. She was wearing a black sweater, black pants, black
boots. No raincoat. Not even an umbrella. Her shiny black
ponytail was looped through the opening at the back of a
black Nike ball cap with a bent bill. "What the hell are you
doing out here?" she exclaimed before she even reached
them.

Joshua Patton and Ashley Robinson both turned to see
who'd shown up.

"The doors appear to be locked," Connor said mildly.
"Weren't you supposed to open up before we got here?"

"I may have to kill Madam President," she said. "The
original plan was for me to be here at nine-thirty A.M. to
get everything ready and make some coffee, but she came
by the studio yesterday afternoon and *insisted* it was *her*
job. Got the keys from me. She didn't call you? Said *she'd*
be here at nine, and you know she's always disgustingly
punctual or even early. Always chirps that stupid cliché
about the early bird. Sheesh—who wants to get up at dawn
to win a worm?"

She glanced at the large face of her wristwatch. "It's
now ten-eighteen. Where the hell is she?"

Ashley's head was turning back and forth between Diana and Connor. She seemed alarmed. Connor didn't blame her. Diana had a commanding presence.

"Joshua Patton, Ashley Robinson, Diana Gordon," Connor said as he yanked his cell phone out of his belt holster.

Patton glowered at Diana, totally ignoring her outstretched hand. Surely he wasn't shocked that a woman wanted to shake hands? Come to think of it, he hadn't shaken Connor's hand either.

Diana glared back at the man, then offered her hand to Ashley, who took it and smiled shyly.

Connor punched Rosemary's number into his cell phone. The thought of yelling at Rosemary made him feel much more cheerful.

He didn't get the chance to yell. He got Rosemary's answering machine instead of Rosemary. She'd evidently read all the instructions in the manual—her message was at least four minutes long, articulated in the tone of voice used when talking to recalcitrant toddlers—"We really value your call," she concluded stiffly. "Be sure to wait for the beep."

As if no one yet knew to wait for the beep. At the last minute, the phone was picked up and a querulous male voice with a thick accent asked, "Why you calling me middle of night? You some kind telemarketer? I don't want any. I tell you that already. I don't need no windshield mended. I ain't got no VA mortgage."

Rosemary's husband suffered from Alzheimer's. It could be quite a challenge to get a message through. "This is Connor Callahan, Dmitri. Remember me? It's the middle of the morning. Your wife was supposed to—" Dmitri slammed the receiver down before the rest of the sentence was out of Connor's mouth.

Connor tried Al Rutherford's number next, but the vice-president of the Arts Alliance didn't answer. Probably he was trailing Rosemary, wherever she was. Three steps behind her, most likely.

Connor twitched his eyebrows at Diana, sighed, and telephoned Rick Langley, Quinn Center's cocky young manager.

Rick arrived within minutes and let them in. "What happened to the keys I gave you?" he asked Diana.

"Madam President took them away from me," Diana said.

Rick rolled his eyes.

Connor was surprised to see that all the lights were on in the windowless main hall where the photographs were displayed. Evidently Rosemary had been there. Diana yelled, "Hello?" but nobody answered. Connor and the judges went to shuck their coats in the cloakroom next to Rick's office. Diana came along.

"Maybe Rosemary's in the ladies' room," Rick suggested.

Diana jogged off to see, came back a minute later to report the rest room was empty. "I guess she didn't show," Rick said as he left. "The janitor might have left the lights on."

The janitor theory seemed most likely to Connor. The air smelled of some kind of freshener. He hoped the janitor hadn't sprayed any of the photos. "Let's get started," he said.

Joshua Patton walked with a kind of shuffling gait like an aging bear. Because of his burns, no doubt. That was probably why he had such a sour disposition. *There's usually a reason behind offensive behavior,* Liz said in his memory. Liz had always made allowances for people.

It was perfectly okay with Connor when Diana took charge of all the duties—pinning the ribbons next to the photographs the two judges selected, listening carefully as they discussed the various entries, taking copious notes. She was a take-charge kind of woman. And a professional photographer, after all, with her own studio. So she knew what she was doing. Probably wouldn't have done him much good to object anyway. And after the way the day had begun, he was content to act as an escort and keep everyone moving right along.

Diana's expression was almost as sour as Patton's. Maybe she was still irritated by the famous photographer's refusal to shake hands with her. Or with Rosemary's no-show. Maybe it was PMS. Sure made women mad when you suggested that though—at least it had made Liz furious.

Six feet two himself, Connor appreciated Diana's height, which was probably around five ten or eleven without her heels. He also appreciated that she seemed comfortable with her height. She carried herself with relaxed but excellent posture, something he was forever lecturing patients about. She didn't have a heavy purse dragging down her shoulder—another pet peeve of his—in fact, she wasn't carrying a purse at all.

Patton was now studying a portrait of a weary soldier slumped in a doorway. "Before you ask," he said, "and sooner or later everybody does, I'm not related to General George Patton."

Connor recognized the reference to the general. His parents had been children during World War II, but it had been the most exciting thing to ever happen to them in their native Ireland. An American base had opened up near their home. The GIs had taught the local kids baseball and given them treats their families couldn't get with their ration cards. This had directly influenced the Callahans' decision to immigrate to the U.S. when they married ten years after the war. Since then, they'd read all the books about the war and taken him to all the movies. Even now, when they were in their seventies, that war still came up regularly when he called them at their home in Peoria, Illinois. "I remember during the big fracas . . ." his father would say, apropos of whatever subject was under discussion. His father hadn't considered either Korea or Vietnam to be real wars, never mind the "minor engagements" in the Persian Gulf countries and elsewhere.

All the same, it wouldn't have occurred to Connor to make a connection between Joshua and the general.

"General Patton was famous," Joshua Patton explained to Diana and Ashley. "I guess you're both too young to know anything about World War II. I wasn't born until nineteen sixty, myself, but my father told me all about General George."

"*My* parents were born a year before Pearl Harbor," Diana offered. "They never mentioned World War II. Went on to become Haight-Ashbury flower children. Probably asphyxiated any childhood memories of wartime with the fog from their bongs."

Connor grinned. *Take that, Joshua Patton!*

Diana Gordon was an interesting woman, he thought as they moved on to the next row of photographs. She looked dramatic in her all black clothing. Connor was wearing a sweater, too, along with his freshly ironed khakis. A white one in the traditional Aran pattern, courtesy of his mother's faster-than-the-speed-of-light knitting needles.

"You've got amateurs alongside professionals?" Patton said suddenly, sounding shocked.

"It's one of the few shows in the state that allows both," Diana said. "Everyone gets their day in the sun. You have a problem with that?"

Her tone said she was ready to deal with him if he did

have a problem, but all Patton did was mutter irritably—
something that ended with ". . . unheard of."

Connor was getting more and more annoyed with the
man. "Admittedly the mixture makes for an uneven show,
but that's part of the charm of it," he said.

Ashley murmured agreement.

"Waste of time judging amateur crap," Patton said. "The
only reason I contacted Rosemary Barrett to offer my services, after seeing ads for the photography show, was because most of these small town shows aren't judged
correctly. People give awards to pictures that aren't fit to be
stuck on a grandmother's refrigerator."

"We even allow nonresidents and tourists to enter," Diana said. Her toothy smile looked dangerous to Connor.

"Tourists!" Patton muttered.

Several Port Findlay residents had nothing good to say
about tourists either, even while they were making profits
from them. Some felt as negative about tourists as they felt
about immigrants. Connor entertained the radical notion
that beautiful places should be available to everyone,
whether they were visitors or people wanting a place where
they could live free of fear. He also agreed with the Arts
Alliance committee that amateurs should be allowed to
compete with professionals. Let the best results win.

He was surprised to learn that Patton had approached
Rosemary. Way Rosemary had talked, he'd got the impression she'd used all the charm at her disposal to persuade
him to come. She'd exhorted the committee to be thrilled
to have his "distinguished" name on the program.

Ashley Robinson was gazing at Patton with an annoyed
expression on her pretty face.

"I'd never been to Port Findlay before I arrived yesterday," she said. "I drove all over. I love the interesting shops

and galleries and bookstores on the waterfront. The parks are beautiful, too, and all those ethnic restaurants, and those tall old Victorian houses on the hill. I don't blame tourists for flocking here. I wouldn't mind flocking here more often myself."

Diana smiled at her. Her smile was magical, Connor thought, it could light up the gloomiest day.

"Only thing is," Ashley added, "if I moved to Port Findlay, I'd be out playing all the time and wouldn't get any work done. It's probably as well for me to live in the city. This show is cool," she added as they all entered another row. "Great lighting. And these stands let you hang a lot of photographs."

She pushed against one of the display stands, nodding approvingly when it didn't shift. "Cool," she repeated as she examined a photo of Oregon coast dunes. "I think we should give this one a third place at least. You could step right in and get sand between your toes."

"Too square," Patton proclaimed.

"What's wrong with square?" Ashley protested. "Look at the light, the little highlights here and there. Look at the mood."

Patton squinted at the photograph. "Could have lost some of that sky. I'd want to dink with that quite a bit."

Diana opened her mouth, then closed it again. Connor understood her frustration. If Patton was going to pick at each choice Ashley made, they could be here all day, and he and Diana had to take the judges out to lunch and then get ready for the judges' reception that night.

Patton finally consented to give the sand dunes an honorable mention and moved on, but he didn't stop arguing. "Lights balance the dark," Ashley would say. "Great form and control."

"Too blocky at the right side," Patton would snap.

·

Connor wasn't surprised at all when Patton disapproved of a montage Connor particularly admired—more for its content than its execution. Titled *The Face of America*, entered by a well-known Oregonian artist named Sheila Strauss, it was a map of the United States, but without divisions into states. Instead, the whole area was filled with stamp-sized photographs—faces whose features revealed all kinds of heritage; European—eastern and western—Asian, Native American, African, Indian . . . Connor even spotted one man whose features were enough like his Irish father's, he might be a relative.

"Fabulous," Diana said.

Ashley agreed.

"Supposed to make some sort of political statement, I suppose," Patton said.

Of what Connor thought was an innovative photograph of an incoming tide, Patton proclaimed, "The horizon should always be straight." And of a beautiful old arched bridge reflected in water so it formed a complete circle— "It needs a powerful central item to overpower the symmetry," he said firmly. A photo of Mount Rainier brought forth only a snort. "Picture postcard stuff," he said, then glanced archly at Ashley. "They call me the Mountain Man, you know, because of my Mount Saint Helens experience. I'm something of an expert on mountain photography, and I practically live in the Olympics."

Connor caught Diana casting her gaze toward the ceiling several times and flashed her several amused *Be good!* commands from his own baby blues.

Both judges liked the nude photos. Another entry from Oregon—Gardner Malone. There were three photos, all in black-and-white, the shading and features showing that the subjects were of African ancestry.

Patton decided the male nude was "a tad overprinted,"

however. Apparently, he didn't have a problem with the female nude, even after he studied it at length.

"Something sleazy about that man," Diana murmured. "Apart from his being a pompous ass, that is."

Ashley loved the photo of the baby. It had been taken from behind, a naked one-year-old boy, sitting up very straight, black hair curling into a V at the tender nape of his neck. There was something poignant about the photo. It looked like a charcoal sketch, Connor thought. Ashley wanted to give it best of show. Patton thought it was too sentimental but finally agreed to give it an award.

Somehow, the two judges managed to agree on first, second, and third place ribbons in each category, with an occasional argued-over honorable mention.

And then, with Diana in the lead, they all trooped into the last row—a single row titled Special Effects.

Diana stopped so abruptly that Patton slammed into her and almost knocked her over, but caught her in time. He didn't apologize. Probably none of his companions would have noticed if he had.

Ashley let out a blood-curdling scream, then froze in place like a statue, both hands covering her mouth as if to block further screams from coming out.

It took Connor a minute to react. Odd how a scene could become suspended in slow motion, he thought afterward. He was suddenly aware of his own pulse hammering in his ears and the sound of cars going past Quinn Center. Rick, the community center's manager, who had gone into his office off the lobby after letting them in, laughed suddenly, shockingly—perhaps on the phone to someone.

At the far end of the row, previously hidden from view by the stands that held the photographs, Rosemary Barrett lay sprawled on her back near the entrance to the kitchen area. Connor was the first to reach her.

There was a small, round hole in the front of Rosemary's tan raincoat, a small amount of blood showing. More blood had oozed out from under her long, slender body and pooled at her side. The unnatural candle-wax pallor of her skin left no doubt in Connor's mind that she was dead.

All the same, he squatted carefully and checked Rosemary's carotid artery. There was no pulse. He had known there would be no pulse. Her neck felt rubbery. Her body was not yet stiff, but it was without life. Her long, dark hair had lost its shine. Her eyes, which were half open, were without color.

"You're a medical doctor?" Patton asked Connor, his voice rough as gravel.

"Chiropractor," Connor corrected.

Patton's upper lip curled. "I don't believe in chiropractors."

Connor had heard that statement before and had developed a standard wiseass answer. *A lot of people don't believe in Santa Claus, but they still celebrate the Christmas holiday.* Which hardly seemed an appropriate thing to say under present circumstances.

Chapter 4

DIANA FORCED HER voice through her tight throat. "We'd better call nine-one-one."

The fear that had hovered like a shadow behind her ever since she'd been shot was permeating her body now, activating adrenaline, making her want to run, hide, get away from this place of death. She concentrated her weight into her legs, imagining roots going through the concrete floor, down into the ground.

Dimly, she realized Connor was calmly and precisely giving the county dispatch center the necessary information.

"Are you sure she's dead?" Patton asked.

Ashley was crossing herself. She stopped. "You think maybe she's not?" There was hysteria in her voice. Without waiting for a response, she dropped to her knees and straddled the body, her short skirt riding up to give them all an embarrassing view of white lace panties. At the same moment, Patton knelt down, put a hand under Rosemary's neck, and lowered his face toward hers. They were apparently going to attempt CPR.

"Don't do that!" Diana snapped. "Look at her! She's been shot. Any idiot can see she's dead."

Patton raised his head, appearing annoyed. Ashley kept pumping.

"Get off her!" Diana shouted. "You're messing up the crime scene."

Both judges jumped to their feet as if they'd been poked with a cattle prod, Ashley automatically wiping her hands on her rear. Diana shooed them back to the center aisle. Ashley was hyperventilating and crying at the same time.

Connor headed to the kitchen area, a few feet beyond Rosemary's body, where he grabbed a brown paper bag from the table that was supposed to hold desserts at the judges' reception. "Breathe into this," he told Ashley and supervised while she followed instructions. Patton was staring at Rosemary's body as though his gaze was a cord joining her to him. One knee of his pants was stained red where he'd knelt on the floor.

Ashley broke away from Connor, her eyes wild. "I think I'm going to be sick," she moaned.

Patton took her by the arm and pulled her toward the back door.

"Don't touch the—" Diana's warning was too late. He'd already flung the door wide and pushed Ashley through. The sound of her retching followed shortly after.

"Jeez," Diana said.

Ashley returned, her face chalk white. Patton closed the door.

"Was that door locked?" Diana asked.

Patton shrugged.

"I need to clean up," Ashley said. Before Diana could stop her, she ran out toward the lobby, stumbling on her high heels.

Diana gazed at Rosemary and shuddered. Connor put an arm around her shoulders. Maybe he'd sensed she was getting ready to run out behind Ashley. "Are you okay, Flash?" he asked.

She couldn't answer right away, but she didn't pull away either. Nor did she object to the nickname as she usually did. "I can't believe this could happen here," she managed after a couple of minutes. "I thought I was getting away—"

"With what?"

She sent a suddenly nervous glance his way. "Not *with*. *From*. Away from, you know, violence, crime—the way cities are. I thought Port Findlay would be peaceful, and it has been. Until now."

Ashley came back, still crying, red-faced. "I told the manager what happened. He said he'd watch for the police to arrive and ran out to the entry all excited. What's he got to be excited about?" She glanced toward Rosemary's body and shuddered as she wrung her hands. "Who would do such a thing?" she sobbed.

Patton put a hand on her back. "I could use a cup of coffee. Let's see if we can get a brew going. I noticed a coffeemaker in the lobby." Just as Diana was awarding Mountain Man points for unexpected compassion, he added, "This scene smells like trouble to me," which stabbed his personality in the foot again.

Ashley probably couldn't hear him over the sound of her sobs, but she let him guide her away, her heels clicking on the concrete floor, one hand holding a tissue to her eyes.

Diana yelled after them not to leave the building—the police would want to talk to them. Without turning around,

Patton gestured with his right hand in a way that signified either agreement or dismissal.

"You sure scared those two," Connor said.

She shrugged his arm from her shoulders. "Some women have hysterics under stress, I get bossy. What can you expect from trailer trash?"

When Connor blinked, Diana went a little pink around the edges. "I meant me, not them," she said. "Sorry. Sometimes my mouth operates independently of my brain." She narrowed her eyes at him. "Apparently I didn't scare *you.*"

"I don't scare easy. But you did surprise me with that talk about a crime scene."

She shrugged. "I guess I sound like a know-it-all. I've probably watched too many episodes of *Nash Bridges*. I'm wild for Don Johnson." She attempted a smile that didn't quite jell. Neither of them could take their eyes off the body.

Rosemary was a well-known fund-raiser and political campaigner, a woman of endless energy, tall and slender, her creamy skin and long dark hair making it difficult to believe her age, which Diana had heard was somewhere around the late fifties. Always beautifully dressed, with great cleavage that surely owed its prominence to Wonderbra, she was forever involved in whatever was going on in the community: chairing the Heart Fund and the local branch of the Cancer Society, not only organizing the bike marathon for MS, but collecting more pledges than anyone else, pedaling madly, exhorting others ever onward. She sang in the choir at the local nondenominational chapel, volunteered for Neighborhood Watch, and was on the city council. It was joked in Port Findlay that no one could hold a board meeting unless Rosemary Barrett was there to pound the gavel.

"You think whoever shot Rosemary could still be on the premises?" Diana asked.

Connor glanced uneasily toward the front of the hall. "You want to search for him? If he has an ounce of sense, he'll be long gone. If he'd had massacre in mind, he'd have shot us in the lobby when we came in."

"You're taking it for granted the killer is a he?"

"I suppose I am. Does that make me a sexist? I'm usually an equal opportunity kind of guy."

She managed a faint imitation of a smile, then they both went back to staring at Rosemary, until Diana caught sight of the large photograph above Rosemary's body. Sidestepping along the back wall, she took care to stay well away from the row of stands. "I don't believe this!" she exclaimed.

Connor had followed her. She gestured at the photo that had grabbed her attention. Amazingly, disturbingly pertinent, it featured a field of huge sunflowers above which the photographer had Photoshopped several evil-looking crows. At the bottom center was a chalked dead body outline.

Diana's voice came out wobbly. "I don't think those red spatters are part of the composition."

Connor swallowed. "I think I agree with you, Flash." Staring at the montage, he pointed at the title on the label next to the photo: *An out of body experience.*

Diana needed air, and once again she wanted to run. For a while after *she* was shot, she'd occasionally experienced this kind of panic attack. The doctor had called it post-traumatic stress disorder. Personally, she'd thought it had a lot to do with Sam Stockman disappearing right after he'd been released. That and Detective Sergeant Morrison of the San Francisco Police Department practically accusing her of having something to do with Stockman's disappearance. Whatever the cause, it had taken her months to put herself back together, one piece at a time. She was okay now. Fine. Just fine.

She took a deep, deep breath and then, to her relief, she heard sounds of voices and a lot of movement in the lobby. The cavalry had arrived.

Chapter 5

POLICE CHIEF SARAH Hathaway was first to appear, which didn't surprise Connor. The Port Findlay police force was not large. Unlike former chiefs who had mostly been political figures, Sarah took patrol duty whenever she could, so she was often first at the crime scene, usually in uniform—the better to put the fear of God into any criminals or would-be criminals who might be hanging around her town.

African-American, around five seven and sturdy, pushing fifty, she took all crime personally. Not that there was a lot of crime in Port Findlay—an occasional meth lab, theft, property damage, some shoplifting by adolescents, domestic violence, DUIs.

Sarah had moved from King County Police Department to Port Findlay in her thirties, sick of big city living. Against everybody's expectations, except her own, she had quickly risen to sergeant, and when the previous chief retired to Arizona in search of year-round sunshine, she was a shoo-in to be his replacement.

She often referred to herself as a tough broad, which she indubitably was, but she had been Liz's devoted friend and was now Connor's. Not today, though, today Connor was a witness, and Sarah had her cop face on.

"Fill me in," she commanded, after Connor and Diana had explained that Rosemary was already dead when they found her.

"Shouldn't you question us separately?" Diana asked. She had her color back, Connor was glad to see. For a minute there he'd wondered if she was going to pass out.

Sarah squinted at her. "You've been reading the police officer's guide? I do things my way, girl. Give me a quick briefing. I'll get your formal statements when I'm good and ready."

They told her how they'd found Rosemary.

Sarah asked only one question. "Did you touch anything?"

Connor owned up to checking Rosemary's carotid artery for a pulse. Diana told about Ashley and Joshua flinging themselves down on the corpse, the stain on the knee of Joshua's pants. Ashley getting sick, Joshua opening the back door so she could throw up outside. Her voice was strong. She was in command of herself again.

"Jeez," Sarah commented.

"Is that blood?" Diana asked, pointing at the photograph with the deadly looking sunflowers.

Sarah squinted. "The crime scene investigators will let us know."

"Does the fact that such a photo is right there, almost above her, seem as weird to you as it does to me?"

Sarah studied the picture for a couple of minutes, one

hand worrying the back of her close-cropped hair, then made a wry movement with her mouth. "Don't know anybody does chalk outlines anymore. Crime scene people measure and photograph and chart and maybe do a video."

Diana had a pained expression. "The dead body outline is an immediately recognizable symbol. It would be difficult to put measurements and charts and so on in a photo montage meant to be artistic."

"You consider this picture to be artistic?" Sarah asked.

"Everyone's a judge," Connor commented.

"You didn't answer the question," Diana pointed out.

Sarah frowned at her. "No, I guess I didn't."

Diana persevered. "You suppose the photograph was accidental, just happened to be there? Or does it have some deeper significance?"

Sarah shrugged.

Knowing Sarah fairly well, Connor guessed she was not about to make any snap judgments. Sarah's methods reminded him of Aesop's fable about the tortoise and the hare: slow and steady wins the race. Diana was more like the rabbit, twitching to get things settled fast.

An emergency medical technician showed up, glanced down at Rosemary's body, then at Sarah. "You might check up on our two judges," Connor suggested. "They aren't feeling too well. They went out to the lobby."

The young man nodded. "They're being attended to, sir."

Connor was never going to get used to being called sir. The respectful form of address had evidently come along as part of the baggage of becoming forty.

"Judges?" Sarah queried.

"For the photo show," Connor said.

"You mean that guy was Joshua Patton? *The* Joshua Patton? I didn't recognize him." Sarah frowned. "Were both judges with you the whole time?"

Connor nodded. "Apart from the two minutes they were outside the back door. Even then we could hear Ms. Robinson and see Patton. And then they went out to the lobby to get coffee."

"Yeah, they're out there now. So they were both with you all the time from when you entered until after you discovered the victim."

"Right," Connor said.

As the EMT moved out, two Port Findlay officers, who doubled as crime scene investigators when necessary, moved in, appearing efficient and purposeful, evidence kits in hand. They were accompanied by some strangers whom Sarah murmured were from the state patrol's crime lab.

Sarah conferred with both teams. Connor followed Diana out of their way and they watched from the aisle as a young male technician took pictures of the weird photograph with the dead body outline on it, then began photographing Rosemary's body from several angles. A slightly older, professional-looking woman wearing latex gloves took down the photo and bagged it carefully, then began making sketches of the scene, while a younger woman measured the distance from the last row of stands to a shiny spent casing Connor hadn't noticed at the foot of the back wall.

Sarah returned to the aisle, smoothing down her uniform jacket.

"How did the state lab people get here so fast?" Connor asked her.

"They're in town for the law enforcement convention at the Holiday Inn—supposed to give some demonstrations this afternoon. I put in a call right after I got the heads-up from dispatch."

"Oh shit!" Diana exclaimed. "I promised Greg Wang I'd take a couple of photos at that law enforcement convention."

Wang was the editor of the *Port Findlay Chronicle*.

"I'd better call him, maybe he can get Victor Newcombe instead."

Connor handed her his cell phone. "Tell him to ask Vic not to squat," he suggested.

Diana's brow creased into a frown, then cleared. "Oh yeah, he took that god-awful photo of you. You should sue. Or at least deck him."

"You're accustomed to decking people?" Sarah asked her.

Diana gave her one of her narrow-eyed glances, but then all three of them were taken by surprise by a sudden commotion that they could hear but not see. Running footsteps and a voice yelling, "Freeze right there," were followed by the sudden appearance of a small woman with messy brown hair at the other end of the row of photographs, a female police officer hot on her heels. Almost tripping over the crouching photographer, the woman flung herself on her knees beside the corpse, calling in a piteous voice, "Mama, Mama!"

"Who?" Sarah asked.

"Melissa Ludlow. Rosemary's daughter," Connor said as two of the crime lab people lifted the woman bodily off the corpse and brought her over to the chief. She hung limply between the two men, her face streaming with tears. "Mama," she kept moaning.

"I'll see to her," Connor offered and the men gladly released her. Putting an arm around her shoulders, Connor led the young woman to a couple of chairs at the far side of the hall. Sitting beside her, he took both of her hands in his and attempted to talk her down. Her hands were clammy.

He didn't know Rosemary's daughter well, had always thought of her as shy and sort of homespun.

As usual she was wearing a long dress, brown with some kind of yellow design on it, plus ankle socks and sensible shoes. Right now there was nothing else sensible about her.

"Take slow deep breaths—in, hold it, out, hold it, in, out. Do as I do. Slower. That's it. Good girl. Keep it slow. Keep it flowing. It's okay. You're going to be okay. You're a strong woman. You can handle this. Keep it steady. In, out, in, out."

After a few minutes, she calmed down enough to talk. "I can't believe it. Who would do such a thing? Who killed her, Dr. Callahan, do you know? Rick Langley said she was shot." Her gaze was fixed on his face, her hands shaking in his.

He kept his voice totally even. *"Apparently* she was shot, yes. We don't know who killed her. I expect Sarah— the chief—will talk to you about it."

"I didn't even know Mama was dead until Rick called me. . . ."

"We just found her," Diana put in over Connor's shoulder. She'd evidently finished talking to Greg Wang. She handed Connor's cell phone back to him. "The chief will find out who did it, I'm sure," she assured Melissa. "Whoever it was will have left some kind of clue. Killers usually do. The chief will want to talk to you, Melissa. She'll need to know if your mom had any enemies, if anything unusual has occurred lately, that sort of thing."

"Don't worry about it now," Connor said as Melissa started shaking again. "Concentrate on your breathing."

Melissa lapsed into silence, drawing in her breath in shuddering gulps.

Once she became calm again, the officer who had followed her in and had been talking to Sarah came over and escorted her out of the hall.

Sarah indicated they should follow her to the lobby. "You were incredibly patient with Melissa, Connor," Diana said as they walked along. "I'd probably have slapped her face when she went into hysterics, like people did in old movies. She's such a twit. I do her kids' photos, so I know. But then with a mother like Rosemary, how could she be otherwise?"

"She'd just lost that mother in a particularly brutal way, Flash. How could I be anything but kind?"

She nodded. "You're right. I'm being obnoxious. I often am."

Her honesty surprised and disarmed him.

"I've heard you're a steady sort of guy," she said, with a glance in his direction. "I see my informant was right. You've sure stayed calm through this whole thing."

"I don't think I'd be too calm if I saw *my* mother lying on the floor with a bullet in her," he said.

She seemed about to comment on that but changed her mind.

In the lobby, Sarah made sure someone was taking care of Melissa—she'd been taken to Rick Langley's office by the female officer. Melissa's husband, father, and doctor had been sent for. Sarah next stopped where Ashley and Patton were sitting on a bench inside the entrance, checked that an officer had taken their individual statements, and told them she'd want to talk to them herself in a few minutes.

Beyond the glass doors, a chubby officer was slinging yellow crime scene tape around anything that wasn't moving. "Quinn Center is going to be out of business for a while," the chief said. She included all four of them in a stern glance. "We don't want anyone talking about that photograph."

Patton gave a slight, arrogant nod. Connor and Diana said, "Of course not," in unison. Ashley's smooth forehead acquired a couple of lines.

"I don't think Ashley noticed the photo," Diana murmured.

The chief glanced from Diana to Connor and pointed upstairs.

An officer had set up headquarters in one of the community center's upstairs rooms. Seating herself, Sarah pulled a notebook out of her jacket pocket and indicated a couple of chairs. Officer Timothy Valentine, Port Findlay's sole detective, was on sick leave, having had his appendix removed, she said. That was why she was doing all the work herself.

"Let's have it from the top," she instructed.

"Again?" Diana queried.

Sarah bridled. "You have a problem with that? I go to court, I want something I can read from as I wrote it down. Anything I don't write down is the first thing somebody's sure to ask me. Besides which, you're past the first shock now, you might remember a detail or two you missed before."

Diana nodded, seeming mollified. "Makes sense. One time when I was—" She broke off, and Sarah glanced at her questioningly. "I must still be in shock," Diana said. "I have no idea what I was about to say."

"Hmm." Sarah sounded unconvinced. The suspicious expression had returned to her face.

"I know how that is," Connor said. "I find myself in the middle of a room in my house, and there's no knowing what I came there to get. I attribute it to moments of mental aberration in a normally superior brain. Not to be confused with the onset of geriatric problems."

Diana raised an eyebrow at him. "You are a hell of a long way from geriatric, Connor."

Sarah gave a fake-sounding cough. "Could we get on with the investigation here?" she suggested, gazing at Connor.

Absurdly pleased by Diana's comment, but composing himself to concentrate and visualize, Connor recounted everything from the moment he'd met Patton and Ashley at the entrance to Quinn Center, then waited for Diana outside, to the time he'd called dispatch.

Sarah made notes, then went over every sentence until she was satisfied he hadn't left anything out. Then she started in on Diana, who answered crisply and efficiently, as if she were used to police inquiries.

"You're very observant," Connor said when she was done. "That's an unusual trait. I don't think you missed a thing."

"Mind like the proverbial steel trap," she said.

"You were late getting here?" Sarah asked, reading over her notes.

Diana nodded. "I'd planned on getting here at ten A.M., but I was a little slow getting going. I wasn't worrying too much about the time. The original plan was for me to open up at nine-thirty, but Rosemary had vetoed that. She'd decided she was the one who should welcome the judges to Port Findlay."

"Had she met either of them before?"

Diana shrugged.

"I gathered she hadn't," Connor said. "She was excited about having Patton. And said she liked Ms. Robinson's work."

"Different strokes," Sarah commented. "If the poster

Ashley Robinson produced for the show is anything to go by, I don't see anything to like. Can't she afford to do color? I believe I've seen her before, but I can't remember where. Kiwanis maybe?"

Connor shook his head. "I don't think so. At least I haven't ever seen her there. It was Rosemary who invited Ashley to be one of our judges. She lives in Seattle. Oh, wait a minute, when she saw . . . Rosemary's body . . . she crossed herself. Maybe she's visited your church? No, that couldn't be, she said she'd never been to Port Findlay before yesterday."

"She's painfully shy," Diana commented. "Rosemary said she had a hell of a time persuading her to help judge the show. I happen to like that poster," she added, with a challenging glance at Sarah. "I like an artist who forces me to see things in a different way. There's a lot of passion in Ashley's work. I find it invigorating. And she *specializes* in black and white, by the way. It's not a question of what she can afford. A lot of us think of black-and-white as more artistic."

She hesitated, then added, "She seemed to enjoy sparring with Joshua Patton." She made a face. "He's such a snob."

"I admire *his* work," Sarah said.

"I'm not familiar with his stuff," Diana said. "If the rest of it is anything like the poster he gave us, it's too artsy-fartsy for me."

Might be a good idea to change the subject, Connor decided. "Here's how it went, Chief. Rosemary told Diana she'd be here by nine to let us into the community center at ten. Nobody else is due in until later this afternoon. When Diana showed up at ten-fifteen and told us she'd given her keys to Rosemary the previous day, I called Rick Langley, the community center's manager. He came over and unlocked the doors."

"You saw nobody else in the building after Rick let you in?"

"Nobody."

"We didn't search the place," Diana put in.

"After we saw the . . . body, we decided the murderer had probably left the area. If not the state," Connor added. "I suppose someone could have been in one of the rest rooms or an upstairs room."

"I detailed a couple of officers to take a walk around when we arrived. They didn't find anyone." Sarah glanced at her notes. "So the front doors were locked when you got here?"

"I tried them," Connor said. "Either Rosemary locked them after whoever else came in, or . . ."

"Or the killer locked them on his way out," Sarah finished.

"His or her," Diana corrected.

Sarah smiled thinly. "As you say." Hostility was back in the air.

Sarah returned her attention to Connor. "The front entry's usually kept locked because tourists have a habit of wandering in to use the rest rooms or see the various displays if the doors are left open. Which is okay during business hours but not otherwise." She frowned. "What about the back door?"

Connor and Diana exchanged a glance. "We don't know," Connor said. "Patton opened it up to let Ashley out when she was about to throw up. Diana asked him if it had been locked, and he didn't know."

"One of my officers checked it," Sarah said. "It has a deadbolt."

"All Patton did was turn the knob," Diana said.

"So it wasn't locked then. Surely it was, usually?"

Connor shrugged. "I guess you'd need to check with Rick. I've never come in that way."

"Rosemary could have come in that way, though," Diana exclaimed. "The keys to both entries were on the ring I gave her. Whoever killed her could have followed her in." She stood up and positioned herself in the general direction of the main hall downstairs where the photographs were on display, where Rosemary's body was still lying.

"I took it for granted she'd switched the lights on from the front, because that's what I would have done, but she could easily have switched the lights on from the back door."

She thought for a minute. "I didn't see her car parked out front, it's probably at the back."

"It is," Sarah said.

"Well then, if someone followed her in the back door, he could—he or she could have shot Rosemary right away. Rosemary would probably head for the kitchen first, that's what I would have done, to put some coffee on. There was a casing right there at the back wall. If someone followed her in and she heard him or her, she would turn . . ."

Stretching her arms forward, elbows slightly bent, left hand folded beneath her right hand as though she were holding a gun, she squinted along her index finger, then looked over her right shoulder and murmured, "That's the direction the casing would have flown."

Apparently becoming aware that both Connor and Sarah were staring at her, she shrugged and added, "Whatever."

Without comment, Sarah made some notes to herself in her notebook, then stood up. "Go on home. I'll be in touch with you both later."

As they stood, she asked Connor, "Who actually knew you and Ms. Gordon and the judges were going to be in Quinn Center this morning?"

Connor sighed. "The entire membership of the Arts Alliance. It was discussed at a general meeting. Which probably means the whole town knew."

"And who knew Rosemary would be here before you?"

Connor glanced at Diana, who answered promptly. "I did, of course."

"Nobody else?"

"There's no way of knowing who Rosemary might have told," Connor put in quickly.

"My assistant, Higby Sanders, was in the studio when she came in to get the keys," Diana said.

"He saw you give her the keys?"

"I don't know. We were getting going on a portrait shoot. A couple from Seattle. They wanted one of the vintage photos. Victorian. Higby was setting up the backdrop when Rosemary came in. I was in my office checking something on the computer. The people were changing clothes. Rosemary came in the back door. Higby may not have seen her."

An officer—Carlos Dominguez—poked his head in the room and told Sarah that Bob Trenery, the county prosecutor who doubled as coroner, had arrived.

"I'll be right there," Sarah said. She stood up. "Either of you know if Rosemary had any enemies?"

After a hesitation on both their parts, Diana answered first, choosing her words carefully. "Rosemary usually acted as if everyone would be bound to love her."

"Did *you* love her?"

"No."

"Did you like her?"

"No. But I didn't kill her, if that's what you are getting at. I don't believe anybody—*anybody*—has the right to take someone's life. Not accidentally, or medically, or carelessly, or neglectfully, or deliberately. Not even if it's state approved."

Connor had thought previously that taken feature by feature, Diana was strikingly attractive, though not necessarily beautiful. But when she was fully engaged, her passion put a light in her face and eyes from within and made her glow.

"Rosemary was a terminally irritating woman," she concluded. Sarah's gaze held on her for a few seconds, then switched to Connor.

"I disliked her intensely," he said.

Sarah's eyebrows rose. "What happened to not speaking ill of the dead? Don't you know it's unwise to express dislike for someone who's been murdered?"

"As you surely know, Sarah, Rosemary is—was—a know-it-all. She had an opinion on everything, always had to out-expert the expert. Gave me a whole lecture on chiropractic once. On top of that, she was unforgivably rude to Liz a couple of times when she was ill. I worked with her when necessary, yes, but I never liked her."

He hesitated. "If I was inclined to kill people for being rude, I'd have bumped off Joshua Patton this morning."

"What did *he* do?"

"Said he didn't believe in chiropractors," Diana answered for him.

Sarah's lips twitched. "Now *there's* a motive for murder. . . ."

"We're not being too helpful, are we?" Connor mulled the original question for a while, then shook his head. "Most people think Rosemary was a perfect woman. Why would anyone kill a perfect woman?"

"For being perfect?" Diana suggested.

Chapter 6

CONNOR AND DIANA emerged from Quinn Center and paused under the porte cochere so Connor could put his parka on. "What's with you and Sarah, Flash?" Connor asked.

Diana tried an innocent expression, but it didn't fool him. He raised an eyebrow to let her know it.

"We have different politics, for one thing," she said. "Remember at Kiwanis when Sarah was program chair for the month, she invited our representative to talk?"

"Brandon Turner?" She saw understanding dawn on his face. "You got in an argument with him about what I believe you called his Draconian and sexist views on unwed mothers. Told him it was way past time to start targeting unwed fathers. Made him sputter, as I recall."

"The man's a throwback. But then he's a Republican."

"I begin to understand," Connor said. "Sarah's a Republican also. And strong on family values. Ronald Reagan was her icon."

"Tell me you're not?"

"A Republican? No, I'm a lifelong Democrat. And you?"

"Hey, I was born in San Francisco. I'm a bleeding heart liberal, what else!"

Diana realized they'd been hesitating outside Quinn Center as if they were reluctant to leave. She looked around, feeling disoriented. Rose Street was full of midday traffic, pedestrians were passing by on the sidewalk, talking, laughing even, as though it was an ordinary day. Which of course it was to anyone who wasn't aware of what was going on inside the community center.

It was still drizzling lightly, but most Washingtonians didn't stay indoors because of the weather. Liquid sunshine, they called the rain.

"How about some lunch, Flash?" Connor asked.

She shook her head. "I still feel shaky. I didn't like Rosemary, but nobody should die like that."

"I'm still fairly rocky myself," Connor said. "That's why I think lunch would be a good idea. Get our blood sugar up."

She considered that. He was probably right. And she didn't really want to go to her studio and work, or even to her empty apartment. The fear was still with her, under control, but hovering around her like a noxious cloud.

Nevertheless, duty called. "I need to pick up address and phone lists at the studio. I'll have to call everyone to tell them the judges' reception will be delayed. Luckily, at this time of the year the photography business is slow to nonexistent on Thursdays."

It would get busier on Friday with tourists coming in for the weekend. Unless news of the murder kept them away.

A sudden memory jolted her thought processes. "We were supposed to take the judges to lunch. We just walked off and left them."

"Do you *want* to have lunch with them?"

"God no. The thought of even sitting in a restaurant . . . And I called them idiots. Heat of the moment. Tact not being one of my major attributes. They *were* being idiots, but I ought to apologize. I'll tell them it's PMS. Which would be the truth." She sighed. "Given the circumstances, do you really think they'd expect business as usual?"

When Connor didn't answer, she glanced at him. He appeared to be mildly stunned. "What?" she asked.

"I'm trying to recover from the surprise of hearing you own up to PMS."

"It's a natural phenomenon. Makes me even crankier than usual. Does the mention of female bodily functions bother you?"

"Not at all. Your outspokenness is always refreshing."

"My last husband put it more bluntly. He called me a pottymouth!"

"Your *last* husband?"

Whoa, what had made her pop that out at him? Not much she could do about it now. "I've only had one," she said. "I just happen to think of him as my last."

"Oh." She could see *his* thought processes working that out.

"Well." He paused, then started again. "Tell you what. Let's hope the judges will figure out for themselves that we weren't up to entertaining them. Their hotel is right next door, after all. How about I come with you to the studio and help make the calls? I'd cleared my calendar for the photo show stuff—the lunch, the reception later."

"Oh God, we have to postpone the whole show." She took a deep breath, deliberately holding it and letting it go slowly. "Okay. One thing at a time."

Connor had cycled to Quinn Center—a new resolution, he told her, one that was liable to wear him out on the uphill stretches. He wheeled his bike alongside as they walked Rose Street, parked it in the lot next to Diana's studio. Diana took him in through Photomania's front door rather than the side street entrance because she always liked entering the way her customers did, seeing her studio the way they did, checking to make sure it still appeared welcoming. She felt in need of something welcoming right now.

Her studio was housed in the lower floor of a two-story stone building that backed onto the waterfront. The entry was an attractive one with mullioned windows instead of the usual plate glass shop window. Her apartment was on the second floor. Next door was the Woolly Bear, a yarn and knitted goods boutique. Beyond that was an art gallery, a bookstore, and Findlay's Landing, a British-style pub.

On the other side of the studio, across the parking lot, was a real estate office, a classy dress shop, an antique store that specialized in Asian goods, and a Greek restaurant.

"Nice," Connor said as they entered the studio's lobby. This was his first visit.

Diana thought it was nice, too. She'd installed a skylight, and her assistant, thirty-two-year old Higby Sanders, had corralled flowering plants in pots behind a white wood fence in one corner of the small lobby. He changed the plants and decorated the area to suit the seasons. Right now the pots were full of tulips. A large weathered bird feeder filled with thistle seeds stood among them, with a pair of realistic goldfinches investigating it.

Diana had expected to find only Higby inside, but what greeted her was the sound of a high-pitched female voice coming from farther inside the building.

Lena Green, the widow who owned the Woolly Bear, was drinking coffee with Higby at an antique table at the side of the prop room. They were great friends but presented a comic picture when they were together, Lena the little grandmotherly type with white hair and small, round glasses; Higby a brown giant of a man with a completely shaved head and a habit of wearing tropical resort clothing.

Higby jumped up to greet them, his usually smiling brown face contorted in a frown. In spite of the cool, damp weather, he was clad in shorts and sandals, but at least he had a shirt on today, even if it was open all the way down the front. Higby worked out constantly and was forever pulling off his shirt to demonstrate his sculpted muscles, polished mocha skin, and the tattooed band of hibiscus that encircled one biceps.

Claiming to be a whiz with makeup and hairstyling, not to mention having a dead-on eye for fashion—"We could advertise glamor shots!"—he had applied for a job the minute Diana opened her studio. He hadn't exaggerated his skills and had quickly become indispensable. He was also wonderful at entertaining kids in for portraits.

"We're talking about the murder," he said. "We heard that you and Dr. Callahan found Rosemary's body. We're distraught, totally distraught. You must tell us *everything!*" Even when he was excited, Higby's voice didn't lose its melodic Jamaican accent.

"I'm guessing you had your police radio on," Diana said.

"Higby called me the minute he heard," Lena said. "We're both devastated." She shook her head, seriously endangering the two short wooden knitting needles that held her silver hair in a bun on top of her head. "I can't believe it. I had an early breakfast with poor darling Rosemary on Tuesday. A mini Arts Alliance board meeting. The top four officers: president, vice-president, secretary, and treasurer. Rosemary, Big Al Rutherford, me, and Eve Bertram."

"Did Rosemary tell you she'd decided to open up the community center this morning?" Diana asked.

Lena's brown eyes opened wide. "I thought *you* were going to do it."

"I was. Rosemary decided it was her duty as president to greet the judges. She came over to get the keys at the studio yesterday afternoon." She turned to Higby. "You didn't happen to eavesdrop did you? I think Chief Hathaway has me pegged as a suspect."

"I didn't even know Rosemary was here," Higby said.

"Great," Diana said with a sigh.

"I can *say* I saw her," Higby said.

"Good God, no, let's not talk of doing anything like that!"

Especially in front of Lena, Diana wanted to add. Lena had an E-mail list a mile long, people to whom she sent every joke, hoax message, charity plea, petition, or smidgen of gossip that came her way, exhorting recipients to send the messages on to everyone they knew. Diana and others had informed her many times that she was in danger of spreading computer viruses, but Lena didn't let that deter her.

All Sarah Hathaway would need was a whisper that Higby had offered to lie for Diana, and Diana would be a dead duck.

"Did Rosemary mention having any problems, or maybe meeting someone at Quinn Center?" Connor asked.

Lena thought hard for several seconds, her plump face tightening into a network of wrinkles. "No."

Diana sighed again. "Well, anyway . . . we came in to get the lists of Arts Alliance members and the photographers who submitted their work. We need to let them know—"

"We have already taken care of that," Higby said. "We telephoned Eve and Big Al and got them started on the telephone tree. They'll have all the members organized by now to call the people who submitted entries. They will be given a brief explanation of Rosemary's tragic death and told that all events are postponed until further notice."

"Luckily we were able to cancel the order at the deli before Marjorie Taylor started cooking for the judges' reception," Lena said, then added worriedly, "Is that what you would have wanted done?"

Diana glanced at Connor. "I don't know why we're called chairs of the photography show. We're obviously not needed."

Higby showed alarm. "Are you mad at us for going ahead before you got here?"

"No way! I'm grateful I don't have to worry about doing it all myself. I hadn't even thought about the deli."

"And you are going to tell us exactly what happened?"

Diana passed that over to Connor, who gave an admirably succinct account of how they had found Rosemary's body. He left out the panicky actions of the two judges and Rosemary's daughter, and obeyed Sarah's order not to mention the weird photograph.

"Higby and I have already decided Dmitri did it," Lena said.

"Rosemary's husband?" Diana said. "You know something we don't?"

"On TV it's always the spouse the police suspect at first," Higby said. "Dmitri's several ounces short of a quart," he added.

"He has Alzheimer's, Higby. That doesn't make him a murderer."

"He's also a Russian—they are always passionate."

"You're Jamaican. That doesn't mean you can sing like Harry Belafonte."

"Or even Kermit the Frog," Higby agreed.

"I called Rosemary's house when she didn't show up to

let us into Quinn Center," Connor said. "Dmitri answered. He thought it was the middle of the night. I doubt he'd be capable of planning and carrying out a murder, then returning home as if nothing had happened."

Obviously he, too, wanted to nip any gossip in the bud. "I expect the police will check up on all leads," Diana offered. "We'd better leave any speculation to them."

"Can you think of anything else that needs doing?" Higby asked.

Diana frowned. "Well, you could maybe get someone to track down the two judges and tell them the reception and the show will be delayed, and I'll call them as soon as we reschedule. They were still with the police chief when we left Quinn Center. Both stayed at the Best Western last night. They may have gone back there. They were going to be here for the duration, but I don't think there's much point in them staying on, unless Sarah wants them to."

She glanced at Connor. "I didn't think to ask the chief to let us know exactly how long Quinn Center would be out of bounds. Probably not too long. I wouldn't be surprised if the crime scene people work through the night. But let's postpone the show for a week at least, out of respect. We can check if the center is available then and let people know. What do you think?"

Connor nodded agreement. "We'll also need to contact the newspapers."

"Done," Lena said. "I called the *Journal* and the *Chronicle*—spoke to Greg Wang himself. He already knew about Rosemary, said you called him."

Ah, that was where the leak had come from.

"He said he'd go talk to Chief Hathaway." Lena sighed. "I don't know how the Arts Alliance is going to function without our Rosemary, bless her heart. Especially as they are probably going to have to manage without me, too."

Diana stared at her in shock. "What are you talking about? You're not leaving Port Findlay?"

Higby patted Lena's back. Lena lifted her chin bravely. "I may not have any choice, Diana. Higby and I were discussing it when you came in. Like I said, Rosemary, Al Rutherford, Eve Bertram, and I had breakfast on Tuesday. Now Rosemary's dead."

"That's it?" Connor asked before Diana could come out on the other side of all that.

"No; there's more," Lena said with great drama. "Eve Bertram's in the hospital because she had pains in her upper abdomen yesterday afternoon!"

She switched her gaze from one to the other of them.

"I'm sorry to hear that, but what does it have to do with Rosemary's death?" Diana finally asked.

"Don't you see? Everything goes in threes. There were four of us, but only one was a man. Three women. Maybe only women are targeted. Two down, one to go. And the last one is me. I'll be the next to die."

Diana managed not to crack a smile. "I don't think the rule of three always applies, Lena. I'm not sure it's sexist, either. If it does apply here, Al's as much in danger as you are. He's a big man, Al. I don't think he exercises. And he smokes. You seem healthy to me."

"Fit as a bug," Higby agreed.

"It's fit as a fiddle," Lena corrected. "But Eve was fine at our lunch. So was Rosemary."

She was evidently determined to look on the gloomy side. But then, Diana remembered, one time when meteor showers were being discussed, Lena had said she was sure someday a meteor was going to drop on the Woolly Bear.

"What about poor Melissa and her kids?" she asked now. "How are they going to manage without Rosemary? I never did think much of that husband of Melissa's. Wayne. Nor did Rosemary."

"More to the point," Diana said, "what did Wayne think of Rosemary?"

"You think he might be a suspect?" Lena asked.

"Well, you said Rosemary didn't approve of him. Maybe he resented that?"

"Wayne's kind of a resentful guy," Lena said.

"Maybe Melissa could use some help with the children," Diana suggested. "She was really shook up. Haven't you sat with the kids from time to time?"

Lena brightened and leaped to her feet immediately. "I'd better go see. Maybe Wayne will be there, and I can see if he looks guilty. Or maybe Melissa will have some ideas about who killed her mom. This is going to be so hard on that girl, bless her heart. She adored her mother, as we all did." She made a hurried exit, obviously delighted to have an excuse to get close to the action.

Connor exchanged a rueful glance with Diana. Neither of them had said anything about Melissa rushing into Quinn Center to throw herself down beside her mother.

There was a silence. Connor looked around the prop room. "Interesting place," he said.

Clothes hung on racks against one wall, mostly the vintage clothes and hats Diana offered to people wanting some of her staged historical photographs. She'd acquired those during the years that portrait, wedding, and special event photography was putting her through college, along with investigative jobs. Over the past year she'd also collected a lot of odds and ends—a couple of boas and some exotic jewelry for Higby's glamor shots, a workout bench and mat with accompanying weights, some fake Grecian columns, antique golf clubs, paintings in ornate frames, even an old stagecoach, a collection of antique guns, and a couple of realistic fake horses that she'd picked up from a movie supply company.

She thought Connor seemed most interested in the guns and stagecoach, but then he moved on to nod approvingly at some of her more artistic work that was hung on the walls—a perfect shot of Mount Olympus; a field of tulips; a sea stack off the Pacific side of the Olympic Peninsula, caught when the combination of light and mist gave the whole scene a glimmering lavender and blue effect.

"I take it you haven't had hordes of people demanding my services today?" Diana said to Higby as Connor headed beyond her darkroom.

"It's been totally dead." Realizing what he'd said, Higby winced.

"You have a beach out here!" Connor exclaimed. "That's a great view of the wharf!"

Diana joined him and opened the back door, gesturing him out to the small crescent-shaped beach beyond.

It had stopped raining. The sun shone fitfully through broken clouds, making the water in the bay glimmer. "This beach is what sold me on the place," Diana said. "I come out here most mornings to practice Tai Chi. On a clear day I can see the Olympics. Very inspiring."

Connor gave her a surprised glance. In the sunlight his eyes were an electric blue.

"It's part of my general exercise program," she said. "Tai Chi improves the relationship between body, energy, and mind. It reduces stress and preserves balance and flexibility. According to Lao Tzu, when the wind blows, the flexible bamboo bends but doesn't break. It's the stiff tree that breaks."

"I'll take that as a warning and keep riding my bike, even if it kills me," Connor said.

Higby stuck his head out. "I'll go find those judges. Unless you want me to hang here?"

"Show yourself," Diana said.

He presented himself in the doorway. His shirt was buttoned, he'd changed into jeans and shoes.

"Go for it," Diana said. "I'll probably go on upstairs. I'm totally whacked. Adrenaline hangover, I guess. I probably need food."

"We both do," Connor said from behind her. "How about lunch at my house?"

Surprised, Diana turned. She liked his face, she decided. How had Victor Newcombe managed to make him look so awful? He had strong features, a frequently wry smile, a Marlboro man jawline. Not exactly a Marlboro man body, but he'd said he'd keep cycling, so he was working on it. Those vivid blue eyes and his newly trimmed tow-colored hair rounded out the whole picture in an extremely pleasing way.

His pants were a bit baggy, though. He was right on the edge of dorky, but put him in tight blue jeans, have him straddle a fence, and she'd love to photograph him.

She realized he'd been watching her as she studied him.

Their eyes met. And held.

She felt a small thump behind her rib cage. She took in a breath and saw that Connor was doing the same. Interesting. She wasn't sure how she felt about this. She decided not to think about it. The day had been emotional enough.

"Lunch?" Connor prompted.

She hesitated, aware that Higby was following this whole exchange with great interest, standing with arms folded across his massive chest like Mr. Clean, moving his bald head deliberately from side to side as if he were watching a tennis match.

"I can't keep on holding my breath, people," he said.

Diana sent him a quelling glance, and he backed away from the door, chuckling.

"Well, I guess I *could* give you and your bike a ride home in my get-away van," she said to Connor. And wasn't sure if her sudden sense of pleased anticipation was a good—or bad—thing.

Chapter 7

WHATEVER CONNOR HAD thought might come to pass from inviting Diana Gordon to his house, he realized it wasn't going to happen the moment he descended from Diana's big red van. Melissa Ludlow was sitting on the steps leading up to the front door of the ultramodern house Liz had been thrilled to find when they moved to Port Findlay.

Melissa was squatting there in her long dress like an abandoned waif in an old silent movie, red-eyed, sad-faced, both arms wrapped around her knees. Her brown hair could have done double duty as a bird's nest.

Before Connor had a chance to unload his bike, Melissa flung herself at him so hard he had to hold on to her or fall over backwards. He sent a pleading glance at Diana, but she just raised her eyebrows.

Melissa sobbed loudly against his chest. He patted her ineffectually, then persuaded her into the house and into his large kitchen.

Diana helped him get Melissa settled in one of the chairs at the glass-topped table, and he tried without success to get her to talk. She was still awash with tears. He put a box of paper tissues in front of her and muttered, "I'll make coffee."

After pouring water into the carafe of the vacuum coffeemaker, he emptied ground coffee directly from the packet into the upper container.

"You don't measure it?" Diana asked.

"Sure I do—two or three shakes of the bag usually makes it strong enough."

Diana shook her head, but she was smiling. Connor liked her smile—a lot—and was beginning to anticipate it. Melissa had stopped sobbing, he noted, though she was still sniffling off and on.

After the water heated, whooshed upward, and then did its journey down, transformed into coffee, he poured three mugs and set two of them on the table.

"That's one scary coffeemaker," Diana said. "Is everything in the house as up to the minute?" She darted a glance around the kitchen, her gaze lingering on the restaurant stove that had been Liz's favorite acquisition. "All this glass and stainless steel are surprising in an old town like this. I guess you like them though."

"Well, yes, sure," Connor said. That wasn't exactly true, but it had always seemed sort of weak in the knees to tell people the house and furnishings had been Liz's choices rather than his. He'd never particularly cared for either the house or its contents, but he'd loved Liz, so he'd given her free rein.

Melissa sipped from her mug in an absentminded way, clutching it with both hands, tears still dripping from her eyelashes. After taking off her Nike cap, Diana sat down, swallowed some coffee, and nodded approvingly. "Great coffee," she said to Connor. "Froth some milk, you could give Java Jenny some competition."

Connor had pulled a large container of homemade vegetable soup and a loaf of sliced Bavarian wheat bread—Liz's favorite—from the freezer. Maybe he should buy a different bread for a change, he thought. Sourdough. Multigrain. Something else. Again, the thought seemed vaguely disloyal.

As soon as the soup was hot and the bread had silently and slowly levitated from the electronic toaster, they all tucked in as if starved. Melissa still wasn't talking.

"Hot soup's always good in a crisis," Diana commented. "This stuff is wonderful. What gives it the zing?"

"A large can of Mexican-style tomatoes, chopped up."

Melissa chose that moment to break her brooding silence. "I want you to find out who killed my mother," she announced without any preamble. Pushing her empty bowl aside, she pulled herself ramrod straight as though she'd suddenly remembered good posture was important. Her gaze nailed Connor with its intensity.

"That's up to the police department, Melissa," he said gently. "Sarah Hathaway's good at her job. I'm sure she'll find out—"

"She's convinced my father did it. She's out to get him."

"She told you that?"

Higby and Lena had jumped to the conclusion that Dmitri was the killer. But he was sure Sarah would wait to see where the evidence pointed.

Melissa squirmed on the Plexiglas chair. She was a singularly unattractive woman, Connor thought. Liz had told him often that he shouldn't judge by outward appearances, but he'd always contended that once people were beyond thirty-five, their inner selves showed on their faces. He judged Melissa to be close to his own age. She was a small, rather scrawny woman with none of her mother's presence, the lines on her face indicating a sullen disposition. Her mouth was a thin gash, pulled tight at the corners. Under sparse eyelashes, her eyes peered out with a wary glint like those of some small forest animal.

Did *his* face put his whole personality on display for everyone to see? he wondered abruptly.

"The chief had me up in that office for half an hour while my poor mama lay there on that cold, hard floor," Melissa said. "Asked me a ton of questions about my dad. When he and Wayne and Dr. Forbes arrived, she said she wanted to talk to my father right away. I told her he's not capable of answering questions. He has Alzheimer's. Did she listen? No."

She shook her head in an exaggerated, dramatic way. Her bird's nest hair appeared to be on the verge of exploding. "She's looking for an easy out. It's simpler to blame my dad than to hunt for the real killer."

That was a lot to assume from Sarah's merely wanting to talk to Dmitri, Connor thought but didn't say. Melissa was still in shock, possibly, not thinking straight.

"Will you help?" Melissa asked again, hands clasped in a prayerful attitude.

"I'm afraid sleuthing wasn't included in my chiropractic training," Connor said mildly.

Melissa transferred her fierce gaze to Diana. "I'm no sleuth either," Diana said. Connor wondered why the statement seemed to make her feel guilty. One of the facets of her personality that he particularly liked was that she usually met people's eyes directly, but right now she was studying her fingernails, frowning as though they might have some terrible flaw in them.

"Sarah would never railroad anyone," Connor assured Melissa.

Melissa gave a laugh that sounded more like a bark, then jumped up, jerking her chair back with enough force to make it topple. Startled out of her silent contemplation, Diana caught the chair a second before it would have hit the tiled floor.

"I should have known you wouldn't help," Melissa said. Her voice had a bitter note in it. "People in this town are all self-centered. Mama always said so."

With that, she stumbled out of the kitchen, ricocheted from the galvanized steel pipe that formed the stair railing, then hauled the front door open. The crash of the door behind her seemed designed to jar the house's foundation.

"At this point my wife would have reminded me that the poor woman lost her mother this morning," Connor said.

Diana put her hand over his on the table. "Knowing on an intellectual level *why* someone says or does something stupid doesn't usually make it easier to take," she said.

He felt tension drain out of him. He also felt—understood. And he liked the feel of her hand on his.

"You don't think it's possible that Dmitri *could* have killed Rosemary, do you?" Diana asked, removing her hand. "I don't really know the man—I guess I've met him twice—he seemed subdued to me. Apathetic. But then anyone married to Rosemary would have to be apathetic, or he'd—"

She broke off.

"Or he'd have had to kill her," Connor finished for her.

She sighed and nodded, then shifted uneasily in her chair. "I feel so damn guilty," she blurted out.

Connor braced himself for whatever revelation was coming.

"No, of course I didn't *shoot* her. But, well, Rosemary and I had a humongous argument during the last part of the photo receiving session. We almost came to blows."

He'd had to quit helping to log in the photographic entries soon after he started, when he was called to his clinic. A patient's fender bender had resulted in a whiplash injury. "Publicly?" he asked.

"Extremely." She paused, shuddering again. "Rosemary didn't want to accept those wonderful nude photos. The photographer was furious. Gardner Malone. He'd come all the way up from Eugene, Oregon. He's this big, bearded guy—a professional photographer—publishes regularly in some of the top magazines. He called Rosemary a racist. Personally, I don't think she wanted to exclude the photos or him for being black, she was excluding the photos because the people didn't have any clothes on."

She sighed. "I reminded her she'd appointed you and me cochairs of this show and there was nothing in the rules to prohibit nude photos. I wasn't about to allow her to shut them out. Rosemary was adamant—with that tight smile of hers in place all the time, of course. Rude all the same. I was rude, too. Mr. Malone was rude. He had his fists clenched as if he wanted to wipe that self-righteous smile of hers right off her face."

She glanced at Connor's face. "I offered to call the clinic and let you arbitrate, but enough of us were on Malone's side she finally backed down, so I didn't have to."

"You're wondering what I'd have said?"

She nodded.

"I'd have said that those nudes are incredibly beautiful, and if I were a judge, I would have agreed with Ashley and given the one of the baby best of show."

She beamed approval at him.

"You didn't tell Sarah about your fight with Rosemary, Flash," he said.

"I hadn't thought about it. I guess I'd better mention it to her before someone else does."

"You think Gardner Malone might have been incensed enough to . . . take it out on Rosemary?"

She shrugged. "People kill people for cutting them off in traffic."

Connor got up and shared the remains of the soup between their bowls, then cleared Melissa's off the table. They ate in silence for a few minutes, then Diana said, "Tell me about your wife. I heard she died of breast cancer before I moved here. That had to be tough."

"Yes."

"People admired her, liked her. They say she was beautiful."

"Yes."

"You still miss her?"

He had to stop answering in monosyllables. "I was angry with Liz at first," he said. "Anger didn't make sense, but there it was. She'd left me, abandoned me. We didn't have kids. She didn't want . . . there was just me."

"You were lonely."

"Still am," he admitted.

"What was she like? Apart from beautiful."

"Good-natured, witty, intelligent, loving, often wise. Gentle. Fashionable. Up to the minute as you put it. Loved this house. Took great care of it and made me do my share. She always said she was happiest being at home. We both loved to cook, enjoyed puttering around in the kitchen together."

Diana sighed. "I guess there's not much Liz and I would have had in common. I'm certainly not gentle or particularly wise, or beautiful, and I can't abide housework or cooking, though I do it when I have to. I have this theory— if we all ate out all the time, we could do away with stoves and refrigerators—whole kitchens, I suppose. I could get by with nothing but a coffeepot. Think of what we'd save on electricity and water bills. No dishwasher necessary. No dishes. I bet we'd come out about equal financially. Think of the employment possibilities for people who like doing that kind of stuff."

She paused. "I do want to have kids. I guess I'd have to cook then. Maybe when I'm forty."

She'd said "forty" as if it was close to the end of life.

"Liz would have liked you, Flash," Connor said. "She admired strong women."

He'd meant that as a compliment. Diana didn't appear to have taken it that way.

"And you certainly are beautiful," he continued. "A different kind of beauty. More casual. More . . . I don't know . . . exotic."

She made a face, contesting the statement. Then stood up. Had he offended her?

Her bowl was empty. So was his. She reached for her baseball cap where she'd left it on a counter and put it on, looping her ponytail through the opening at the back. "Thank you for lunch. That was wonderful soup."

He realized he didn't want her to leave. "Would you like to see a picture of Liz?" he asked.

She tilted her head to one side as if considering. "Sure."

He led the way to the bedroom, hoping she wouldn't think his invitation was a ruse. Why should she think that? Had the suggestion sounded like a ruse? Or was he worried it had because he was suddenly overly conscious of her being in his bedroom?

She picked up the photograph of Liz from the dresser that ran the width of the room. "Lovely woman," she said, then glanced at his face. "I guess you loved her a lot."

He nodded.

Setting down the photograph, she glanced at the king size bed with its all-white coverings, then headed back to the hall. "What about you?" he asked to keep her from leaving. "Why is your ex-husband your last husband?"

Her face clouded. "I didn't enjoy being married, don't ever want to do it again. He expected me to account for every single thing I did. He didn't like my part—" She broke off. "He was jealous of the people I worked with, didn't approve of me socializing with them. Didn't like me working, wanted me to quit. Put guilt trips on me if I worked late. One evening I caught him checking out the underwear I'd put in the laundry hamper. That's when I realized the marriage was never going to make it. I suggested he'd be happier if we were divorced. He didn't agree. I left him, then had to get a restraining order to keep him from stalking me."

"Did he stay away after that?"

She fingered the edge of a black lacquered Japanese tray on the white pedestal hall table. Liz had left mail there for him to post on his way to the clinic.

"No," Diana said finally. Her gaze met his in the mirror above the table, and she turned to face him. "I had to be constantly alert for quite a while. He was somewhat . . . let's say *uncertain* in temperament. I wasn't sure what lengths he might go to. But luckily, he fell for someone else and finally left me alone. It was a relief when he stopped showing up at the—office."

Why the hesitation, he wondered, and remembered she'd left gaps in information before.

"You said something about your parents living in Haight-Ashbury. Were you living there before you came here?"

"Parents? That was a joke for Mountain Man. I was raised by wolves. Werewolves. Stick around, you might hear me howl at the moon."

"I'd like to," he said. "Stick around."

Their eyes met again. Whenever that happened, he felt a connection.

"I'm glad you moved to Port Findlay, Flash," he said.

She nodded but shifted her gaze, obviously feeling awkward. "Me, too." She sighed again. "Except it was better before Rosemary was murdered. It felt . . . safer."

"I don't believe there's been a murder here for a number of years," Connor said. "Probably there won't be another for quite some time."

"Let's hope not." She held out her hand, and he held it for a long moment. Then she said, "I'd better make sure Higby saw to the judges. And I should give the chief a list of the people involved in setting up the show yesterday— she'll probably want it. I can tell her about my fight with Rosemary at the same time."

"And Rosemary's fight with Gardner Malone," he suggested. "Want me to come with you?"

Their eyes met again. She glanced away first. "It's not necessary."

He bowed to the inevitable and opened the door. "It's stopped raining."

He regretted that their dialogue had suddenly become stilted, knew it was probably due to his prying, but felt they could not get anywhere as friends, or more, until she began to trust him.

Quite suddenly, he felt extremely tired. Aftershock, he thought. But there was one silver lining that had turned up today: Diana Gordon no longer protested when he called her Flash.

Chapter 8

"THIS IS PHOENIX," the man said into his cell phone. All of their code names were of cities they'd never lived in.

Denver didn't answer, but Phoenix could hear him breathing.

"I killed the wrong woman," Phoenix said.

The silence at the other end of the phone was like a deep black hole that was waiting for him to fall into it.

He tried not to stammer. It didn't do to show any signs of weakness. "I'll get the right one next time."

"That would be advisable." The words were fairly cordial, but the familiar voice was as chilling as a cold wind from the arctic.

Phoenix thought of explaining that it wasn't his fault, that circumstances had changed, that he hadn't been given a photograph, and the woman had appeared to fit the description. Someone should have told him . . .

"I'll have to wait a while," he said instead. "Have to let

the fuss die down. She was some kind of pillar of the community. The dead woman. The woman I shot. A do-gooder."

Silence. Obviously there was no interest in the dead woman. She wasn't the *right* dead woman.

"I may have to wait until after the photo show is over. The . . . murder, the . . . death . . . is getting too much attention now. Television, newspapers—reporters hanging around downtown."

"Don't wait *too* long," Denver advised softly. A moment later the line went dead.

Phoenix shivered slightly, even though the sun through the window of his office had been spreading heat all morning.

Chapter 9

A COUPLE OF days after the shooting, Sarah and Connor went for an early morning walk in Bromley Park, named for a shipbuilder who had been one of Port Findlay's original nineteenth-century pioneers.

Out of the blue, Sarah had suggested Connor might like to share her ritual. They had enjoyed friendly relations ever since Connor and Liz moved to Port Findlay. At one time she had walked every weekday morning with Liz. She had trusted Liz enough to talk freely to her. Perhaps, Connor thought, he was about to inherit that trust along with Sarah's company. In any case, if he walked regularly, he could give up riding that damn bike uphill.

Yesterday's rain had given way to sunshine. Connor enjoyed the feeling of its warmth on his head as they walked briskly along the manicured trail.

"Ms. Gordon gave me a list of the people involved in setting up those photographs," Sarah said soon after they started out. She sounded exasperated. "I suppose you know how many there were."

"At least a dozen," Connor said. "Twenty if you count the people who handled the photos during the receiving session. Then there were a couple of our brawnier citizens who brought the stands out of storage and put them together. The rest of the helpers hung the photos on the stands."

"Not to mention the people flinging themselves on top of the victim." Sarah sighed. "I understand Ms. Gordon yelled at them."

"She did indeed."

"Good for her," Sarah said, but grudgingly. "The crime scene guys picked up a lot of stuff. Anyone present at a crime scene leaves something or takes something away—fibers, hair, fingerprints, whatever—in this case *everyone* left something. There's no knowing what they took away. Too much stuff altogether. It's going to be next to impossible to figure out what's important and what's not. It would have helped if the janitor had cleaned up thoroughly the night before the murder, but he'd been told not to because he might accidentally damage the photographs."

"I thought I smelled cleaning solution."

"I did, too. Evidently, the janitor mopped the outside aisles only. So everybody's everything is still all over the rest of the place. And that's a concrete floor—we didn't come up with any handy-dandy footprints. Oh, and the janitor hadn't bothered to clean the doorknobs on the back door—usually did those once a week, he says. So all *they* yielded was a bunch of smears. Fingerprints on top of fingerprints."

"Who told the janitor not to clean the whole area?"

Sarah gave him an approving glance. "My question exactly. I asked it of the janitor, and he named your friend Diana. Ms. Gordon says it was Rosemary Barrett's idea, she merely passed it on."

There was a suggestive note in her voice, but he declined to comment.

"How well do you know Diana Gordon?" she asked.

He raised an eyebrow.

"It's only a question, Connor."

"A friendly question, or a police question?"

"Sometimes I'm not sure myself," she admitted. "Probably, official questions don't belong on a friendly walk. So let's say I'm curious as your friend."

"Okay. And as Diana's friend, who wouldn't mind becoming more of a friend, how would you suggest I answer?"

She cocked an eyebrow. "You're *interested* in her? Like *that?*"

"Like *that.*" He hesitated. "I don't know a whole lot about Diana. Probably less than you do."

"You and Diana were together when you discovered Rosemary's body."

"So?"

"She was late showing up."

"And she explained why."

"I have to examine all possibilities, Connor."

"I realize that. But I don't want to go there, okay?"

"Fair enough for now. Later I may get pushy."

After walking in silence for a while, she offered some more information. "The prosecutor/coroner called in the Snohomish County medical examiner. He came across by boat from Seattle to do the autopsy Thursday afternoon."

"Where?" Connor asked, realizing he'd never known, had never needed to know.

"Fenwick's Funeral Home, where we've always done autopsies. Got everything we need right there. Stainless steel table. I'm not surprised you wouldn't know about

that. This is the first homicide we've had in several years."
She sighed. "The ME estimated Rosemary was probably
killed somewhere between eight A.M. and ten A.M. on
Thursday morning. That fits well with what Ms. Gordon
said about Rosemary Barrett expecting to arrive at Quinn
Center around nine A.M."

She paused and squinted at him. He wondered if she
might be hinting that therefore Diana Gordon had known,
was possibly the only person to have known, that Rosemary was going to be at Quinn Center at that time. He decided not to comment.

"Ms. Barrett was killed almost at the spot where she was
found. Seemed as if she might have tried to crawl away but
didn't live long enough to do it, fell over on her back.
Forty-caliber bullet, fairly close range."

She glanced up at his face as though checking for a reaction.

"Your friend Ms. Gordon came pretty close with her
imaginary scenario."

Had she put some emphasis on the word *imaginary?*

"It appears that the shooter came in through the back
door, probably surprised Ms. Barrett soon after she'd
switched on that whole bank of lights. Probably, she turned
around and he, or she, as Ms. Gordon would have me add,
shot her right below the sternum. Bullet hit some major
blood vessels, exited her body, sailed between a couple of
stands, missing the photographs, lodged in the side wall
near the kitchen entrance. Some blood spatter on that one
photograph only. Bizarre all around."

Connor winced. "Flash—Diana and I weren't sure if the
red spots were part of the special effects design."

"*Cosmic* design maybe. It's blood spatter all right. We
haven't yet determined that it was Ms. Barrett's blood, but

it seems most likely, unless the shooter cut his finger on the pistol and waved it at the photo."

Connor glanced at her sideways, but there was no discernible humor showing on her face. He was fond of Sarah, Liz had been fond of Sarah, but while most cops he'd known shared a dark sense of the funny side of life, or death, Sarah seemed to have been shortchanged.

"Ms. Gordon gave me the name of the person who entered that photograph—Milly Schreiber," Sarah added. "Unfortunately, Karen Destry, the woman who logged that particular photo in, didn't get Milly Schreiber's address. There's some kind of law, probably related to Murphy's, that says if one time you don't get the information you absolutely should get, that's the information you're gonna need. Ms. Destry remembers only that the woman was from Portland, Oregon, says she was so horrified by the photo, hardly wanted to touch it even, she passed it on to the people doing the hanging fast as she could."

"You think it's significant? The photo?"

Sarah shrugged and let out a breath. "Who knows? Things I find impossible to believe happen all the time."

"That's almost a line from the sound track of *Cinderella*," Connor said, hoping to lighten things up and get her off the Ms. Gordon track. "The little daughter of a neighbor of ours used to play the CD a lot."

Sarah's expression was blank. "I still haven't tracked down Milly Schreiber," she said. "Portland P.D. couldn't come up with anyone with that name. I talked to Karen Destry again, who said she vaguely remembered one of the people entering photos saying she was going to be out of the country, so she didn't want to bother filling in her address. She'd be in touch when she returned, she said. Ms. Destry thinks that might have been Milly Schreiber. Naturally, the woman didn't pay the entry fee with a check. She paid in cash."

They had reached the waterfront section of the park. A couple of people waved from their sea kayak, Connor waved back. The Cascade mountains were in full view in the east this morning, etched sharply against the sky. The water was choppy, the breeze picking up.

Connor and Sarah circled the snack bar and rest room area and headed out of the park.

"Ms. Destry told me that Rosemary Barrett hated the Schreiber photo as much as she did, but had already had a fight with Diana Gordon over some nude photos and didn't want to waste any more energy. Ms. Barrett's very words, I believe. Fortunately for her, Ms. Gordon had already told me about her fight with Rosemary Barrett."

He was relieved Diana had told her. "There were three nude photos," he said. "Rosemary didn't want to admit them. The photographer—Gardner Malone—was upset. Diana and others persuaded Rosemary to relent."

"You were there?"

"No, I'd been called out on an emergency. Diana told me about the incident after our interview with you."

"She said she'd forgotten about it."

"That's what she told me, too. When she remembered, she left immediately to let you know."

"Hmph. You know this Gardner Malone?"

"No, he arrived at Quinn Center after I left. I expect he'll be at the judges' reception when it's rescheduled. And at the show, of course."

"A week from now, Ms. Gordon said. We can only hope Milly Schreiber turns up, too. I may have to talk to Malone before then." She went quiet and appeared to be ruminating. "I'd been there, I'd have sided with Ms. Barrett," she said at last. "I've never seen any need for people to show off their naked bodies."

Connor decided not to go there either. But he couldn't resist asking if she'd told Diana that.

"I did. She told me that in the interest of artistic freedom, Port Findlay and the Arts Alliance were lucky I wasn't running the show."

He managed to keep a straight face. Diana Gordon was not huge on tact.

"So where does the case seem to be going?" he asked as they came close to the end of the long downhill stretch to downtown and the police station parking lot where they'd met up earlier.

"Too early to tell," Sarah said.

"Melissa Ludlow's afraid you're going to try to pin it on Dmitri."

"So she told me, in between sobs. That young woman's going to drown herself crying."

"Her mother was shot, Sarah," Connor pointed out.

"I remind myself of that whenever I'm around her. But I do believe by the time people are full grown they should show some self-control. She acts like she's in the middle of a soap opera." She shook her head. "By all accounts Ms. Barrett was devoted to her husband and daughter and vice versa. Also, Ms. Ludlow informed me Dmitri Barrett has Alzheimer's."

Connor nodded. "You might talk to Dr. Forbes about him. Rosemary brings—brought Dmitri to me for chiropractic care, but Forbes is his medical doctor."

"Was a time we would automatically suspect the spouse first," Sarah said. "Used to be most homicide cases involved the victim's nearest and dearest or at least someone known. But nowadays the percentage is way down. More strangers getting into the act. As a criminologist put it a while back, we've taken the home out of homicide."

"Why would a stranger kill Rosemary?"

"Fair question. One of the reasons I'm not ruling Dmitri Barrett out." She laughed shortly. "Questioning Dmitri is like entering a house that's been abandoned for a long time—so long it's full of cobwebs and creaky floors. One minute he's telling you his wife should have been canonized, the next you're pretty sure he suspects she's down below shoveling coal into the devil's furnace."

As they paused in the police station's parking lot, where Connor had parked his Jeep Cherokee, she said, "Thanks for walking with me. There aren't too many people I can talk openly with."

"I enjoyed it, too," he said. "And I do need the exercise." He smiled at her. "You set a good pace."

She was frowning, turning away. He thought that possibly she hadn't heard him. "Be careful who you talk to, Connor," she said, suddenly turning back. "Best probably you don't talk to anyone. We're getting some newspaper interest that isn't local."

"In Rosemary's murder? Hardly seems sensational enough."

"Anything can seem sensational once the media gets on the warpath."

He was still pondering Sarah's last comment as he drove to Java Jenny's for a coffee fix. As he parked, he noticed a large group of people milling around with picket signs outside Quinn Center. Why would anyone picket the community center, he wondered, until he got close enough to read some of the signs.

Port Findlay Is a Racist City.

Don't Spend Your Dollars in a Town That Discriminates.

Boycott Racist Port Findlay.

Black Bodies Are Beautiful.

As he watched, a pickup truck drew up near the pick-eters and a couple of men in cowboy hats got out and started waving a Confederate flag. The picketers immediately formed themselves into a phalanx ready to do battle.

"Jeez!" the young barista said. She was hanging out of her drive-up window. "Are we going to have a riot right here in downtown Port Findlay?" She seemed to relish the idea. "What's it all about, Dr. Callahan?"

Not wanting to say anything about Rosemary Barrett trying to refuse nude photos—black nude photos—or even about her at all, Connor hesitated, and heard sirens. A couple of black-and-whites hurtled along Rose Street. Sarah Hathaway climbed out of the first one and faced off with the group, arms folded. Connor saw her mouth move but couldn't hear what she said. Within a couple of minutes the cowboys had climbed back in their pickup and the picketers were dispersing. One tough lady, Sarah!

Chapter 10

THERE HAD TO be a good chunk of Port Findlay's population crowded into the flower-filled nondenominational chapel, Connor thought. Rosemary, of course, had sung in the choir and worked tirelessly at most of the chapel's events.

Probably the presence of the Seattle TV Channels' vans in the parking lot also had something to do with the turnout. Although the picketing outsiders had folded in the face of Sarah's warning, media attention to the as-yet-unsolved murder had kept interest high during the intervening days. Connor couldn't imagine that anyone would expect something to happen at Rosemary's memorial service, however.

"This is some kind of circus," Diana Gordon murmured as she sat down next to him.

He hadn't seen her since Melissa Ludlow's visit. Things had been busy at the clinic. Well, that was his excuse anyway. Truth was, he'd been scared by the strength of his own feelings that day. He'd thought the cause might be the extra emotion connected to Rosemary's murder. All the same, though he'd been tempted to stop in at Photomania on his way to lunch a couple of times, he'd resisted the idea.

Diana was wearing a long, narrow, black-and-white patterned skirt with a tailored black jacket. Her hair was tied back low on the nape of her neck with a black ribbon. She looked elegant, but it didn't seem appropriate for him to tell her so here and now. All the same, he was glad he was dressed well himself today, in his best suit, a charcoal gray, complete with the required white shirt and sober tie. Probably unseemly to even think about it, he thought.

"Did you hear about the picketers?" Diana asked.

He nodded. "Sarah scared them out of town."

She made a face. "So I heard. That woman would quell anyone's fun. She should have let them fight it out. Free speech and all that."

She'd called herself a bleeding heart liberal, he remembered.

"She's the chief of police, Flash, she's supposed to preserve the peace."

"I suppose." She sighed. "Evidently someone called a local reporter and told him about the demonstration. When he showed up, he got three or four different stories about Rosemary banning the nudes. Mostly grossly exaggerated. Someone told him the man who entered the nude photographs in the contest was mad enough at Rosemary to kill her, but another man had pulled him off her. AP picked up on the whole story."

Connor groaned.

"Did you see Joshua Patton?" she asked.

"Patton came? Are you serious?"

"He's sitting right down front."

Connor craned his neck. Diana was right, Patton was

sitting near Dmitri and the Ludlows. The pastor didn't approve of a separate room for the bereaved family. Being among friends was better for them, he always said. Connor didn't remember much about Liz's funeral, so he couldn't vouch for the veracity of the theory.

The service was long, with much emphasis on Rosemary's devotion to Port Findlay's community activities. After the service and hymns sung by the choir Rosemary had belonged to, several people accepted the minister's invitation to say a few words. Al Rutherford spoke at length, mopping his forehead with a large blue-bordered handkerchief from time to time. He was as loyal to Rosemary in death as he had been in life. There was no doubt Rosemary deserved to be canonized for all she had done for the town. "A woman for all seasons," he concluded, mysteriously.

Melissa, tearfully and with great drama, read a poem she had written for her mama—a bad poem.

"It might not have been so awful if it hadn't rhymed," Diana breathed in Connor's ear. "Coupling saint with ain't was unfortunate."

A moment later, she apologized, still in the same breathy whisper that stirred the hair behind his ear. "I shouldn't have made fun," she said. "The poor little woman is really suffering."

Connor nodded, then reached over and took hold of her hand, to show he wasn't sitting in judgment, and also because he wanted to hold her hand. She didn't seem to mind.

Melissa concluded by announcing that her father hadn't felt well enough to attend the brief service preceding his wife's cremation, but he wanted to say a few words now. People should bear in mind that he was afflicted with Alzheimer's disease and might not remember why he was here.

Dmitri stood up at the podium for a long, silent moment. Older than Rosemary by a decade or more, he was a tall man, sturdy but pale. The shirt beneath his dark suit seemed too tight in the neck.

"My wife was wonderful woman," Dmitri said as people were starting to get restive and exchange embarrassed glances. "Loyal, kind, always concerned with other peoples."

Connor frowned. The man's voice was stilted. He had never, in Connor's experience, had much to say, but he'd not previously sounded quite so . . . rehearsed.

Melissa approached her father and took his arm. He gazed at her questioningly as if she were a stranger, then shook her off. "Meanest woman ever lived, Rosemary," he said into the mike. "Never know when she will blow up. Wicked woman. Make my life hell ever since marriage."

A shock wave swept through the entire gathering. Melissa and Al were desperately trying to pull Dmitri away from the microphone. For an older, supposedly sick man, he was exhibiting some strong resistance.

"My daughter tell you I probably not remember anything to say," he continued with surprising force. "You want know what I don't remember? I don't remember asking Rosemary marry me, no time. She grabbed on to me. Made me change name, said nobody would know how pronounce Baratynsky. Where's problem with this? Say like spelled. But no, I have to change, make Barrett instead. What do I know, immigrant, lousy English? What do I have Rosemary wants? Money. Family money. Rosemary like money."

The pastor had finally come out of his stupor and had eased Melissa aside and taken hold of Dmitri's other arm. Together, he and Al hustled the old man away from the microphone and into the waiting hands of portly Dr. Carl Forbes, who was Dmitri's physician. Chief Sarah Hathaway showed up about the same time, and the pastor greeted her with apparent relief.

With a signal to the organist, Pastor Reynolds got the choir going on "Amazing Grace" and started signaling each row to leave the chapel, while Melissa was telling the gathering over the microphone that her father hadn't known what he was saying, his grief and the Alzheimer's had affected his brain, making him paranoid.

Arts Alliance members surrounded her, offering sympathy and comfort, finally persuading her away from the podium. Someone announced there would be a reception with refreshments in the adjoining meeting hall.

"Wow!" Diana said once they were outside. "That was quite a mouthful. Poor old Dmitri. You think he was telling the truth? He sounded quite violent. Almost makes me believe he might have killed her."

"I've an idea everyone who was in the chapel is going to think it's possible," Connor said, noticing that Dr. Forbes was getting into the back of a police car driven by Sarah Hathaway. Dmitri Barrett was sitting bolt upright in the seat next to him.

Hearing loud voices nearby, Connor turned, then nudged Diana to get her attention. A few paces away, Joshua Patton was being interviewed by Art Wellington, one of the better-known Seattle TV reporters.

"Yes, most unfortunate," Patton was saying. "I was the one who found her, you know. Right there in the Special Effects lineup of photographs, on the floor beneath . . ."

He paused. "Beneath the easels," he finished smoothly.

"He was going to tell about that awful photo," Diana whispered.

Connor nodded. "Good thing he thought better of it."

"It was a terrible shock," Patton agreed with the reporter. "At first, I didn't realize the poor woman had been shot. I even tried to resuscitate her. Gave it my best . . . effort. But it was too late." He shook his head sadly. "No, actually, I *hadn't* met her before. But I talked to her on the phone when she invited me to judge the show. Charming lady. Refined, articulate. I regret I didn't have a chance to meet her while she was . . ."

He let his voice trail away again.

"But of course," he said in reply to the reporter's next question. "Life goes on, the show must go on also. We've rescheduled the photography show for Saturday. I'll be coming in early to finish judging the last section."

"Where the body was found," the reporter intoned solemnly.

"Exactly," Patton agreed.

He made eye contact with the camera. "You should all come!" he said enthusiastically. "There are some wonderful photographs, some amateur, some professional. This is one of the few shows in the state that permits both. Everyone gets their day in the sun."

"I ought to sue him for plagiarism," Diana said. "And what's up with that '*We've* rescheduled?' Like he's doing all the work?"

Connor didn't answer. He was speechless. Not with indignation . . . with sardonic amusement for the strange ways people had of behaving.

Patton moved on toward the next building, evidently intending to attend the reception, nodding as he passed in recognition of Connor, ignoring—or not noticing—Diana.

"Prig," she muttered under her breath. Or maybe it was "Prick."

Just as Connor was thinking this was a good opportunity to offer to buy Diana lunch, she said briskly, "Well, so much for our 'not General Patton,' " then patted Connor's arm. "I can't stay for the reception the Arts Alliance is putting on. I have two separate families coming in for portrait shoots." She consulted her watch. "First one's due in about ten minutes."

Her gaze swept him from toe to head. "You look nice. Smart. I'd better scoot. Thanks for the moral support in there."

That was probably a reference to his holding her hand in the chapel, he decided. *Nothing moral about it,* he wanted to say. He watched morosely as she walked away.

Nice. Smart.

Dull. Is that what she'd meant?

After a solitary lunch in Brady's Cafe—everyone in Port Findlay must have gone to the potluck—he drove uptown to his clinic, relieved that he'd managed to avoid the reception and any further meeting with Melissa Ludlow or "not General Patton."

He was surprised when Tammy Griffith, his office manager, informed him a visitor was awaiting him in his office; amazed and concerned when Melissa Ludlow popped up from the chair on the patient's side of his desk the moment he entered. "Now will you believe me?" she demanded.

"Believe what, Melissa?" he asked.

"Didn't you see Chief Hathaway glom on to my dad? She's taken him off to the police station. She's probably giving him the third degree. He's not responsible. He's confused—out of his mind with grief."

"Shouldn't you be with him, then?" Connor asked hopefully. "What about your children?"

Melissa was shaking her head before he finished the last sentence. "I've sent Wayne to take our attorney down there. My neighbor took Mabel and Douglas home with her. I want you to come to my house with me right now, Dr. Callahan," she continued without pausing for breath. "I have something to show you. Something that belonged to Mama."

"I'm sorry, Melissa, but this is a clinic, remember. I have patients—"

"Your girl said you don't have any appointments this afternoon. You never do on Thursday afternoons she said. You play catch-up on records and so on."

He hoped Tammy had heard herself being referred to as his girl. It might make her think twice before she let someone ambush him again.

"All the same, I'm afraid I do have to take care of—"

Melissa burst noisily into tears.

"I could come up later," he said hastily. "Four o'clock maybe." Her husband and kids should be home by then, he thought. No way was he going to Melissa Ludlow's house while she was alone.

She seized his right hand in both of hers. "Oh, thank you, thank you, Dr. Callahan. I knew you'd help me, thank you."

"Yes, well . . ." Connor had no idea how to deal with this excess of gratitude. He was afraid she was going to kiss his hand or fling herself at his chest again.

Fortunately, Melissa must have decided it would be best to leave before he changed his mind. "Four o' clock," she called back over her shoulder as she hurried out.

Tammy's face appeared around the doorjamb at the same second the clinic door slammed. "You sure you know what you're doin', Doc?"

He let out a breath in a long-suffering sigh. "You got me into it, telling her I wasn't busy. You doing anything at four o'clock?"

"Water aerobics at the Y," she said and rapidly withdrew.

He'd give Diana Gordon another try, he decided as he

took off his suit jacket and removed his tie. Time to get back to work.

A little under a couple of hours later, he approached Diana's studio, a couple of tall, iced caffe lattes in hand, hoping the beverage would predispose Diana in his favor.

Photomania's lobby was empty. Chairs in the waiting area had been strangely arranged, one behind the other in a row. Connor walked into the studio and tracked voices to the back door, which was held open against any draft by a stuffed duck. He went through to the little crescent-shaped beach at the back.

Realizing Diana and Higby were in the middle of a photo session, he stopped abruptly on the threshold. "Sorry," he said.

"Stick around, Connor," Diana said, glancing over her shoulder. "We're almost through here."

She had changed into a white tank top and skinny jeans. Sexy. Some impressive cleavage there. The general atmosphere around Connor seemed suddenly charged.

The photographic subjects were five children ranging in age from about a year and a half to eight. Asian children. Three girls and two boys. Four of them were building a sand castle, the older boy was holding a kite. They were beautiful kids, all dressed in T-shirts and shorts, a natural backdrop of mirrorlike water and blue sky with puffy white clouds behind them.

Connor recognized the Matsuyama family immediately, and stepped back again, but it was too late, the oldest boy had seen him.

"There's Dr. Callahan," he shouted, and all the children jumped up and ran to him. The two younger girls started climbing him as if he were a tree.

After distributing hugs all around, he apologized to Diana and Higby and the children's mother.

"I guess they know you," Diana said, smiling, evidently not at all annoyed that in the children's mad dash, the sand castle had been flattened, the kite trampled.

"Dr. Callahan adjusts us," the oldest boy said proudly. "He cured us of wetting the bed."

Connor laughed. "I should use you in a TV commercial, Thomas."

With his big hands, Higby had the castle rebuilt in no time, while Diana dusted off the kite. "Places, everyone," she said.

But as Diana took the shot, the smallest girl, Emi, climbed out of the sandbox and wandered off. "There she goes again," Diana said cheerfully.

Connor watched as Higby returned the tot to her place, talking to her patiently and lovingly, letting go and backing off as Diana stepped to one side, holding onto the cable release attached to the camera.

"Say cheese!" The children's mother, Tina Matsuyama, a petite, dark-haired woman, was standing with her back to the wall of the building.

"Tina!" Diana protested.

"Oh sorry," Tina said. She waved her hands at her children. "No cheese, okay? Forget the cheese. Miss Diana doesn't want you to say cheese, ever, remember? Too unnatural. You aren't advertising toothpaste, Miss Diana says."

Diana laughed. The little girl wandered off again.

Higby brought the child back into the group, then stood poised on the sidelines. "Let's all sing," Diana suggested. "All together now: 'I'm a little teapot, short and stout, here is my handle, here is my spout. When I get all steamed up, hear me shout, tip me over, and pour me out.'"

Higby and the children all sang along with her, one little boy waving his spade in time to the beat.

"Yay!" Diana yelled. The children all giggled, and she clicked off several shots.

Connor stood by while each child hugged Diana and was hugged in return, after which they all had to be hugged by Higby and then Connor. Tina shepherded them all into the building, then into the rest room and out again. Higby told her to come back in half an hour to see the proofs on the computer. "Me, too, me, too!" little wandering Emi kept saying as they all went out into the street.

"That was one of the most amazing things I've ever seen," Connor said.

Diana smiled. "Aren't they great kids? Emi's a kick. Tina was so thrilled when she started walking last month. She was a bit late, and we were all worried. Well, you probably know all that. Now Tina's not so sure it's such a blessing."

"I'm guessing you like children as much as I do."

"Love them. Good ones and naughty ones. Little ones and big ones. Going to have some of my own someday."

Higby was clattering chairs around in the waiting area. "I guess the kids were playing train out here," he called.

Connor handed Diana one of the lattes he'd bought. "You are a lifesaver," she said. "Higby fixed me a sandwich when we got back from the service, but we didn't take the time to make coffee."

Connor took a sip from the other cup, pleased with himself. And her. "You do whole families often?"

"Whenever they buy one of my package deals—each child's birthday and special holidays like Easter and Christmas, complete with Higby Bunny or Higby Claus."

"Not forgetting Higby Pumpkin at Halloween," Higby called.

Diana laughed. "We started with the Matsuyamas on

Emi's first birthday. Great family, aren't they? Lovely manners!"

"And always affectionate," Connor added.

She smiled and led the way into her small office near the back door, seated herself at her computer, and set down her coffee container. "Thank you for this, you're a wonderful man. Did anyone stage any new demonstrations for the TV cameras in the wake of Dmitri's revelations?"

"Not as far as I know. I didn't hang around after you left."

"The noon news from Seattle featured a few sound bites from a couple of interviews outside," Higby said from the doorway. "They didn't get inside to hear Dmitri, God be thanked, but they brought up the whole race issue again. They're making it sound as if all of us in Port Findlay are members of Ku Klux Klan."

Diana glanced up from the computer. "I don't think anyone would mistake you for a Klan member," she said.

The lines on Higby's brown face lifted into a smile, then rearranged themselves into a frown. "Too bad Empress Rosemary didn't get to see the damage she caused, making such a fuss about those photos," he said.

"I thought you liked Rosemary," Diana commented.

"I *tolerated* Rosemary," he said. "Those news stories weren't altogether wrong, Diana. Ms. High and Mighty was a racist through and through. 'What do I call you?' she asked me once. 'Do you prefer black or African-American?' I was taken aback because of the tone of her voice and the way her lip curled. 'Neither,' I said, trying to make a joke of it, not to be rude like her. 'For one, I am Jamaican, and for the other, I am brown.' She waved a hand, 'Brown, black, what's the difference,' she said, still with that smile she always had."

He paused. "I read about some survey put out by Stanford University. Said people become nicer as they get older. I guess Rosemary didn't read the article. 'You may call me Mr. Sanders,' I told her. But she never did. One way or another, she dissed me enough times there was no possibility of liking on my part."

"Why didn't you tell me she said all that!" Diana said.

"You'd have punched her lights out."

"I would." She swallowed. "I guess somebody did." She frowned ferociously at the computer screen.

"You do all your work on the computer?" Connor asked to change the subject.

She shook her head, still fingering keys. "Straightforward digital portraits like this, sure. But I still prefer the results I get with thirty-five millimeter when it comes to anything artistic, or for my vintage photos. The vintage photos are always black-and-white or sepia. In my opinion, doing them in color would be like colorizing old black-and-white movies—losing all the artistic values."

She hesitated. "I love old movies, and old television shows. I watch reruns whenever I get the chance. When I was a kid—"

Connor paid attention, but she went back to the original subject. "Earlier, before Tina and the kids came for their portrait session, I had another family in, here on vacation. The Wallingford family. Great group. Higby and I set up a Wild West stagecoach robbery. People love that! I do, too!"

"I saw that set last time I was here," Connor said. "I liked the old French dueling pistols, and wasn't that a blunderbuss I saw?"

She laughed. "It was indeed. For those photos I'll do my developing the old-fashioned way. In a darkroom. My last husband . . ."

She grinned up at him briefly. "You'll remember him, I

guess. He was a photographer. I inherited some of his old photographic equipment. I could send my thirty-five-millimeter stuff to a lab the way everyone else who's still using it does nowadays, but there's something about film and paper. Besides which, digital cameras require more light, and though digital prints really come alive on the computer and you can send them all over the world if you want to, they don't have the fidelity of image I can get with film materials when it comes to printing."

She hesitated before going on. "The higher truth here is that I'm a romantic. . . . I *like* messing around in a dark-room."

She grinned mischievously up at him, obviously realizing she'd said something that sounded suggestive.

Smiling back, he felt that some kind of clock inside him, a clock that had stopped a couple of years ago, had begun to tick again. Maybe it was blood moving through his veins again. *Veins?* he repeated to himself. *Is that what I'm calling it now?*

Higby had discreetly retreated to the other end of the studio, where he was putting a new set together.

"I need to talk to you, Flash," Connor said.

"Talk away, Callahan," Diana said. "I can do this and listen."

"I was hoping you might do me a favor."

"Always happy to oblige, but I have to get these proofs ready for Tina."

"I can wait. I'm through for the day. Would you possibly be finished by four o'clock?"

Her profile showed a sideways grin. "You doctors are all alike. Dr. Forbes, Dr. Parker, Dr. Callahan. Days off on Saturday and Sunday. Morning appointments only on Tuesday. Golf on Thursday."

"I'm not a golfer, and I work all day Tuesday." He

laughed, then admitted, "I usually take Thursday afternoons off. Sometimes I go fishing. I've even fished with Gary Parker. But not today."

"Hmmm." Her attention had returned to the computer. After a few seconds she said, "I'd promised myself I'd tidy up the prop room when I got through here. Why don't you tell me what's on your mind?"

He took a deep breath, followed by another mouthful of milky coffee. "Melissa Ludlow wants me to go up to her house."

Her fingers stalled on the keys, and she gazed up at him.

"She says she wants to show me something."

"Ho-ho! What do you think she has in mind?"

"She *said* it has to do with her mother."

"So, are you going?"

"I don't want to go alone."

"You are as wise as you are wonderful." Her smile faded. "You're asking me to go with you." She became extremely busy on the keyboard, then swore softly as she evidently made an error. "I don't want to get involved with anything more to do with Rosemary's murder, Connor."

"Me neither, but I feel sort of obligated."

"Why?"

"Because she asked me, I guess."

"She has a husband, she could ask *him*."

He decided not to press his luck by saying anything more.

After a few minutes, she turned the computer monitor so he could see the screen, clicking keys to show him several poses. The final one was a great photograph, and he told her so. Every child had come alive with joy. The little wanderer was especially adorable.

Liz had been unable to have a child, hadn't wanted to consider adoption.

Connor felt guilty for even remembering that.

"Okay," Diana said abruptly.

"It's beautiful," he said, thinking she meant the photograph.

"Okay, I'll go with you to Melissa Ludlow's house," she said.

"Thank you, Flash," he said, his voice loaded with relief.

"You really were scared to go alone, weren't you?" she said as she pulled a tan cord shirt over her tank top an hour later.

Tina and family had been and gone in the meantime, after choosing several of Diana's photos to be printed.

"Terrified," he admitted.

Chapter 11

MELISSA LUDLOW'S BUNGALOW was as neglected inside as the patchy dry lawn that surrounded it. Colorful plastic toys had been abandoned in the entryway and what Diana could see of the living room beyond. A layer of dust lay over the cheap furniture, a laundry hamper on wheels stood next to an easy chair, the chair itself was full of clothing that was apparently waiting around to be folded. Melissa wasn't the neatnik her mother had been. Diana was not an obsessive housekeeper, but she was usually tidy.

Melissa herself was as disheveled as always. She'd changed out of the long black dress she'd worn to her mother's memorial service, into the same dress she'd worn the day her mother died. No, it was a different color. Navy blue with little yellow flowers. Maybe long, dowdy dresses were all she had in her clothes closet.

Melissa had lost her mother one week ago, Diana reminded herself. Give her a break.

Nah, this mess was a lot more than a week old.

"I got Wayne to take Mabel and Douglas to the movies after he came home," Melissa said after smiling gratefully at Connor, ignoring Diana. "I don't want him to know I'm talking to you."

"I'm not sure it's a good idea to keep it from—"

"Mama never liked Wayne. He's an automobile mechanic, you know."

"A good mechanic," Connor said. "He's worked on my SUV a few times."

"Yes, well, Mama never thought he was good enough for me, she kept on telling me to wait for someone better, but nobody better was interested in . . ." Her voice trailed away on a sigh, and she gestured him into the living room.

Diana figured she'd somehow become invisible, but she trailed along anyway.

Connor twitched his eyebrows at her. She raised one of hers back.

Melissa hoisted the pile of clothing off the chair and dumped it into the hamper, then tipped another chair to remove a large tabby cat. Reassembling itself on a nearby sofa, the cat began scratching itself behind the left ear with a rear paw. Melissa gestured a vague invitation to sit. Connor sat. Diana followed his lead after a moment's hesitation, it having occurred to her to wonder if the cat had fleas.

She became aware that all the chairs in the room pointed in the direction of the biggest TV set she had seen outside of Costco. A huge stack of kiddy videos had toppled onto the floor from a shelf at one side. A whole parenting story right there, she thought.

"I still want you to find out who killed my mother," Melissa said to Connor, picking up where she'd left off a couple of days earlier, still ignoring Diana.

"The police—" Connor began.

"I have something for you to start with," Melissa interrupted. Picking up a laptop that had been leaning against a wall, she placed it on the end table next to Connor's chair. "This belonged to Mama."

She stood back, arms and lips folded, as if nothing more needed to be said.

Connor raked one long hand through his tow-colored hair as though trying to stir up some kind of response. "I'm not sure I . . ." was all he could come up with. Diana wasn't sure she could help him out. What a nice man he was to come this far, she thought.

"Mama brought that computer to me some time ago," Melissa said, flopping down on the sagging sofa next to the cat. "She said if anything happened to her, like if she ever died of a heart attack the way *her* mother did, or if she had an accident, I was to do something to it."

"Do what?" Connor asked.

"I can't remember. Something to do with the hard drive. I wasn't paying much attention. I don't know anything about computers. Don't want to. But this morning I remembered what she'd said and wondered if she'd had some kind of premonition that something *would* happen to her. So then I thought there might be a clue in the computer."

"Did she say anything about anyone threatening her?" Diana asked.

Melissa shook her head, then started to cry. "I thought she was being silly about maybe having a heart attack, the way her mama did. Though she never was, really. Silly, I mean. But I couldn't imagine Mama ever dying. She was so strong always, much stronger than me."

She swiped at her nose with the back of her hand.

Standing, Connor picked up a box of tissues from the top of the enormous TV. Handing it to Melissa, he asked, "Why did you want me to come over, Melissa? You should give the laptop to Chief Hathaway. She would probably have access to a computer forensic specialist. There might even be one on staff—the officers all seem to have several areas of expertise."

"Mama didn't like you or your wife, but she always said you seemed like an honest man," Melissa said. "I never heard her say that about anyone else in this town. I don't know why she didn't like you. You've always been nice to me. I like you a lot." She gazed hungrily at him.

Connor showed alarm. Diana coughed to hide a strong desire to laugh. Melissa switched her gaze. "Mama didn't like *you* one bit either."

"Thank you for sharing," Diana said faintly.

Connor leaned toward Melissa, his hands curling as if he wanted to shake her. "You have no business being rude to Diana," he protested. "She was kind enough to come here simply because I asked her to help me help you. You must apologize to her at once!"

Melissa took refuge in tears. "I wasn't being rude. I was repeating what Mama said. I don't know anything about Diana."

"Your mother didn't know anything about me either," Diana said. "Why would she *say* something like that?"

"I don't know." Melissa was whining now. "I'm sorry I said anything. I'm sorry I told you. Please don't be mad at me. I can't bear it when people get mad at me."

Diana pulled herself together. Probably, the stupid little woman had made up the statement out of some kind of spite. Obviously she was interested in Connor for other reasons than the hope that he'd help her father. She could be jealous of Diana, upset because Diana had come here with Connor.

"Okay, Melissa," she said. "There's no need to make a big deal out of it. Let's forget it ever came up."

Melissa appeared relieved. She turned to Connor. "Don't you be mad at me either, Dr. Callahan. I didn't mean to make you mad. I want you to help me. I *need* you to help me. I'm so afraid for my dad, and you were kind to my dad when he wandered off that time."

Connor frowned. "I happened to see Dmitri on the wharf in his pajamas when I was heading toward the ferry—"

He broke off, shaking his head.

"Maybe your mother wanted you to erase the hard drive," Diana suggested. "I agree with Dr. Callahan, by the way. You should take the laptop to Chief Hathaway."

"I want Dr. Callahan to poke around in the laptop and see if there's anything anybody should know about," Melissa whined. "That's not much to ask, is it? All Mama's private business is on there. I don't want the police pawing through that."

She gazed at Connor with wet, pleading eyes. "Please, Dr. Callahan. I'll pay you. I have money, my own money, I sell stuff on eBay sometimes. You'd be surprised . . . whatever it takes . . ."

"I'm not holding out for money, Melissa," Connor said stiffly. "I wouldn't dream of accepting money from you."

He had taken up a position with his back to the TV, hands pushing back his suit jacket to take refuge in his trouser pockets, frown lines creasing his forehead. Diana liked the lines on his face. They made him appear good-natured even when he was frowning. "I don't think—" he began.

Melissa sat forward. "Lena Green told me when she came to baby-sit that you taught her how to use her computer."

He shook his head, apparently irritated now. "I showed

Lena how to get on the Internet. That hardly makes me an expert."

"You don't even have to tell me what's *on* the computer," Melissa said, starting to cry again. "Just see if there's any kind of clue . . ."

Connor sent a hunted glance Diana's way. She held out a moment longer, then remembered that the reason she'd become a private investigator was because justice was important to her. She'd never told anyone that because it seemed pretentious to think she could have that important an effect on crime. All the same, no matter how she felt about stupid little Melissa, if tough lady Sarah Hathaway really was inclined to shove Rosemary's murder off on poor old Dmitri . . .

"I'd be willing to help if you want to have a go at it," she said to Connor.

Connor studied her face a moment, then said, "Okay." To Melissa, he added, "One condition. I have to warn you that if we do find anything important, we'll have to turn the laptop over to Chief Hathaway."

Melissa frowned. "Oh well, do whatever you have to." Standing, she picked up the laptop in its case and thrust it into Connor's reluctant hands. "Thank you," she said fervently. A minute later, he and Diana were outside the door, which was closing behind them.

"Speaking of being railroaded," Diana said, but she really wasn't as grouchy as she sounded. She was actually feeling quite pleased with herself.

Why was that? she wondered as she and Connor climbed into his Jeep and fastened their seat belts. Could it possibly have anything to do with the prospect of having agreed to spend some time with Connor Callahan?

* * *

"ROSEMARY BARRETT WAS an inexhaustible wonder woman," Diana said an hour and a half later, pushing an errant strand of black hair away from her forehead.

They had been sitting at Diana's desk in the little office at the back of her studio, roaming through Rosemary's laptop. The office setting had been Diana's idea. Connor had suggested they might work on the computer at his house, but she'd remembered how nervous she'd felt in his bedroom, in the presence of Liz's photograph. Not only had she wanted, for one mad moment, to tell him all about her past life as a private investigator, which she didn't want *anyone* in Port Findlay to know about, she had also had a physical and indisputably sexual response to the mere fact of the two of them being in the same room as a bed. She was now afraid to trust herself alone on his territory, worried that she'd suddenly feel compelled to jump his bones.

The only thing that had saved her before was the huge bed itself. All that empty space. All that virginal white: pillowcases, coverlet, blinds, chairs.

While they were on the way to Photomania, she'd finally allowed herself to admit—to herself—that she was extremely attracted to Connor Callahan, but she still wasn't sure if she wanted to do anything about it, or even how she felt about it.

Perhaps more importantly, she still wasn't sure how *he* felt about it. It was fairly obvious that he had an idea or two on his mind where she was concerned. But if he was still hung up on his wife, it would be a huge mistake for her to get involved with him.

One thing in his favor, she thought now, Connor's late wife's photograph had been a five by seven in a stand-up frame. He hadn't sanctified Liz by commissioning some huge portrait done in oils, framed in gold, and hung on the wall to gaze suspiciously down on any woman with designs on her husband.

Connor was scrolling again through the titles of the various directories listed under My Documents, in Rosemary's computer.

"Do we need to go through the garden club notes?" he asked.

"We did that," Diana reminded him. "It was mostly lists of plants people had volunteered to bring for sale at library benefits."

They had also gone through Rosemary's records of Quinn Center's board meetings, city council board meetings, the boards of a couple of charities, Arts Alliance member lists, the year's calendar, and choir schedules.

"All work and no play . . ." Connor commented.

"To some people work is play," Diana pointed out. She certainly couldn't criticize that attitude; she spent most of her time working.

"There's one thing notable about this schedule," Connor said.

Diana stared at the screen. And suddenly saw what he meant. "There's nothing happening on Tuesdays."

"Right."

"So Rosemary took one day a week off. Maybe she was human after all."

"The woman wrote down which days she did laundry and when she rotated the plates from top to bottom on the shelves in the kitchen cabinets," Connor pointed out. "Why would she skip Tuesday altogether?"

Diana shook her head. "I guess we'll have to ask Melissa."

Connor groaned.

"I'll do it now," Diana said and reached for her office phone.

"Of course Mama did something on Tuesdays," Melissa said. "She did stuff every day. Board meetings, working at the food bank, or the hospital, or yanking the stupid bear grass out of the library flower bed. Whatever. Mama never, ever, took a day off."

"Well, why wouldn't she put whatever she did on Tuesdays on her schedule?"

Melissa sighed. "Mama didn't tell me everything. But I do know this: my whole life she was never home all day, hardly ever home at all, once she got her chores done."

Diana repeated the conversation, such as it was, to Connor. "There was a lot of emphasis in her voice on that bit about Rosemary hardly ever being home Melissa's whole life. Makes me wonder how Melissa felt about that. How she really felt about her mama. Whether she was really as devoted a daughter as she wants us to believe."

"What are you thinking here?" Connor asked. "You're thinking maybe *Melissa* killed Rosemary?"

"Well, it wouldn't be the first time a daughter got tired of having her chain yanked."

Realizing she'd sounded rather forceful, she added, "Trouble is, I can identify. So I'm not sure how much of my response is due to my own experience, rather than Melissa's."

"Your mother didn't tell you everything?"

"My mother was hardly ever home. Well, she was home, but hardly ever home for me."

"You told Joshua Patton your parents were flower children in Haight Ashbury. You told *me* they were were-wolves."

"All true."

He was listening attentively. He did that. As if he'd been

waiting a long time to hear whatever she had to say. It was a beguiling trait that tempted her to bare her soul. Hard to resist.

"Well, they didn't grow hairy coats like the *Star Wars* Wookiee, but they frequently howled at the moon."

"They were high?"

"Should have been flagged as a danger to air traffic."

His hand covered hers, which were clasped on the desk. "What happened to them?"

She laughed shortly, bitterly. "They survived. Gave up drugs. Became vegans instead."

"You made a crack about being trailer trash. The day Rosemary was murdered."

"You always remember what anyone says?"

"Only if the person matters to me." He was gazing at her with complete concentration, his blue eyes warm, as though he hadn't been put off by her description of what other people referred to as family.

"Yes, well, we lived in a trailer. I left when I was sixteen, never looked back."

She paused, then laughed wryly. "Well, obviously, I do look back, I just did, but I try not to."

"You turned out extremely well," Connor said.

"You don't really know me," she countered.

"I would if you'd let me."

She took in a deep breath and let it out. What she really, really wanted to do, this minute, was to lean over against the warmth of him, to accept his caring, to let go and see what would happen.

"I think I'm punchy," she said abruptly. "Let's call it a day, okay?"

"Okay." The word was fine, the tone filled with obvious reluctance. After clicking out of the word processing program, Diana shut down Windows and closed the laptop's lid.

As Connor reached for the computer, Diana became abruptly aware of how large and shapely his hands were. She pushed her chair back and stood up. "We can tackle this again another time, maybe."

"Maybe we could—" Connor began.

"Another time," Diana repeated.

He had stood up, too, and was showing disappointment. "Okay," he said again. Evidently he wasn't going to push at all.

So why was she now disappointed?

Hormones "R" Us.

She walked him to the studio's lobby. She was about to unlock the front door when he put his free hand over hers, leaned forward, and kissed her on the mouth without touching her in any other way. It felt wonderful. She kissed him back. Sometimes hormones weren't all that bad.

"Maybe we need to think about this," she said after they'd separated and were staring at each other.

"I've *been* thinking about it," he said.

She nodded. "Me, too." As his smile widened, she added, "I'm not ready, Connor."

"Okay," he said, one more time.

Chapter 12

"BECAUSE OF THE unusual circumstances, Al Rutherford and the other Arts Alliance officers have decided to forget about tradition," Connor told Liz.

Never a bad idea, he imagined her responding.

It was early Saturday morning, a couple of days after Rosemary's disastrous memorial service. Connor was back up at the cemetery.

"Rather than delay the photography show another day, we're having the judges check that last section—Special Effects—before the judges' reception at ten o'clock today, then we'll open the doors to the general public at noon. That way the judges don't have to hang around an extra day. Flash and I want the damn show to be over."

No response in his mind from Liz, but he was sure she'd have understood their wanting to put the events of the past nine days behind them.

"Dangerous Dmitri's still at large," he said. "Sarah

couldn't get any sense out of him, but I'm pretty sure it wasn't the Alzheimer's talking at the memorial service; that was Dmitri being truthful. It seems likely that Rosemary the do-gooder had a whole other persona we didn't know about. If you remember, we saw some of that in the way she treated you when you were sick."

Still no Liz talking in his mind. Was his conscience bothering him, drowning out the memory of her voice?

"I'm getting a bad case of the hots for Diana," he blurted out.

That stirred up some brain activity. *Surprise, surprise!* he imagined her saying. At the same moment the wind came up, rattling the leaves of the trees, blowing right at him, making his hair stand straight up. "Okay, okay," he said, not altogether jokingly. "I get the message."

"ASHLEY ROBINSON'S DOCTOR says she's suffering from post-traumatic stress syndrome," Vice-president Al told Connor and Diana. "I spoke to her father. He said she's been having terrible nightmares. The murder scared her so much she doesn't want to come back to Port Findlay ever again. Sorry to let us down and all that, but she'd never seen a dead body before."

Diana sighed. "I guess that explains why she didn't show up. It would have been nice if she'd let us know."

"Joshua Patton did a good job on the Special Effects section," Al said. "He's a fine photographer," he added, echoing Rosemary's sentiments as always.

"Sure he is," Diana said with a hint of sarcasm in her voice. Turning her back on Al she said to Connor, "Milly Schreiber hasn't shown either."

Connor sighed. "Not much we can do about that, I guess."

She smiled at him. He was wearing a black, long-sleeved shirt with tan chinos. A great combination. Sexy.

A large group of people who had entered photographs in the show, including Gardner Malone, were trailing Joshua Patton as he hobbled around the hall. Patton stopped by Connor and Diana and smiled at both as though he were totally delighted to see them again.

"Here I am," he said. "Ready and willing to comment on my choices, and Ashley Robinson's, too."

Another big smile.

Diana bit back the remark she really wanted to make. "That's generous of you," she said, her voice neutral.

At that moment, Big Al joined the group. Diana and Connor decided to follow along and keep a wary eye on Patton. They weren't going to put up with him hurting anyone's feelings with overly blunt remarks.

Surprisingly, their fears were not realized. Patton handed out compliments right and left. He even said nice things about Gardner Malone's nudes—not a word about overprinting or the baby picture being too sentimental. And he kept *smiling* at people!

He had sent flowers to Dmitri, according to Lena Green. And after the potluck reception that had followed Rosemary's memorial service, he'd told Big Al that he deeply regretted not having met Rosemary Barrett, she had sounded so delightful on the telephone when they made arrangements for him to judge the show.

Diana still thought he was a pompous ass.

There was a feeling of suspense in the air, she decided. People peered over their shoulders as they poked along through the display. Some of them had gathered in little knots in the space beyond the last row and wondered audibly where exactly Rosemary's body had been found.

But gradually they all began to relax and help themselves to the fruit and vegetable appetizers Taylor's deli had put out as a stopgap until the main buffet opened.

"Isn't that tall, bald guy a Seattle reporter, Flash?" Connor murmured, directing Diana's attention to a man standing at the end of the row they were in.

She recognized him. "Gary Thorne. Don't point him out to Patton, he'll be telling him how he's responsible for getting this whole show on the road. I guess Gary's watching us all for signs of racist behavior. Let's hope nobody displays any."

She need not have worried. The reception went off without a hitch. And at noon, when the doors were flung wide, people flooded in. A record crowd. Probably generated by all the news stories, not to mention Patton's TV invitation.

At one-thirty P.M., after joining Joshua Patton and Big Al for lunch in the Quinn Center lobby, Connor and Diana saw Patton off the premises. His good manners during the reception had evidently been something of a strain; he'd had little to say during lunch and seemed as pleased to be leaving as Connor and Diana were to see him go. Though the two cochairs would have to stay on the job until the show closed the next day and all photographs had been returned to the people who had entered them, or set aside to be mailed to those who hadn't been able to attend, their main responsibility—the judging and its aftermath—was finally over. And they would never have to put up with Mountain Man Patton again.

"Sheesh," Diana said as they watched Patton drive his Land Rover out of the parking lot.

"Miserable man, great car," Connor said, then excused himself to go to the rest room.

While she waited for him, Diana wandered over to where Lena Green was pouring tea at one end of the lobby.

Lena presented her with a full cup and a beaming smile. "It gives me so much pleasure to see you and Connor together," she said. "You make a lovely couple. He's a grand-looking guy, and you're almost as tall as he is. Are you wearing heels today?"

Diana admitted she was. Which had nothing to do with Connor, she pointed out. Her wrapped skirt was long and would drag the floor if she didn't wear pumps.

"We're cochairs, Lena," she said firmly. "Nothing more." The last thing she wanted was Lena gossiping about her and Connor.

Lena paid no attention to that statement. "I've been so worried about him," she said.

"Connor? Worried? Why? What's wrong with him?" If there was anything, it might be a good idea to find out now, before . . . *Before what?* she asked herself.

As if she didn't know.

"Well, he seems so lonesome. He goes up to the cemetery all the time, you know, to talk to her."

"Who?"

"His wife, of course. Liz."

"But his wife's—"

"Dead. Yes. He talks to her *grave!*"

Diana stared at the older woman.

"Don't you think that's sweet?" Lena asked.

"I think it's majorly weird," Diana said.

"Well, I suppose he *thinks* he's talking to her spirit, or something," Lena said. "All I know is I've seen him up there at the cemetery, talking out loud. I go up there myself, you see, to take flowers to my late husband's grave. Ted's been gone a long, long time, but it seems a nice thing to do, to take flowers, don't you think? Connor takes flowers up, too. But I don't talk to Ted. Come to think of it, we didn't talk all that much when he was alive, so it's no wonder."

She turned pink suddenly and smiled at someone beyond Diana's shoulder. "Hi, Connor, want some tea?"

"No thanks, I'll get some coffee later. Diana?"

Still bemused, Diana set her cup down and turned with him to go back to the main hall. But as they walked past the dining area, Sarah Hathaway signaled to Connor to join her at one of the tables. She didn't include Diana in the gesture, but Connor took hold of her arm and moved her along with him.

Sarah, wearing smart civilian clothes—a loden green jacket over a tan and green dress—was sitting with a frail, elderly lady who had cotton candy white hair, a pink-and-white complexion, and bright green eyes that matched her pantsuit. "This is Milly Haliburton," Sarah said, without any inflection in her voice. "She uses her maiden name on her work."

"Milly Schreiber," the woman said with a sweet smile, shaking hands as Connor and Diana seated themselves. She had an empty plate in front of her, along with a cup of Lena's tea. Connor poured himself a glass of water from a pitcher in the middle of the table.

"I came to pick up my photograph and discovered the show had been delayed," Milly said. "Chief Hathaway has been telling me all about the kerfuffle you had."

Milly's accent sounded British, which she confirmed a moment later by telling them she'd been out of the country, visiting cousins in England.

Diana hadn't ever thought of a murder as a "kerfuffle," but she supposed that's what Milly was referring to.

"I've had to inform Ms. Schreiber that her entry is being held as evidence and couldn't be shown today," Sarah said.

"No problem, my dear," Milly said. "As long as I get it back eventually." She flashed a bright smile at Diana and

Connor. "My entry has blood on it, you know," she confided. "The police call that blood spatter."

Diana nodded, not quite knowing what to say. Connor was also silent.

"I'm dreadfully disappointed my photograph didn't win an award, of course," Milly went on. "I think though that from what the chief tells me, the spatters might add quite a bit to the work."

"Add what?" Connor queried.

"Ambience," she said. "And value, of course." Her voice was completely matter-of-fact. "I'm thinking it might fetch a good price on eBay."

Connor and Diana exchanged horrified glances. Sarah narrowed her eyes and put her cop face on.

"That's real blood, ma'am," Connor said. "Mrs. Barrett was shot. Fatally."

The woman nodded solemnly. "Well, now, of course, the chief told me that. That's what I'm talking about. All of that certainly makes the picture unique, don't you think?"

Sarah's eyebrows had climbed, but she seemed as unable as Diana or Connor to come up with a response. Standing, she said, "Please remember that for now I don't want that photograph mentioned anywhere."

"Oh, my lips are sealed," the woman said at once, adding with a little tinkling laugh before getting up and walking away, "Let me know when I can pick it up, and when it's all right to reveal all."

Diana was trying to assimilate all of this on top of the surprising information Lena had given her about Connor. She felt as if she'd entered an alternate universe.

"I'm not sure I'm understanding all that I hear," she murmured.

"Piece of work, Milly Schreiber," Sarah said, apparently thinking she was agreeing with Diana. "Didn't express any sympathy as far as Rosemary Barrett was concerned. No curiosity about who might have killed her. No expressions of concern for the family. All she was interested in was when she could get that damn photograph back."

Diana made an effort to bring herself to the surface. "You classifying her as a suspect, maybe?"

Sarah looked at her directly. "Right now, everyone's a suspect."

Including me, obviously, Diana thought.

After a moment, Sarah went on. "Ms. Schreiber probably doesn't qualify, though. Supposedly she left the country the day after entering the photograph. Said she was staying with relatives in a place called Uxbridge."

She pulled a small notebook out of her jacket pocket. "County of Middlesex, England. We'll check it out, of course. But you wouldn't expect anyone to lie about something like that. Too easy to track. But she sure is . . ."

She paused as though she was at a loss for words.

"Bizarre," Diana suggested.

"That, too," Sarah agreed. "I was about to come up with nutty as a fruitcake, but I think bizarre about covers it."

"Maybe you could accidentally *lose* that photograph," Diana suggested.

Sarah gave her the first approving smile she'd ever bestowed on her. "Don't think that idea hasn't crossed my mind."

"Unbelievable," Connor said as Sarah walked away.

"I need more tea," Diana said. "Having met Milly Schreiber, and exchanged glances with Chief Hathaway and . . ." She hesitated, adding in her own mind the little tidbit Lena had provided. "I'm feeling drained."

"Maybe Milly's a vampire," Connor said, taking her arm again and turning her toward the opposite wall of the main hall, where the buffet table had been set up. "You should have something in common with her," he added with a sideways grin. "Aren't werewolves along the same lines?"

Touché. Maybe she was bizarre herself. "My werewolves were harmless compared to Miss Schreiber."

His expression had become quizzical.

"We can discuss my parentage some other time," she said. *Among other things. Like what's all this about talking to your dead wife?* "Let's relax and be glad it's so peaceful."

Unfortunately, after the early birds left and new visitors arrived, the peace was shattered.

Hearing raised voices, Connor and Diana hurried to the area the sounds were coming from and discovered Gardner Malone, apparently defending his controversial nudes to a man Diana recognized as Otto Schmidt, a longtime resident of Port Findlay and one of the more opinionated members of the Arts Alliance.

Otto was at least eighty, a tough-appearing individual, sporting as much hair on his face as Malone, though his was gray where Gardner's was jet-black. He'd assumed a pugnacious pose, hands in classic, and comedic, boxing mode. Gardner's fists were clenched at his sides as he squinted at Otto.

"Well, I'm sorry she's dead," Gardner was saying as Connor and Diana worked their way through the small crowd that had gathered. "But I still say she was an interfering old biddy. She had no right making insulting remarks about my work. I've won prizes for my work."

"Well, for your damn information," Otto said, dancing a little from side to side, "Rosemary Barrett wasn't the only person who objected to people, includin' an innocent little baby, being displayed nekkid in a family show."

"Family show?" echoed Gardner. "Nobody told me anything about a family show. This is supposed to be Disney? I don't think so. Supposed to be an art show. Photographic art, I believe the advertisements said."

"Well, none of the advertisements asked for pornographic art," Otto said.

"Pornographic! You're calling my work pornographic!"

"There's plenty of talk goin' round about forbiddin' disgustin' crap like that in future shows," Otto said, dancing again, spraying a little spit along with 'disgustin'. "I'm draftin' a petition myself. Goin' right to the city council with it."

Dropping his fists, Otto turned to face the crowd. "Anyone wants to can come by my house and put their John Hancock on the petition to keep garbage like this out of our town."

With that, he grabbed the photograph of the woman off the stand and flung it to the ground.

Gardner let out a howl of rage, and before anyone could intercede, the two started throwing punches at each other, though luckily with little degree of accuracy.

"Do something," Diana said to Connor.

"Why me? I got my main philosophy of life from *Star Wars*: 'Let the Wookiee win.' "

"One's as hairy as the other. Which one's the Wookiee?"

Connor stepped forward at the same moment as Diana. Otto immediately turned his flailing fists on Diana, who simply leaned back to avoid them. Connor moved in, picked the much older man up, and pulled him aside, getting punched in one eye for his trouble.

While Connor was pressing his hand against his eye,

Gardner made as if to push Diana out of the way. It was obviously a complete surprise to him to find himself on his knees, shaking his head, a split second later. It was a surprise to Connor, too. As far as he'd been able to tell from Diana's rapid movements, she had deflected Gardner's shove with her left arm, pulled him down by *his* left arm, while her left hand came up and knocked his head to one side. For a second she remained poised and ready, but then relaxed as Gardner sat back and gazed up at her, apparently stunned speechless.

Sarah had appeared out of nowhere. She stared sternly down at Gardner. "You and I already had our talk, right? You and I had an agreement. I'd believe your story about being innocent of all harmful acts, and you would keep your temper under control. You going to settle down, or do I have to take you in?"

Gardner got slowly to his feet. Picking up the photograph Otto had thrown to the floor, he set it carefully back in place on the stand.

Otto shook his fist at Gardner, but from a distance. "I'm gonna sue your black ass and the other two's white asses for assault and battery," he said.

"I'm the one who got punched in the eye," Connor protested. "Besides, my ass is pink."

Diana laughed. "Mine's sort of an olive tan," she confessed.

Sarah was obviously shocked.

"Nobody asked you to put your face in the way," Otto shouted at Connor.

"*I* didn't even touch you," Gardner said.

"Okay," Sarah said. "It's now or never. Behave yourselves or leave. Those are your choices. Unless you'd prefer cooling off in the city jail."

Still growling, Otto stalked away.

"I'm staying," Gardner said to Sarah. "I've got to find out when I get my trophy."

"About a half an hour from now. A few minutes before closing time," Connor told him. "There'll be a ceremony."

Gardner nodded. "I'll be there, don't you worry."

"I wouldn't have laid a hand on you if you hadn't pushed me," Diana said by way of apology.

To her surprise, Gardner grinned at her. "Hey, I almost forgot, you're the one made the old biddy take in my photographs. You are one tough chick, girl. I don't know that I've ever been taken down so fast. Put me in my place real good."

"Skirt slowed me down," Diana told him cheerfully. "Next time, I'll wear pants."

"Lord help me."

"I THOUGHT YOU did Tai Chi for exercise," Connor said as they walked away. "Balance, you said. Flexibility. Bending like bamboo."

"It was a simple little single whip was all. Willy Cornfoot taught me that move when I was fifteen. He lived next door."

"In the trailer park?"

"Tai Chi is deceptive," Diana said, to avoid answering. "It's slow and graceful when it's done for exercise, but all the moves can be speeded up and used in self-defense. There's even one called *dim mak*—which translates as *death touch*—where you bunch all your fingers together in a certain way and go for some vital spot."

She smiled at the expression of alarm on his face. "It's always a good idea for a girl to know a few self-defense moves, don't you think?" she said sweetly, then relented and added, "Did it upset you that I waded in?"

"Not at all." He made eye contact. "It turned me on."

So maybe the expression hadn't been alarm after all. "I always knew Tai Chi would come in handy someday."

She waved off the people who were crowding around to offer sympathy and help. "We're okay. Better off than the other guys." She tapped Connor's right arm. "Let me see your eye."

He moved his hand away. The white of his eye was bloodshot, and the surrounding flesh was red. "We should get you some ice."

"We're closing up now," Higby said, appearing suddenly beside them. "It is only a few minutes before we intended to. Seems a good idea to do it now."

Diana nodded agreement. "You have enough help?"

"More than enough," he said. "Big Al is going to present the awards. And Chief Hathaway has promised to stick around. That will make everyone think twice about any more disturbances." He grinned. "All the volunteers are agog. After the ceremony, once we have this place cleared out, they can't wait to sit down with a coffee and talk it all over."

He sent a meaningful smile Connor's way. "You two go home. You have had enough excitement." He grinned at Diana, then at Connor. "She showed them, didn't she, Dr. Callahan! That is one strong lady!"

"Yeah, sure," Diana said, clasping the side of her neck and moving it gingerly. "This particular lady now has a pain in the neck."

Higby gave her a smug smile. "Well now, Diana, you are standing next to a chiropractor. Can you crack her neck for her, Dr. Callahan?"

Connor winced. "Chiropractors would rather not use the word *crack,* if you don't mind. An *audible release* is the preferred term."

He gazed at Diana with some concern. "Did you walk over here this morning?"

She nodded.

"I'll drive you to my clinic then. Tammy should be there. Our office manager. Our physical therapist is working today until six, I believe."

Diana moved her neck again, and flinched. "Whatever it takes."

FOG HAD ROLLED in to blanket the water while they were in the community center, not an unusual occurrence in Port Findlay. So far, land visibility was okay. "Have you been treated by a chiropractor before?" Connor asked as he parked at the back of his clinic.

"When I was in—before I moved here," she said.

"You've already told me you used to live in San Francisco," he reminded her.

"Oh, yeah. Sure." She was so used to being secretive, it had become second nature.

Connor opened the clinic door for her. "So you haven't had an adjustment in a year?"

"More than. But I've worked out. I thought I was in good shape. I need to practice that single whip move with more care! I must be doing something wrong."

The office manager, introduced as Tammy Griffith, was a large, pretty woman with bright red hair that seemed to crackle with life. She expressed interest in Connor's discolored eye, and at first jumped to the conclusion that Diana had given it to him and that's how she had hurt her neck.

"We fought side by side, shoulder to shoulder," Connor informed her. "We are allies. All for one, one for all, that's our motto."

"What did the other guys look like?" Tammy asked.

Connor filled her in as briefly as possible, while Diana studied the colorful fish swimming in a large aquarium mounted in one of the waiting room walls.

Shaking her head, Tammy whipped out a clipboard and forms for Diana to fill out. "Who knew a photo show would put you in harm's way," she said. "I'm glad I didn't get involved."

A couple of minutes later, Diana handed over her medical history, which wasn't quite complete. She hadn't seen any need to mention the bullet wounds.

She followed Connor into his X-ray room. "I didn't know I was going to cause so much work."

Connor raised his eyebrows, wincing as his right eye evidently protested. "You thought I'd simply reach over and straighten you out, right there in Quinn Center?"

"Something like that."

He grinned. "Sorry, Flash, we have certain rules of behavior here. If I'd been a medical doctor visiting Quinn Center, you wouldn't have expected me to have you take off your clothes so I could examine you then and there, would you?"

"Well, it might have been interesting."

They gazed at each other fairly intensely following that remark. Connor didn't wince at all, Diana noted.

Connor turned official, very serious, as he finished with the X rays and got her on the table. His hands were cool, gentle, as he stroked her neck. "Here?" he asked, pressing a finger on the spot that was hurting. "You've got it," Diana exclaimed.

With a swift and sudden movement, he adjusted her neck and, for good measure, had her turn first on her right side, then on her left, and on her back, so that he could adjust her spine.

"That was some kind of audible release," she joked as

he helped her off the table. She was completely free of pain, she realized. "You're pretty good at what you do, Callahan. That was amazing."

He smiled at her. "I'm glad it helped. I won't be able to adjust you again, though. I'll refer you to my colleague, Jomo Smith. You'll like him."

"Hey, I have insurance, I'm not a deadbeat. Was it something I said?"

They had reached the reception area. He spoke quietly. "If you were to become my patient, it wouldn't be ethical for me to date you."

"You're planning on dating me? You haven't asked me yet." She narrowed her eyes. "Define dating!"

"I thought we might begin by adjourning to Findlay's Landing. After that, we can see how it goes."

Tammy was following their conversation with as much avid interest as Higby had displayed.

"Well, I suppose we *could* get some fresh ice for your eye from Mac the bartender," Diana said.

A narrow band of sunlight shone through a side window and lit the side of Connor's face. His eyes really were a vivid blue in spite of the damage to the right one.

FINDLAY'S LANDING SERVED a mixture of Scottish and Irish food and drink, as well as the best pizza in town. It was usually crowded, but it was early yet, only a little after six o'clock. Most of the people in there were tourists, it being a weekend. Diana was glad there weren't any locals, at least none she knew, to gossip later about her and Dr. Callahan drinking together.

Mac was happy to supply not only the ice but a proper ice bag to put it in, though he insisted on hearing the full story first. "We'll be getting more press about Port Findlay's racist attitude, for sure," he commented, then took their orders for a Guinness for Connor and a Columbia Crest Chardonnay for Diana.

They sat back and relaxed for a few minutes, looking out at the fog, which appeared to be thickening. Findlay's Landing was on the other side of the wharf from Diana's little beach. All they could see was white foam rippling over the pebbles.

"I'll call Gardner Malone later and apologize properly for all the trouble over his photos," Diana said after a couple of sips of the excellent wine. "And for getting involved in a knock-down-drag-out fight with him."

"You were defending yourself," Connor said, then hesitated. "It's probably a good idea to call, all the same. There's no doubt the man's been badly treated, first by Rosemary, then by Otto. I don't think he even realized he was threatening you, he was so damn mad at Otto."

"I'm damn mad at Otto myself," Diana said.

"Yes, well, he's not too popular with me either," Connor said, still holding the ice pack to his eye. He lifted it away. "Should I ask Mac for a raw steak?"

"Ice is cheaper," Diana said. "The swelling is going down, but you're definitely getting a shiner."

He put the ice bag back in place. "Diana," he said in a meaningful voice that seemed to signify something important was about to be said. Not Flash. Diana.

She was suddenly nervous, but fortunately, that was as far as he got before the pub door opened, letting in some tendrils of mist. Higby, Lena Green, and Al Rutherford walked in.

"Well, look who's here," Lena cried gladly, and settled herself into the chair on Connor's left without any suspicion that she might not be welcome. Droplets of moisture glittered on her silver hair. "I heard you both got into a brawl and came out on top."

Lena had a direct line to all Port Findlay gossip, so it wasn't surprising she'd heard about their episode. "Have you eaten yet?" she went on cheerfully. "What did you have? I'm starved."

A waiter was hovering nearby. "I think I'll go for the Forfar Bridies," Lena told him. "No gravy though."

Something sounded a chord in Diana's memory. She thought about it after the waiter had taken all their orders, and it crystalized when he brought Lena's food.

"That breakfast you and Al had with Eve Bertram and Rosemary," she said to Lena. "Didn't you say that was on a Tuesday?"

Lena started right in on her meal while the waiter was serving the rest of them. "The board meeting, last week," she said around a mouthful of the meat pasty. "It's usually on the first Monday of the month, but it was put off until the Tuesday because I had a doctor's appointment on that Monday. I had a sore place on my shoulder. I was sure it was cancer, but the doctor said it was probably my bra strap rubbing." She sighed. "I can only pray he was right. There's a lymph gland right there, you know. And so much has been going wrong everywhere. I blame it on Mars— ever since that planet came so close to Earth, we've had all kinds of problems."

She chewed for a while. "Tuesday, yes, two days before . . ." Her voice trailed away. "Eve's home by the way. They say she's going to be fine. I guess that means I'll be around a while longer."

"With any luck we'll have you around until you're a hundred," Al said in that smarmy way he had. Maybe now that Rosemary was gone, he was going to suck up to Lena instead.

Lena blew him a raspberry, but she was obviously pleased by the implied compliment.

Be nice, Diana instructed herself.

Connor had caught Diana's point. "What was Rosemary going to do the rest of that Tuesday?" he asked Lena.

"She said she was going to Seattle."

"Did she often go to Seattle on Tuesdays?" Diana asked.

Lena frowned. "How would I . . . wait a minute . . . she did mention at a couple of Monday board meetings that she was going to the city the next day. Maybe more than a couple."

Al lowered his fork and glared at Diana. "Why the hell do you want to know?" he demanded.

Connor picked up the thread while Diana was cutting her beer-battered fish with far more vigor than the tender food required, her mouth closed tightly over the nasty retort that was trying to emerge.

"Diana and I wondered if Rosemary had gone anywhere or done anything that particular day that might have led to . . . well, if she'd met someone or annoyed someone . . ."

"I don't know what she did in Seattle," Lena said. "For all I know she might have had an assignation."

"Lena!" Al protested.

"You think Rosemary had a lover?" Higby said. "*Our* Rosemary? Do tell."

"I didn't say she *had* a lover," Lena said, sounding irritated. "I said she *might* have had an *assignation*. It was a joke."

Diana swallowed a forkful of fish and leaned forward. "Maybe it was something she said, something you heard, that made you think that was possible. Try to remember, Lena. It's important."

Lena shrugged. "I don't know anything, really I don't.

It was just—" She broke off again, her eyes going out of focus.

"What?" Diana demanded.

"Well, she was really nicely dressed that morning. That Tuesday morning. Rosemary always was well-dressed, but she had this pretty dress on, and usually she wore suits with skirts or tailored pants, you know how she was. This was a flouncy sort of dress, and she had her hair kind of pinned up real pretty. Then Eve asked if she could hitch a ride to Seattle—she'd love to do some shopping in the city—and Rosemary said she was sorry, she wasn't going anywhere near downtown, and she seemed a bit uncomfortable. And then Eve made some comment about her being secretive, and I said well, maybe she had an assignation, and Rosemary blushed."

"Did she now," Diana marveled, trying to imagine such a thing.

Al was squirming in his seat. "You've no right to say such a thing about Rosemary. She was a married lady, a good Christian woman."

Diana regarded him with interest. *Is it possible that Al and Rosemary . . . surely not.*

Connor was gazing at Lena around the edges of his ice pack. "I don't understand why you would even *think* of Rosemary having a lover."

"That would be because our Lena has one," Higby said matter-of-factly. "Ever since she started dating on the sly, she's convinced everyone else has a lover, too."

If Rosemary had blushed as scarlet as Lena was doing, Diana could see why Lena had jumped to her conclusion. A wave of color had come up the older woman's neck all the way to the roots of her beautiful silver hair. "You don't have to tell the world," she said to Higby.

"You didn't tell me it was a secret," Higby said.

"I didn't think I had to."

"Who?" Diana asked, but Lena had closed her mouth firmly and was glaring so ferociously at Higby, he raised his hands in surrender and wouldn't say another word. Al was in total shock. All this talk of lovers was obviously upsetting him.

It wasn't long before Lena decided she was ready to go home, and she made Higby leave with her so he'd have no chance to gossip. Al left with them. As they walked by the windows on the way to the parking lot, Lena had her head tilted way back so she could look up at Higby. She was obviously haranguing him. Al was striding ahead, ignoring both of them.

"Interesting," Connor said. He set the ice pack down on the table and grinned at Diana. "Do you suppose Lena's right? Everyone has a lover?"

Diana had finished two pieces of fish and half of her french fries. Restaurants always did serve too much food. It was evidently their mission in life to bulk up the entire population of the United States.

"Yeah, right," she said, setting her plate aside. "Sin City, that's Port Findlay to a T."

"Do *you* have a lover?" he asked.

She looked him in the good eye. "I'm emotionally shut down," she lied.

"Really?" His wry smile said he didn't believe her.

"Really," she said firmly.

Chapter 13

DIANA WATCHED SEATTLE'S channel five newscast and *CNN Headline News,* read for a while, then soaked in a hot, lavender-infused bathtub, cleaned and flossed her teeth, moisturized her face and hands.

She was putting on her red plaid pajama bottoms and a white T-shirt when she realized she was still too wired to sleep. That's what came of drinking wine, hanging out with an attractive albeit slightly dorky man, sending him home alone. The apartment—the whole building—seemed too big, too empty.

The fog had ventured in over the land, lowering the temperature to well below chilly. Rather than turn on any heat, Diana pulled on what she always referred to as her "pink thing," a fleecy pink robe that looked as if it ought to have bunny slippers to go with it. It had been a gag gift from Brad Jeffers, her former partner, when she was recuperating from her bullet wounds. It wouldn't win any fashion awards, but it was so comfortable she often wore it when there was absolutely no chance of anyone seeing her in it.

Far from feeling sleepy, torn between checking E-mail on her computer, turning on the television again, or reading another magazine, she decided instead to go down to her darkroom and get started on the Wallingford family's stagecoach photos. She'd used four rolls of film. Film was cheap, she was always generous with it. It would take a while to develop the film, but the process would relax her.

She suspected that Connor Callahan would have been happy to help her relax. That knowing smile when she'd said she was emotionally shut down. And he'd given her the chance to change her mind when he'd asked if she really wanted to be dropped off at her apartment.

He'd expressed disappointment when she'd made an excuse about them both having to get up early for the second day of the photo show.

Sometime soon, she thought as she went downstairs, switching on lights on the way, her footsteps echoing, she was going to have to make up her mind about Connor Callahan. She'd been getting pretty close to a decision when Lena threw her that curve about him talking to his dead wife. She didn't like the sound of that at all.

Tomorrow evening, after the show was over, she and Connor had a date to examine Rosemary's computer again. They would be through with the show then, other volunteers would be dismantling the stands, making sure the photographs that hadn't sold got back to their creators, and the photographs that had sold were picked up by their new owners.

She'd think about it tomorrow, she decided. Tomorrow, tomorrow . . . Scarlett O'Hara channeling Annie!

Laughing at herself, she peered out through her little office window. All she could see in the whiteout were the halos around next door's waterfront light, and the lights on the wharf. In the studio, she switched off the overhead light. It was a good habit, even when there was nobody around to open the darkroom door and ruin her film.

She took her time, carefully winding each roll of film loosely onto a reel, placing it in the developing tank, turning on the amber safelight, pouring in the solution, enjoying the whole process as she always did.

She could hear the muffled sound of the town's foghorn as she worked. Two blasts within five seconds, repeated fifteen seconds later. She was never sure if foghorns and train whistles sounded romantic or ominous.

A couple of times, she was vaguely aware of a slight scratching sound beyond the wall. Last year wasps had built a nest in one of the walls, but it had been an outside wall. She'd had to get an exterminator to come and take the nest out. He'd killed the wasps first. She'd hated that. The nest had been a marvel of construction, like papier-mâché honeycombed with little holes.

She wouldn't want to go through that again. She still felt guilty.

Mice maybe, she thought when she heard a different sound sometime later. If she had mice, she'd buy the kind of trap a Japanese friend had used in their college dorm. A *nezumi tori*. Michi had caught two mice in the fairly large cage and carried them out. Diana hadn't asked what she'd done with them, but she knew what she would do, she'd take them under the wharf and turn them loose.

By the time she had the negatives developed, fixed, and washed, and was through hanging the strips to dry, she was thoroughly relaxed and getting sleepy. She was also in need of water; the wine at the pub had made her throat dry.

Turning off the safelight, she yanked open the door of

the darkroom and walked straight into a totally unexpected, brilliant beam of light directed right to her eyes. In
a split second, her heartbeat went from 76 beats per minute
to at least 120. Blinded, disoriented, she tried to retreat, but
before she could grab the darkroom door to close it, the
beam of light went out. In the sudden blackness, a hand
grabbed the front of her fleecy robe and pulled her vi-
ciously off balance. Something hit her hard on the side of
her head.

As she stumbled against the darkroom's doorjamb, a
pair of hands covered in some kind of gloves reached
around her throat, thumbs closing on her windpipe.

The hands were strong. The pressure on her throat was
unbearable, she couldn't breathe. Certainly, she couldn't
yell, always the first method of defense, and there was no
weapon at hand, the second choice. Fear was all around
her, paralyzing her.

Faintly in the back of her mind, she heard a former self-
defense instructor's voice saying, "Somebody assaults you,
give 'em hell. Don't let it happen! Punch, kick, gouge, yell
your head off! Do what you have to do!"

Galvanized, she let herself go loose in the knees, as
though she was weakening, then brought her right knee
sharply upward where she judged the man's groin to be.
There was an "Oof!" from the intruder, and his fingers
slackened, letting go altogether when she kneed him again,
right on target. She pushed past him, but he recovered
quickly and shoved her to one side, knocking her to her
knees. Sensing that he was about to kick her, she reached
wildly around and managed to grab his leg and yank on it,
sending him crashing to the floor.

He swore, then reached for her as she was getting up.
But she managed to evade his hands and ran to her office,
spotting the cordless phone by the light on the answering

machine. Scooping it up, she jabbed at the 9-1-1 keys in the faint light coming through the window from the real estate office's waterfront light. Something crashed down on her head as a voice spoke in her ear. "Nine-one-one, what are you reporting?"

The phone dropped out of her hand. Pain rocketing through her head, she crumpled downward into a darkness shot through with dancing flares of colored light.

Quite suddenly, there was no more light at all.

"Ms. GORDON? DIANA? She's not responding. That ambulance better get here soon."

She was lying on her back. The voice had come from somewhere above her. "Don't need ambulance," she muttered.

"You're not in any condition to make that decision," the voice said. A male voice. Not a threatening voice. A familiar voice.

"Be still, Diana," he said. "We don't want you moving until the medics get here."

"I'm okay," she said.

This was a lie. There was a rushing sound in her ears, and her eyes didn't seem to want to open. A band of pain across her forehead had zipped them closed.

A minute or an hour later, she felt herself being handled. Forcing her eyes open, she saw six foot five police officer Adrian Lawrence, and the much shorter Officer Carlos Dominguez, gazing down at her as an emergency medical technician strapped her onto a board and another one padded her head and neck.

"Somebody broke in," she told the faces as they lifted her and the board onto a gurney.

Adrian nodded. "We gathered that. Place looks like your 'somebody' tossed it."

"I dropped the phone," she said, just as it rang. The sound pierced her forehead.

Adrian answered the phone. "Hi, Higby," he said. "You been listening in on your police radio again?"

Diana held out her hand for the phone. Adrian hesitated a second, then held it to her ear.

Higby had heard the call go out to the police department, along with the Photomania address. "The police are here, I'm fine. EMT's here, too," she assured him.

He wanted to come in to the studio and check on everything himself. "No way," she said. "Morning will do. And I don't want you talking about the break-in, not to Lena, not to anyone."

"You're thinking it's not an ordinary burglary, then," Higby said.

"Why would you think that?" she asked.

"If it was an ordinary burglary, you'd want all the neighbors to know about it so they could be more alert."

"I have to go, Higby," she said weakly, knowing she couldn't argue with his reasoning.

"Did you get here in time to catch the guy?" she thought to ask the officers.

They shook their heads. "Minute we found you, I went out to the beach," Carlos said. "Thought I saw some movement in the fog under the wharf, but when I got there, nobody was hanging around waiting for me. Same with the parking lot. No extra vehicles. Guy was either on foot or parked somewhere and hoofed it in. I came in, searched all through the studio and up into your apartment. Nobody around. Any idea who he was?"

About to shake her head, she realized she couldn't. Wouldn't have been a good idea, anyway. "Never did see him."

Carlos said he had examined the front and back doors,

and as far as he could see, neither had been tampered with. The front door had been locked and bolted on the inside. The intruder had fled out the back door. It was standing open when the officers arrived, Diana facedown in the doorway.

"That's got to be where he came in," Diana said. "I remember locking the front door before I went upstairs." She frowned. "Maybe the back door wasn't locked. I sometimes forget to check on the back door. I leave it standing open most of the day when the weather is good."

"Unlocked doors at night are not a good idea, even in a low-crime area," Adrian lectured. "Too much of an invitation." He glanced down at his clipboard. It didn't seem to have much on it. "You get any idea of height, or weight, hair color, smell, anything?"

"Nothing. It was too dark in here." She explained about coming out of the darkroom, the flashlight blinding her. "I didn't notice any smell about him, but my nose was full of fixer smell, it tends to numb the olfactory nerve. His hands were big. I guess he was fairly strong—when he pushed me aside, I went flying. It slowed him down when I kneed him, though."

Both officers winced.

"Yeah, it would." Adrian's sideways glance was admiring. "We'll report it at the morning meeting," he said. "Not much to go on, but we'll ask around at neighboring businesses. Most of them are closed, but we'll check Findlay's Landing and the Greek place."

"We need to get going," the medical technician said.

"Where?" Diana demanded.

"The hospital. We need to check your head." He segued into lecture mode. "The skull bones are pretty hard, and they do a fair job of protecting the brain, along with the layers of tissue that contain cerebrospinal fluid and form a cushion for the brain. You don't have any cuts, so no bleeding, but you've got a fair-size lump, and you were unconscious when the officers found you."

"I'm talking," she pointed out.

"You're a woman," Adrian said.

The EMT grinned, then sobered immediately. "We're sure you're okay," he said. "In spite of what this jerk said, you are making sense and your pupils are okay. Your memory appears to be functioning well."

About to protest that in that case she'd as soon stay home, Diana restrained herself. Obviously it would be stupid to refuse to go to the hospital. Blacking out even for a minute was not a good sign. Nor was the present sensation of someone zapping her head with a cattle prod. She felt nauseated, too. And cross-eyed.

She was annoyed with herself for letting the intruder get away. She had no idea who he was, or what he looked like, or what he'd been after.

The technician put an ice pack against the lump and told Adrian to hold it in place, then he shone a penlight in each of her eyes.

"I think the guy hit me with a flashlight," Diana said, blinking. "That was before he tried to throttle me."

"You're not having a good day," Carlos said, scribbling on a clipboard.

"What I'm saying," Diana said, then paused to tell the EMT guy, "Hold it, I'm thinking."

After lumbering through the fog that seemed to have moved inside her head, searching for the spark that was suddenly glinting in the distance, she said to the officers, "If he was strangling me, he had to let go of the flashlight."

Carlos went to poke around the area near the darkroom and came up with a hefty flashlight, which he handled by the business end.

"He had gloves on," Diana told him. "Latex, I think. They felt like latex."

"What do you think he wanted?" Carlos asked.

"To cut off my ability to breathe," Diana said. "Way I feel right now, he came close." She laboriously processed another thought. "If he dropped the flashlight, what the hell did he hit me with?"

"There's a lot of sand by the back door," Adrian offered. "Plus what appears to be the remains of some kind of stuffed animal. Though I wouldn't have thought that would be enough to knock you out."

Diana groaned. "It was a stuffed duck. A doorstop. As well as the sand, it had a bunch of ball bearings in it to make it heavy enough to hold the door open, even if the wind blew through."

Carlos gestured at a closet next to the darkroom door. "Appears your guy had something in mind here."

Diana swiveled her eyes sideways. She kept packets of contact sheets, boxes of photos and negatives, and other photography supplies in that closet.

A box had fallen to the floor. A few photos had spilled out. The box itself was empty. It had been full. Which meant photographs were missing.

At her request, Carlos brought the box to her. She squinted at the label. San Francisco. That seemed significant. She had no idea why.

"Anything important?" Adrian asked.

"Probably scenery."

"Your scenic photos are good enough someone would want to clobber you on the head and steal them?" Adrian asked. He smiled at her. He had a nice smile. Was something more personal flickering there? He'd asked her to go to the movies with him once.

She suddenly realized she was still wearing her pink thing. Good Lord. She had to be imagining the flickering.

"Not good enough to strangle me for," she said. "I doubt he'd get much for them on eBay."

SHE WAS IN the ambulance, which was wending its way slowly through the mist on the way to the hospital before another spark ignited in her brain. "What?" Adrian asked, evidently recognizing some semblance of life in her face. He had elected to ride along with her. Maybe it *was* personal.

She hesitated. If she told him the pictures might have been connected to her previous investigative life, she'd have to tell him she'd *had* a previous investigative life.

"My head hurts," she said to throw him off.

She hadn't brought much in the way of photos with her when she left San Francisco. Brad had decided to keep their business going, so she'd simply turned over her files to him. She was pretty sure the photos that had been stolen had dealt with a case she'd thought she might write about if she ever had time to do it. A large gang of young men and women had formed a profitable business staging traffic accidents. One would drive a car in busy traffic, then stop suddenly so that the car behind would have no time to prevent a fender bender. Then the driver in front would sue the innocent driver behind for damages, whiplash, migraine, inability to function—whatever creative but hard-to-disprove problem he could dream up, maybe with the connivance of a couple of well-paid doctors who hadn't paid much attention to the Hippocratic oath.

Conveniently, there would always be a witness who would swear to the rear driver being the one to blame. Most times, the insurance companies would settle out of court. The members of the group took turns being the driver and shared the loot.

"Didn't you get in a fight at the photo show?" Adrian asked, his voice amused.

"That would be earlier today if it's not midnight yet."

"It's not." His grin flashed. "I may have to run you in for disturbing the peace."

"I'm the victim here," Diana protested.

"Who was the fight with?" Adrian asked.

"Connor Callahan and I got in a dustup with Otto Schmidt and Gardner Malone—a photographer from Oregon. It wasn't all that serious. The chief calmed everyone down. Otto went home; Gardner stayed long enough to pick up his award and then went back to Portland."

"You think your intruder might have been one of them?"

"No. Otto's scrawnier, Gardner's big, but he's nice."

"So we're looking for a guy who's big, not scrawny, not nice."

"You've got it, hotshot."

"Ought to be easy to find. Stand-out description like that." He peered at her neck. "Guy had a good grip. Your neck's red. You'd better have someone check it while you're in the ER, or wherever you end up."

Privately, she thought she might need to consult a chiropractor.

At least she had acted, she told herself as she was wheeled along an empty, echoing hospital corridor. She had been afraid, but she'd acted in spite of the fear. Which was some kind of triumph—over the fear and over the intruder.

All the same, fear was still lingering in her mind: a larger fear now, looming like a dark cloud, a fear she didn't want to acknowledge to the police, or anyone else, but one she was going to have to face. Soon.

Tomorrow, she thought. *Tomorrow.*

* * *

BRAD JEFFERS HAD always been an early riser, so Diana
felt no compunction about calling him at 7 A.M. the next
day, the minute she got home from the hospital. The sun
was shining in a clear blue sky.

"Hey babe," Brad said in a pleased voice. "I was thinking I should call you."

"Sure you were."

"No, really. I was talking about you. I was down at the
police station, and I ran into Detective Sergeant Morrison,
remember him?"

She wasn't really ready for a complicated conversation.
She'd come a long way since midnight. The CAT scan results had revealed no serious trauma, and all her vital signs
and responses to sensations had checked out, but the doctors had felt she should stay a few hours for observation. A
nurse had watched her for signs of any problem and had
kept waking her up to make sure she could. She needed a
shower and a cup of strong coffee before her brain could
begin to operate.

"How could I forget Morrison?" she said. "He as good
as accused me of knocking off Stockman."

"Yeah, well, Stockman is still among the missing. But
I've got Morrison half convinced of your innocence. I keep
reminding him you weren't through convalescing when
Sam took off. Anyway, I have a theory why Stockman
hasn't turned up yet. You'll remember that Hedrick Insurance made noises about suing him for fraud, after they saw
your photos. I talked that up, trying to convince Morrison
that's probably why Stockman decided to vanish."

There was a silence while she tried to digest all of this.
It didn't sound good to her, especially as the photographs
that had been stolen by last night's intruder were from one
of the San Francisco boxes. The Stockman photos were not

among them, but the intruder had no way of knowing that. She'd actually never seen the photos of Stockman herself. All she'd thought about was getting away, leaving San Francisco. But before getting shot, she'd followed Sam Stockman for days. She knew what he looked like. He was a big guy. About the same size as last night's intruder.

"So were you calling me so you could sit there and breathe?" Brad asked.

She didn't want to get into last night's events. "I wanted to check up on you, see how things are going."

"Going good. Got a thriving climate of crime. Plenty of business. I miss you, babe."

"I miss you, too."

"So how are things going in Nowheresville?"

"Port Findlay's a great little town, a beautiful location. The views of the mountains alone—we're so lucky to have two ranges, the Cascades and the Olympics. From my beach, on a clear day—"

"I heard you had a murder up there. Anyone you know? Somebody on TV said something about a photography show."

She decided not to tell him she'd found the body. "It made the national news?"

"CNN ran a brief piece on it. I happened to be watching. Said you had a racial problem up there. What's up with that?"

"We have nothing of the sort. It was blown way out of proportion. Two cowboys in a pickup truck—that was it."

Silence dropped again. Then she asked, trying to sound casual, coming out stilted, "You still have the photos of Stockman?"

"Sure do."

"I'd like to see them. I never did, you know."

"Yeah?"

"It still gripes me the police said there was no evidence. I want to see for myself there was no gun."

"It sure doesn't show up in the pictures, babe. Believe me, I looked. Hard."

"I'd still like to see them."

"I'll burn a CD for you."

She said a few more things about Port Findlay, asked about his wife Yvonne and their two sons, then they hung up. She'd sensed that he still had questions. It had to have seemed strange to him that she'd suddenly ask for those photos a year after the fact. But he hadn't asked outright why she wanted them. He knew her well enough to know that if she'd wanted him to know her reason, she would have told him.

Chapter 14

THREE HOURS LATER, helped by more of the acetaminophen the ER physician had prescribed, Diana showed up at Quinn Center. Higby was full of concern when he saw her, but swore he hadn't told and wouldn't tell anyone about her intruder.

Connor noticed she wasn't too sprightly and asked her if she was sick, but she just said she hadn't slept too well the previous night, which was certainly true. She got out of answering any more questions by making a fuss about his eye, which was less swollen but turning a vivid black and blue.

Enough had happened in this so-called merry month of May to last her all year, she thought, and it was only three days past the halfway mark. She wasn't sure how she made it through the day. Unfortunately, four of the people who were supposed to help hand out the photos to the photographers who had entered them didn't turn up, and she and Connor had to stay on and help.

The crew that was dismantling the stands so they could be put in storage had also mislaid some volunteers—Rosemary's murder had made a lot of people jittery—and the two cochairs had no choice but to help out there, too. When they were finally able to leave Quinn Center, Diana wasn't sure she'd ever want to enter the place again.

With little discussion—they were both exhausted—they agreed to postpone any further detecting until the following day, then enjoyed some wonderful Szechuan chicken and vegetables at the Chinese restaurant on Water Lily Street.

"I like your hair down around your shoulders like that," Connor said, setting his chopsticks across his plate to indicate he was finished. "The ponytail is fine, cute, but this is softer."

She'd left her hair down to cover the lump the intruder had left her with. "Cute? Soft?" she said. "I'm not sure I want to be either."

"Why am I not surprised?" he said, then lapsed into silence for a while. Neither of them had shown any interest in the fortune cookies.

"Okay, Flash," Connor said, after the diminutive waitress had cleared the dishes away and they were finishing up their second pot of green tea.

Diana thought he meant he was ready to leave, and started to get up, but he put his hand on her arm and said, "First tell me what's going on, and what it has to do with the police."

She sat down again. "Who told you something was going on? Higby? Did he tell Lena? God, it will be all over town. Or was it one of the officers—"

"Nobody told me anything."

"Then how did you know?"

"I didn't. I don't. However, my mother would say you

look like death warmed over. You're far too pale, and your eyes are as narrow as a nervous cat's, plus something is preying on your mind, and you don't really want to share it with me."

"You have a crystal ball?"

"I know clues when I see them. Higby hovered over you all day like a mama bear with a cub. Officer Adrian Lawrence came in and spoke to you seriously. Sarah came in and spoke to you seriously. When I was carrying stands out to one of the trucks, Carlos Dominguez came by in his patrol car and asked if you were feeling okay."

"Did he tell you—"

"I asked why you wouldn't be, and he said airily that he was just checking. I've been waiting, hoping you'd volunteer some information. You're supposed to tell friends when something's wrong. We are friends, aren't we?"

"Of course we are," Diana said immediately. "I didn't want to worry you. I wanted to pull my weight and get the job done."

Bending her head, she pulled her hair aside.

"What happened?" he asked after gently examining the area.

She told him from start to finish, including the fact of the missing photographs. She also told him she had no idea who the intruder had been, except she was sure it was a man and he had probably thought she wasn't home. Her van had been parked in the side lot, which she shared with a real estate office. Maybe he hadn't seen it because of the fog. Maybe he didn't know the get-away van was hers. Maybe . . .

"Why would he want the photographs?" Connor asked. "What were they?"

"I'm not sure," she said, which wasn't completely true.

"He walked right in? Don't you have a burglar alarm?"

"Sure I do. But I kept forgetting to turn it off when I came in, and I figured the neighbors were probably getting tired of the noise, and anyway, there didn't seem to be that much crime around here, so I let sleeping alarms lie."

He rolled his eyes but didn't pursue the subject. "Why would he attack *you?*" he asked.

"Maybe he'd heard about Melissa asking you and me to look into Rosemary's murder. Maybe he had something to *do* with Rosemary's murder."

"Nobody attacked *me*," Connor said. "I feel so damn responsible."

"You didn't hit me."

"I got you into this. I should never have asked you to help, gotten you involved. From now on—"

"I'm not completely sure this came about because of our investigation," Diana said. "Can you stand one more maybe? With the understanding that in this case, I may really be as paranoid as Lena?"

"Lay it on me," Connor said.

She sighed. "I was supposed to open up Quinn Center for you and the judges, remember? It was discussed at the Arts Alliance general meeting. There was no reason for it to be a secret. Someone could have mentioned it and been overheard."

He gazed at her for several seconds before reading between the lines. "You think the murderer made a mistake?"

"Think about this. How would you describe me?"

He frowned.

"Go on, pretend you're telling someone to watch for me. Give me a general description."

He shook his head. "Okay, let's see. Tall, of course. Long dark hair. Slender. Thirties."

"And how would you describe Rosemary?"

"She was a lot older than thirties. And her hair was probably dyed."

"But it was about the same color as mine. And you wouldn't be able to tell she was nearer sixty than thirty if you weren't up close and personal. Even fairly close, she looked good. She worked at it."

"So why would someone want to kill you? What possible reason . . ."

She could feel her face getting hot. "Why would he kill Rosemary? If he got it wrong the first time, wouldn't it make sense for him to try again?" She laughed shortly. "Who knows what evil lurks in the hearts of men."

He regarded her quizzically. "You're not old enough to remember the Shadow."

"I was quoting my father, who was probably quoting the bible. Who's the Shadow?"

He leaned forward. "Let me get this straight. You believe it's possible that the man who murdered Rosemary intended to murder you, and he came into your studio last night and assaulted you?"

"I haven't got as far as believing. I don't even know if I'm *thinking*. I'm *imagining—wondering—*"

"But he didn't stick around to try to finish the job—if that's what he had in mind."

"I think he might have stayed to duke it out if I hadn't punched in nine-one-one as soon as I had light to see by. That's when he hit me again and hit the road. He'd know Dispatch would get the location the minute they answered and could have someone there PDQ. He wouldn't want to be caught in the area."

"But who would *want* to kill you, Flash? Do you have any enemies in town? Surely not."

She shrugged with as much nonchalance as she could

conjure up. Nerve pains shot along the familiar path of the scar on her back. To be companionable, a few jagged knives stabbed her head. The dark cloud pressed closer. She thought maybe she should wait to examine it until she was alone. "It's probably like I said—paranoia."

She reached for her shoulder bag, hanging on the black lacquered arm of her chair. "On me this time," she said.

He didn't protest, but kept gazing at her in a concerned way while little Su was working out their bill. She wasn't sure if he was concerned because he believed she might have been in danger, or concerned that she was imagining more extreme danger where none existed. Maybe the latter was the correct interpretation: she was turning into another Lena—she'd be worrying next about getting targeted by meteor showers.

They had driven to the restaurant separately. Connor insisted on following her van home, going in with her, and checking out each room. The studio had been put back together again. Higby, of course. She'd have to be sure to thank him.

Connor finally left, reluctantly, and only because she insisted she had to get some sleep and only after making sure the burglar alarm was programmed and the doors were locked.

After a good hot shower and a couple of the doctor's pills, Diana fell asleep the minute her still-aching head settled into the pillow.

Much refreshed, she managed to make it through Monday's appointments, including some yearbook photos she and Higby had agreed to do at the high school. It was a bright spring afternoon. She put on a wide-brimmed straw hat to protect her face from the sun, and it seemed to help hold her head together. She also wore sunglasses. Normally she avoided them on a photo shoot, for obvious reasons, but she seemed to be light sensitive as a result of the intruder's violence.

The rhododendrons, azaleas, and lilac on the school grounds were in full bloom, the kids were happy to be outside, and the session lifted Diana's spirits immeasurably. The kids enjoyed themselves, too. Higby always had a good time.

Late in the afternoon, when her brain seemed to be functioning again, Diana called Connor at his clinic and suggested they visit Dmitri and see what he might have to say about Rosemary's Tuesdays.

He still had a couple of patients coming in, he told her. One of them was a new patient. New patients always took more time, but he'd be happy to accompany her as soon as he was through. "Are you sure you're up to it?" he asked. "How's your head?"

"Okay. How's your eye?"

"It's not too bad. I have to admit I'm getting tired of people making jokes about it. If one more person asks what the other guy looks like, I'm going to go lock myself in the X-ray room."

He paused. "Don't think I haven't noticed that whenever I mention your health and welfare, you change the subject to mine," he said before hanging up.

After changing into fresh jeans and a clean white T-shirt, Diana waited an hour, then realized it could be another hour before Connor showed up. Her unusual patience had been tested as far as it could go, she decided. Phoning Tammy Griffith, Connor's office manager, she asked her to tell him to meet her at Rosemary's house, or call her on her cell phone. She dictated the number.

Stopping only to buy a box of "homemade" chocolate chip cookies at Molly's Market, she drove on up to the corner of Violet Street and Hornbeam Avenue, the latter named for the large round-headed trees that marched up each side of it.

Afterward she excused herself on the grounds that it wasn't her fault Dmitri was as careless as she sometimes was. She had, after all, rung the doorbell. Twice. And she had tried the brass latch only to make sure the door was securely locked. And discovered that it wasn't. Worried about Dmitri's welfare, she had entered only to assure herself that he was okay, locking the door behind her.

Dmitri was nowhere to be seen.

Naturally, she was interested in Rosemary's home. She had never been in it before. It was excessively tidy— charming in a cottagey sort of way. Rosemary had been the high queen of taste, according to just about everybody. Diana thought she might get some ideas on how to improve her own large but fairly boring apartment if she took a look around.

The kitchen had obviously been designed for someone who liked to cook regularly, though without the rather sterile steel appearance of Connor Callahan's kitchen. Polished copper pans hung by their handles from racks attached by chains to the ceiling. Utensils in ceramic pots and electric gadgets were lined up on one long counter with outlets all along it.

The living room was painted magenta. A surprising color, but it worked well with the creamy woodwork and carpeting, flounced drapes, squishy furniture, and the botanical prints on the walls.

There was a chaise in the master bedroom.

Mistress bedroom would have been a better name for it. There was no sign of anything masculine in the two large closets behind the silently gliding mirrored doors. Diana reminded herself she was no longer a licensed investigator. She wouldn't have snooped this much without proper cause, even when she *was* licensed. But there was always the chance that the intrusion into her studio had come about because of some mysterious connection with Rosemary's death.

So, she rationalized, she was *protecting* herself by sticking her nose into Rosemary's private sanctuary.

That's what the bedroom felt like—a sanctuary. The walls were a deep forest green, the covers on the bed flowered like the living room upholstery.

There was a big dressing table, uncluttered, with only a matching walnut jewelry box and tissue container on its polished surface. There were several drawers. Diana set the Molly's Market box down on a nearby chair.

Everything was as Diana would have expected it to be. Extremely neat. Modest. White Jockey panties, white bras—a couple were Wonderbras, as she'd always suspected. Panty hose in one drawer, socks in another. Cotton and silk tops, neatly folded.

Diana always folded her own tops, too; hangers made bumps in the wrong places. She came across a pair of cotton gloves, the kind you can wear at night if you've slathered moisturizer on. It seemed a good idea to put them on.

The bottom drawer yielded some surprises. A whole stack of lacy lingerie, white, cobalt blue, black. A red garter belt. Black stockings that required something to hold them up. Two thongs.

Thongs!

Rosemary?

She tried to imagine Rosemary Barrett wearing these garments for Dmitri, but the picture refused to take shape in her mind.

Perhaps Lena hadn't been too far off base after all.

Maybe Rosemary *did* have a lover. Did she entertain him here? Was Dmitri so far gone he wouldn't have noticed?

Diana had replaced each lacy item as neatly as she'd found it when she suddenly experienced the eerie, neck-prickling feeling that someone was watching her. Wondering how the hell she was going to explain rooting through Rosemary's drawers, she whirled around and saw Rosemary's orange cat sitting in the doorway, regarding her with the unblinking stare that cats come by naturally.

"Hey," Diana said, letting her breath out.

The cat lifted a lazy paw and began licking it, as though to indicate that Diana's presence was of no interest to her—him? Hadn't she heard that orange cats were usually male? Or was she thinking of calico cats, which were always female?

While she pondered this earthshaking question, the cat stiffened and turned in the opposite direction, tail up and twitching, and Diana realized she was hearing scrabbling sounds. Someone was opening the front door.

Heart hammering in her chest, she cautiously closed the drawer, grabbed the cookies, and peered around for an escape route. She found it immediately in the sliding glass doors that opened to a side yard.

As she stepped out and started sliding the door closed, the cat went with her. There was no time to pick the cat up, she could hear footsteps coming toward the bedroom. She eased the door closed, realizing as she did so that she was still wearing Rosemary's gloves.

Yanking them off, she tucked them in her jeans pocket, ducked her head, and ran to the side of the fence that divided the area from the front yard. To her horror, she discovered that there was no gate. The fence was high and smooth, with few footholds. All the same, it was the only way out. After balancing the box of cookies in the top branches of a nearby holly bush, she reached for the top posts, placed her feet flat against the wood and duckwalked up, scratching herself on the holly and acquiring a couple of splinters in her right hand, which she had no choice but to ignore.

But as she peered over the top of the fence, wondering if it would be any easier to go down the other side, she saw that the Barretts' neighbor was hauling a hose off a huge reel and heading for the grass on this side of his driveway. All he had to do was glance up, and they would be eyeball to eyeball.

Dropping back down into the Barrett yard, she ran the perimeter of the fence, searching for another way out, but there were too many shrubs too close to the boards. At the rear of the yard was a glassed-in gazebo with a hot tub inside it. She actually considered hiding in there but realized that eventually she'd have to come out, and she'd still be faced with the problem of getting over the fence.

The cat was sitting on the door mat, watching her. Diana reminded herself of her personal slogan: attitude is everything. Recovering the box of cookies, she headed directly for the sliding glass doors to the bedroom and tapped loudly on the glass. She heard a toilet being flushed, waited until it stopped, then tapped again.

This time Dmitri appeared on the other side of the windows.

Waving and smiling, she pointed down at the cat, then held up the cookie box. "Hi, Dmitri!" she called.

He frowned but slid the door open.

"I thought I'd drop in and check to be sure you are getting along okay," she said. "Is this cat supposed to be outside?"

Even as she spoke, the cat leaped into the house and disappeared under the bed. "I brought cookies from Molly's Market," Diana added.

Dmitri regarded her without recognition or fear. He didn't seem to have noticed the cat. Then he caught sight of the box and seemed more interested.

"The cookies are for you, Dmitri," she said.

He nodded, took the box from her, and started to close the door. "May I use the bathroom?" she asked in desperation.

He thought it over. "I suppose is all right, sure," he said at last, and she was able to pop herself inside.

"I'll only be a minute," she said.

When she came out, having relieved herself, plucked out the splinters, washed her hands, and replaced Rosemary's gloves in her dressing table drawer, Dmitri was standing in the middle of the kitchen, still clutching the box of cookies.

Diana's heart stopped beating. Sitting on a high stool on the other side of the kitchen island was Connor Callahan. He was dressed nicely in his work clothes: Dockers and a nice shirt with the long sleeves rolled partly up. His fair eyebrows had climbed about as high as they could go.

Dmitri's disordered mind might not try to figure out how Diana Gordon had managed to show up at the sliding glass doors to his late wife's bedroom, but Connor's mind was crystal clear. All she could hope was that one, he didn't know there was no gate to the side yard, and two, that she wasn't blushing.

Attitude, she reminded herself. Taking the cookie box from Dmitri, she put it on the table in front of Connor, along with a square flowered plate she grabbed in passing from a cabinet, talking the whole time about the house and how pretty it was, how well Rosemary had decorated it, and how lonesome Dmitri must be.

The orange cat showed up in the doorway to the living room, fixing her with a malevolent stare. *I know what you've been doing,* the stare seemed to say.

"Put the cookies on the plate, will you?" she asked Connor. "I'll make some coffee."

"I don't like coffee," Dmitri said.

"Tea, then. You met up with Dmitri somewhere?" she said in an aside to Connor, as she opened cabinet doors.

Spying a box of Empress Hotel afternoon tea, she took it down. Rosemary had spoken often of her admiration for the luxury hotel and had made numerous trips to Vancouver Island's Victoria to visit it. She'd acquired an English brown teapot with the Union Jack painted on it, too, and an electric kettle.

Diana put these useful things together as Connor got Dmitri seated on a stool on the other side of the kitchen island, then she pulled over a stool opposite the two men.

Connor was gazing at her chest. She didn't mind—anything that would distract him was good—until she glanced down and saw there was a holly leaf clinging to her left breast. Darn, why hadn't she noticed that when she was in the bathroom? She brushed it off and assumed an innocent expression as Connor's gaze came up.

His lips twitched. "Dmitri's a patient of mine," he said. "He was my last patient of the day. After I got the message you left with Tammy, it seemed a good idea to tag along with him."

"You've been to the house before?" she asked with dread.

"Several times. I've even supervised Dmitri's sessions in the hot tub when Rosemary wasn't around. He loves to use it but forgets how long he's been in there if nobody's with him. Rosemary keeps—*kept*—it locked. Such a nice private yard, isn't it?"

His eyes were meeting hers levelly, his voice showing no particular emphasis. He knew, obviously, that she had to have entered the premises illegally. But without malice aforethought, she wanted to assure him.

"Chiropractic is good for general health," he continued in that same even tone. "It helps Dmitri feel a lot better."

During this dialogue, Dmitri munched steadily on the cookies Diana had brought, humming tunelessly as he chewed.

Diana certainly didn't want to say how long she'd been here or give any hints about finding something interesting. Sometimes Dmitri's wires straightened themselves out, and he caught on to things. Nor did she want him to suddenly wonder how she got into his yard. He probably wouldn't appreciate the truth—cookies or no cookies.

As though he'd heard his own name as it wended its way through her thoughts, Dmitri glanced up at Connor. "What happened to your eye?" he asked.

"I walked into a door," Connor said.

"I do that all the time," Dmitri said and went back to humming.

Connor caught Diana's eye. "I guess you couldn't wait for me?"

"I got antsy," she admitted. "How come you didn't tell me Dmitri was coming in to see you?"

"I hadn't gone over the schedule. No problems last night?"

"None at all. Your eye looks better."

"How's your head?"

"My head hurts," Dimitri said, as Diana said, "It's fine."

"I have headache all time after Rosemary died," Dmitri continued.

"It's been tough on you," Connor sympathized.

"You must miss her," Diana said.

Dmitri met her gaze. His blue eyes were even paler than usual. Watery. "Not much, no."

He hummed for a while, and they left him in peace, but then he suddenly said, "It's like when people give up coffee. I heard about on television show. People say coffee not good for, so give up. People have bad, what you call—symbols."

"Withdrawal symptoms," Connor suggested.

"Like you say. Headaches. So is like that with me with Rosemary."

Diana and Connor exchanged a glance, both trying to follow Dmitri's circuitous reasoning. He'd given coffee up and had headaches. He had another headache. Because he'd given Rosemary up?

"We need to tread carefully here," Connor said under his breath.

"Oh yes," Diana breathed.

Diana turned toward Dmitri. "Are you saying Rosemary was bad for you?"

"You got it, missy."

"In what way?"

"Yelled at me, for one thing." His expression turned sly. "Not supposed to talk about. Melissa said. Everybody mad what I say already."

"We're not mad at you, Dmitri," Connor said softly.

Dmitri smiled.

"You said for one thing," Connor said. "What was another thing?"

Dmitri hummed. "She hit me sometime."

"Rosemary?" Connor sounded totally shocked. Diana wasn't sure *she* was. She'd always mistrusted perfect people. Her mother had been "perfect." She'd never hit Diana, but she'd had a wicked temper and had come awfully close, usually for no reason. The strain of being perfect probably caused major amounts of stress.

"Make me mad she hitting me," Dmitri said.

"Mad enough to kill her?" Connor asked, again very quietly.

"I thought about."

"Did you do it?"

Dmitri's brow furrowed in thought.

Neither Connor nor Diana were breathing.

"I don't think so," Dmitri said. "Besides, Rosemary feed me and help me get around and stuff. Who else going to do? Who will do now?"

"Well, I would think Melissa—" Diana began.

Dmitri put his lips together and produced a rude noise, then his whole face squeezed into a frown. "I know who are you," he said, peering over his teacup at Diana. "You woman take all time pictures."

She nodded.

"Rosemary not like you."

She thought she could take that as a compliment. "Who was she like?"

Confusion showed on his face. "Not that kind like, the kind she not want to be your friend."

Nothing surprising there. "Why not?"

"She say you not who you say you are."

Wordless, Diana stared at him, her stomach tightening into a knot.

"What did she mean?" Connor asked.

Dmitri shook his head hard. "How I know? Rosemary say things like that about people around here all time." He hummed for a while. "She find out things. Secrets."

"What secrets?" Connor asked.

Diana was afraid to take part in this discussion.

"Secret things people do."

"Why?"

"To put in computer. So she can get them. The people."

That was too much for Diana. "She wanted to *get* me?"

"Sure. Can I have more cookie?"

"Help yourself," Diana said, pushing the plate toward him.

"How did Rosemary get people?" Connor asked. "Did she make any of the local people mad? How was she going to get Diana?"

There was no answer. Dmitri's period of lucidity, if that's what it could be called, had passed, and he'd settled into humming and munching again. The light that had briefly shone in his eyes was gone.

Chapter 15

"WHAT WAS ALL that about?" Connor asked. They were standing outside the Barrett house, next to Diana's big red van.

"All what?" Diana asked, though Connor was sure she knew exactly what he meant.

"Rosemary saying you weren't who you said you were."

"Oh that!" Diana shrugged, a little too elaborately. "I would think it was about Dmitri having Alzheimer's. Didn't make any sense at all. Poor old guy. We didn't see anybody's secrets in Rosemary's computer."

Connor decided to postpone further personal discussion.

"Seems to me Melissa has some kind of agenda here," Diana said. "This isn't about protecting Dmitri from the police. I get the impression Dmitri doesn't think Melissa has a whole lot of filial affection for him."

"You may be right. I'm not sure whether to believe him about Rosemary beating him up though. Did she ever seem that vicious to you?"

"Rosemary?" Diana laughed. "Sweetest woman ever was. Everybody says so. Goddamn Pollyanna. Me, I'm a cynic from way back. I'm inclined to believe Dmitri. I hadn't heard a whisper about her having racist tendencies either. You never can tell about domestic violence. Like alcoholism, it happens in the best of families. I remember several cases—"

She broke off.

Connor decided once again to let it pass. "I think what we need to do is go back into Rosemary's laptop. See what we missed."

"Why don't you let *me* have the laptop for a while," she said in what was evidently supposed to be a casual tone. "I'll take a look-see and—"

She was avoiding his gaze. A faint tracing of red outlined her high cheekbones, adding not only to her attractiveness but the certainty that she was hiding something.

He interrupted. "We'll tackle it together. Whatever we find, we'll each have a witness." He regarded her in silence until her dark eyes rose to meet his gaze. "Is that why you want to go it alone? You don't really *want* a witness?"

"Connor—"

Again, he interrupted. "You broke into the house, didn't you?"

"No. I would never do that. The door was unlocked. I rang the doorbell, I thought maybe Dmitri didn't hear me, so I went on in."

Apparently he didn't quite believe her. He appeared to be disappointed in her. Her stomach lurched.

"When the opportunity came up," she said, "I thought it was important to take a look around. And I did find something interesting. We're supposed to be investigating a murder here. In my opinion, anything goes, under these circumstances."

Some of the tightness left his face. "I do appreciate it when you are straight with me, Diana. Which brings me to something else that's been bothering me. Your reluctance to talk about your past."

"I don't know anything about your past either, Connor," she pointed out. She hated that he was calling her Diana.

"Tell you what we'll do," he said. "We'll go to my house. We'll *both* talk about our past lives. After that, we'll get to whatever you think may have been the cause of your experience last night and why you think it's possible someone might have wanted to kill *you* rather than Rosemary. And then we'll dig into Rosemary's laptop and try to find out why Rosemary would say you aren't who you say you are, or if Dmitri was spaced out."

He paused, fixing her with those vivid blue eyes that a person could get lost in. "We have reached a point where we need to know each other, Flash."

She let out a long breath. "Okay."

He insisted on fixing dinner for both of them first. After opening up a bottle of Washington State's own Ste. Michelle Chardonnay, he brought out ingredients and started chopping things up with a large, obviously sharp knife. "I'm making queasy dillers," he told her.

"Catchy name. I'm already queasy watching you with that knife."

"My hands are my living. I use them with caution." He started peeling an avocado with that same huge knife. *"Quesadillas,"* he translated. "Two flour tortillas with whatever you have on hand in between them like a sandwich, okay?"

She nodded. She'd heard of quesadillas but had never been sure of what they were and didn't remember ever having one.

Connor laughed. "A couple of years back, I saw an ad in

a catalog for an electrical pan for making quesadillas, which are among my favorite specialties. One of the problems with cooking quesadillas in a skillet is that you have to turn them over, and that can result in a hell of a mess. I'm no good at tossing pancakes or omelettes either. So I sent for the pan. Liz was keen on the idea because she liked that you didn't have to use any fat. You put the tortilla sandwich in there, put the lid down, and it cooked both sides. Nothing to it. Except that the tortilla tasted like cardboard flavored with chalk. Sometimes you need that fat."

As he talked, he was shredding a cooked chicken breast with his long, strong fingers. "I called up the company and asked how to return the pan. Gave the catalog page number and the item number. And the guy on the other end said, 'Oh, you mean the queasy diller maker?' "

Diana laughed. "So ever since you've called them queasy dillers."

He grinned.

Some of Diana's married friends had shared jokes like that. It seemed to be a common factor in happy marriages. In jokes nobody else could understand, part of the bonding process. Once again, she reminded herself to be wary of getting too involved with Connor Callahan despite his great personal charm.

The resulting queasy dillers were wonderful, all the same. He'd added chopped onion to the chicken and avocado, covered the whole thing with grated mozzarella before putting on the top tortilla. And he managed to turn each one over without spilling a sliver of onion. He served them with salsa and a huge salad, followed by cookies-and-cream ice cream and chocolate chip cookies.

"I have died and gone to heaven," Diana said when they were done.

As they drank coffee made in his designer coffeemaker,

Connor started telling her how he'd become a chiropractor. She supposed he was preparing the way, so she would also tell all.

He'd meant to become an engineer, like his father. He'd found the studies boring, but he admired his father, loved his father, and thought his father would be pleased if Connor followed in his footsteps.

But then Mel Weaver, his college roommate, who was from the Seattle area, had invited him to his home for the Christmas vacation, promising him some great skiing at Snoqualmie Pass and Crystal Mountain.

Following a week of skiing, his friend had decided he needed to visit his uncle, a chiropractor, who had also adjusted Connor, after X-raying him. "The whole process fascinated me," Connor said. "I felt good. As if I were standing taller, straighter. Dr. Weaver explained the philosophy and techniques of chiropractic. He had a whole wall of photographs sent by grateful patients."

He shrugged. "Okay, that was a bit hokey, but what it said to me was that here was a man who spent his time with people, helping people. And engineering began to seem even more boring to me, though funnily enough, Mel found it exciting and thought I was out of my mind when I told him I was going west to the same chiropractic college Dr. Weaver had attended, as soon as I graduated."

"What did your father say?" Diana asked.

"Well, he wasn't thrilled that I was leaving Illinois, but he'd guessed I wasn't too happy, and he wanted me to do work that would make me feel fulfilled."

He poured more coffee for both of them, then added, "Liz and I had been going together for a couple of years, so we decided to get married and travel to Oregon together. Fortunately for us, Dr. Weaver knew of a chiropractor in Portland who needed an office manager, so Liz went to work for him. With her income and some fairly horrendous loans, we managed to get me through."

He grinned at her as he stood up. "My purpose in telling you this boring story is to show you how easy it is to talk about past lives."

In spite of the smile, she sensed he was making a serious point here. "I get the picture," she said. "It's payback time."

Connor insisted they leave the dishes where they were, escorted her into the living room, and sat her down on a long sofa covered with black leather that barely yielded when sat upon. It was flanked by a pair of matching chairs upholstered in white. She could photograph this whole house using black-and-white film. Taking up a position at the opposite end of the couch, Connor gazed at her expectantly.

"This is a really unusual house," she said nervously. "All those roofs and windows going off at different angles."

It definitely wasn't her kind of house, but she could hardly tell him that. The dream house she carried in her mind was old-fashioned, homey, peaceful—with bay windows, fireplaces, antiques, Tiffany lamps, chairs stuffed with down and upholstered with some kind of blue-and-white fabric she'd seen once that featured people doing things in bucolic meadows. "It must take a lot of work to keep the place up. So much white. And all these tile floors."

"Liz liked white. And I have a crew of three who come in for three hours one day a week." He held up a hand as she started to ask another question. "My housekeeping was not on the agenda. The next item on the agenda has to do with your past."

"You don't really want the whole biography, do you? I wouldn't know where to start."

"The cliché answer to that comment is—begin at the beginning."

"Oh. Okay. Here we go then. I was born thirty-four years ago, on a dark and stormy night . . ."

He held her gaze and she faltered. "I guess I'm being facetious. I do that. It's a defense mechanism."

"I've noticed. How about you start with San Francisco. That's all I know about you—that you came from San Francisco. You lived in a trailer. And your parents were either hippies or werewolves."

She stood up and walked over to the wall of windows that looked out on a beautifully landscaped garden. Violet-green swallows swooped back and forth, inspecting a couple of birdhouses, apparently hoping to set up house-keeping. At least a half dozen American goldfinches were blending right in with a gorgeous tree that was hung with dozens of yellow tassels. Diana could recognize many birds, having photographed more than a few since her arrival in Port Findlay. She'd illustrated a calendar for the local Audubon Society for next year.

"I guess they know Washington State chose the goldfinch as the state bird," she commented.

"My wife loved to watch birds."

His voice was matter-of-fact, not mushy, but she felt a quiver of concern again, remembering what Lena had told her about him talking to his dead wife.

"Did your wife garden?" she asked.

"No. Liz wanted to put in a Zen sand garden surrounded by rivers of stones with shrubs here and there. I'm the garden fiend. I planned that whole area on paper, brought in dirt, added compost, peat moss, bulbs, perennials, shrubs, trees—that laburnum is one of my favorites."

Diana had always wanted a garden. Living in the city,

all she'd ever managed were some indoor pots and a hanging basket or two out on her veranda. This garden was a little too tidy, she thought. She'd prefer an old-fashioned garden with wallflowers, hollyhocks, roses—masses of roses. She wouldn't have any idea how to go about making such a garden though.

Connor's lawn was the incredible green of an exclusive golf club that allowed only wealthy members. All kinds of colorful flowers grew in banked soil around the edges, along with mounds of mossy stuff and other mounds of heather. Stepping-stones of exposed aggregate were scattered around. She knew something about aggregate, having had a boyfriend who worked in research and development in the concrete industry. He'd been concrete in his thinking, too.

"Flash?" Connor prompted.

She turned around and came back to the sofa, perching on its edge. "You've kept it up well," she said. "The garden."

"I don't do it alone. The guy who takes care of that pocket park—Rainbow Park—near the elementary school moonlights for me in exchange for chiropractic care."

He gazed at her directly. "I'm going to sit right here until you answer my question, Flash."

She sighed. "When I was a little girl, I used to pretend I lived in a castle with a moat surrounding it. There were sharks in the moat, armed guards keeping watch behind the portcullis, which was usually down and locked. Nobody could get in."

She glanced at him in obvious apology and held up a hand in a helpless gesture that moved him tremendously. "I'm not purposely avoiding your questions. I've always been afraid that if I were to start talking about my past, I might never stop."

He held her gaze, and after a moment she took a deep

breath, then let it out on a long sigh. "My parents were hip-pies, yes." Her mouth twisted. "A writer named Peter Fryer defined a hippy as a 'product of the Haight-Ashbury dis-trict of San Francisco. Anarchic successors to the Beat generation. Essential beliefs—protest, legalized drugs, opting out. Not to be confused with conventional youths who like to dress up at weekends.' I memorized that from a dictionary of slang. Mom and Dad to a T, barefoot and waving flowers, dining on psychedelic drugs. Not only were they hippies, they were religious hippies, practicing what they called "natural" religion. Lots of Bible reading to go along with the smoke. They met during the famous summer of love, founded a sort of cult, named it Edensong. They had a lot of followers. They were—are—charismatic, I guess. I can never see them clearly, there's too much chaotic history between us."

She stood up and paced a while between the sofa and the French windows. "That really is an extraordinary gar-den," she said, stopping to gaze at it again. "This whole house is amazing. It's not at all like the others in town."

"You were telling me about your parents."

"Oh, yeah. The summer of love. I was born three years after they met. We lived in a sort of trailer park on an empty lot at the edge of the Haight."

After another silence, she started walking around the room, checking out the art. Most of the works were Liz's choice. She had liked abstracts, which of course went with the house best. Connor had been happy to let her have her way, though he would prefer something more accessible. The Impressionists. No, they'd hardly go with the furni-ture. Landscapes though. Maybe photographs. Josef Scaylea. Ansel Adams. Diana Gordon. *Not* Joshua Patton.

Diana turned around to face him, her back to the wall. Literally and maybe metaphorically.

"Actually, it wasn't quite as bad as it sounds," she said. "Most of the trailers were double-wides and nicely furnished. The trailer park was minimal as far as landscaping went, but it was clean. There were showers, flush toilets, laundry facilities, all the amenities. Could have been any fairly upscale trailer park, U.S.A. Except that it was a commune. Residents shared everything."

"Everything?"

"Pretty much. Chores, money, food, gardening, spouses. I was definitely the product of my mother and father though. They assured me they didn't start swapping around until after I was born."

He was suddenly horrified. "They didn't—"

"No, none of them touched me. They knew I'd deck them if they did." She laughed shortly, bitterly. "I was always a tough cookie. A rebel. Have you ever seen *The Munsters* on TV?"

He shook his head, wondering if she was going off track again.

"There's this great TV channel. TV Land. I watch some of the old shows there: *Welcome Back Cotter*, *Andy Griffith*, *Happy Days*. Ron Howard was so cute then! Anyway, in *The Munsters*, everybody in the family—Herman, Lily, Grandpa, Eddie—is a monster except for Marilyn. She is what we would call normal, but the rest of her family think there's something wrong with her. They apologize for her. To them, *she's* the monster. I was Marilyn. All kids rebel, sooner or later, don't you think? The joke here is that I rebelled myself straight, drugless, smokeless. Even sexless until I found someone "outside" to marry. As I told you, that didn't work out. But at the same time it wasn't a waste. It got me out of Edensong and the trailer park, and Larry, my husband, was an avid photographer. He taught me a lot.

I helped him out on shoots the way Higby helps me. It was an interest that developed, if you'll pardon the pun, out of circumstances. When I threw Larry out, I kept all of his photographic equipment, including his darkroom stuff. So when I needed money to put myself through college, it all came in handy for doing weddings and school pictures."

"It was an early marriage then."

"I was eighteen, he was thirty-two, well on his way to being an alcoholic. I thought I could help him, change him. Ha!"

Connor decided it was best to forget about the ex-husband. The *last* husband. "Your parents still live in San Francisco?"

She shook her head and came back to sit on the sofa. "When I was about halfway through college, the neighborhood brought in a developer who wanted to buy the land and build high-rise condominiums on it. He offered a ton of money, which I think the neighbors probably all contributed to, they'd never stopped hassling. The entire commune voted to accept the offer. My parents moved the whole kit and caboodle to Idaho. They call every other year or so, when they remember me."

She laughed. "They don't remember much. But then, like Grace Slick said, 'If you remember the sixties, you weren't there.' "

She hesitated, and he got the idea from the undecided expression on her face that she was debating how much more to let loose.

"So what did you do *after* college?" he asked to help her along.

"Insurance," she said.

"That's rather vague."

"You've noticed."

She was warning him off, he recognized, but he persisted anyway. "I can't see you working in something as prosaic as insurance."

"Prosaic? Gosh, no, insurance can be real exciting. Life, accident, dismemberment, not to mention dental."

Much too breezy to be true, and she was suddenly avoiding eye contact.

"Well, okay, it was boring," she admitted with a false-sounding little laugh. "But it paid well, and I kept up the photography. And gradually, the photography took over."

Head tilted, she gazed at him with a challenging air as if daring him to find anything wrong with her story.

"That's about it," she said, when he didn't respond. "Was it worth swimming across the moat?"

He was quite sure she hadn't told him the half of it, but judging by the set of her mouth, it wasn't worth trying to get any more information out of her. He had no desire to get bitten by those sharks she'd mentioned, or shot down in flames by the armed guards. And of course, it was no damn business of his, except that he wanted to make *her* his business.

"Isn't it time we got to work?" Diana said.

"You were going to tell me about last night."

"I already have."

"You haven't told me why you think someone might have killed Rosemary thinking she was you."

She laughed. "Say what?"

"Okay, that didn't come out too clearly. Let me put it this way. Why would anyone want to kill *you?*"

"I don't know."

Her gaze was straying again.

"Then *who* would want to kill you? Your ex-husband?"

"He doesn't know where I am. As far as I know. And he's inclined to be lazy, so I don't think he'd go that far.

Last I heard he was getting married to the woman he hooked up with after I put him out. I expect he's sniffing *her* panties now. Speaking of which, when I was at Rosemary's house—"

"Are you going to keep changing the subject?"

"Hey, I was about to tell you an interesting Rosemary story. But if you don't want to hear it . . ."

"Later," he said. "Right now I'm more interested in who else might have it in for you."

"Everybody makes enemies sooner or later, Connor."

He gave up, then stood up, fully intending to go get Rosemary's laptop.

But she gazed up at him, her face wan. "Are you shocked by my unpretty background?" she asked. She seemed suddenly desperately weary and lonely, which was exactly how he often felt. Automatically, he reached out a hand to her, and she took it. As she stood up, he pulled her gently but determinedly into his arms and kissed her on the mouth. Thoroughly. Earth trembled on its axis. A few planets shifted to other areas of space.

"Wow," Diana said, when she came up for air. Her hands cupped his face and her gaze met his with an intensity that matched his own.

"Wow indeed," he agreed. Then he added, "To answer your question, yes, I'm shocked that you had to go through such a dreadful childhood. I'm also impressed that you had the courage to break away and to make your own way. I admired you before, Flash. I admire you even more now."

His mouth brushed her mouth again, slowly, moving lingeringly over hers, his tongue tracing her lips. She tasted clean and warm and pine-scented as though she had recently come out of the deep woods.

Her hands traveled to the back of his neck, to his shoulders, to his neck again. Her hips swayed against his, wanting to get closer. No, he was the one who was moving, his hands clasping her lovely, firm bottom.

"Once in a while, when I was in college, I'd get a crush on some guy and agree to a date," she said. "Sooner or later, he'd kiss me and it was like—nothing. No feeling, no emotion, no nothing. The only reason I married the man I married was that I felt some stirrings. I'd really given up on feeling anything strong."

He smiled.

She smiled back.

A moment or a minute later, he didn't know which, he took her hand in his, kissed it, then eased her into the guest bedroom, avoiding the bedroom where he'd slept with Liz, where Liz's portrait stood on the dresser, and Liz gazed directly out with her eyes wide open.

They watched each other undressing, without speaking, but also without awkwardness, and he thought he had known since the first time he met her that eventually they would come together like this.

At the last minute, he remembered to be responsible and searched for and found the proper protection. There was no way to see discreetly if there was an expiration date on the package, but he was fairly certain the contents would still work. She smiled at him with obvious approval and no hint of embarrassment. He sensed that she would always be straightforward about practical things. If it needed to be done, it would be done.

She had a wonderfully firm body, with well-toned muscles and skin like silk. It was obvious from the start that she was going to be an equal partner in their lovemaking. No lying back and letting him have at it. He wasn't at all surprised by this. She was on top, on her side, now yielding, now demanding, now giving, with as much urgency as he was feeling and demonstrating, the two of them tumbling together and loving with a kind of desperate lust at first, but then settling into a gentle rhythm, a dance as old as life itself. He liked that she watched him the whole time, her dark eyes wide open and hot.

Afterward, he stroked her face with the back of his hand, feeling drained, yet at the same time filled with a deep tenderness. She regarded him with equal tenderness.

Equal was a word that kept occurring to him, he realized. He wasn't sure he and Liz had always been equal. He'd loved making love to her, but he'd never felt quite as . . .

He killed his disloyal thoughts.

"When you want to distract a guy, you really distract him," he said. "Are you ever going to tell me what it is you suspect about the man who broke into your studio?"

"I don't really know what I suspect, Connor." She smiled. "It's all probably in my imagination. Once I brought it out in the open by mentioning it to you, it sounded incredibly stupid. That's why I didn't want to get into it too much. I guess my subconscious doesn't like dramas I don't have a part in; it has to cast me as the lead character without any real evidence."

She yawned charmingly like a kitten, then touched his cheek. "If I lie here much longer, I'm going to nod off. So if you are quite through with me, I guess we should shower and dive into Rosemary's laptop again."

"Mmm," he agreed, but didn't move.

"You aren't through with me?"

"The spirit is willing," he said.

She laughed, yanked the top sheet out of the tangle of bedding, pulled it around her, and sat up on the side of the bed.

"Diana," he said, and she turned. Her ponytail had come undone, and her dark hair hung like a curtain around her face. She was so lovely, so softened around the edges, so unlike her usual somewhat remote self, he wanted to drag her back into his arms.

"Just when I got used to you calling me Flash you had to turn formal," she said.

"Not formal, serious," he said.

She appeared alarmed. "Let's not get too serious yet, okay? We have to get used to this, see how it's going to play out."

"I wasn't going to propose," he said with a grin.

"Good. See that you don't. I have a lousy track record with men. Don't say I didn't warn you."

He sensed that the sharks were swimming around in the moat.

"So what did you want to say that was so serious?" she asked. She sounded amused, but she had turned away at the same time.

"Whatever this does turn out to be—between you and me—I would hope it would be joyful. Without angst."

"Angst isn't in my vocabulary," she said.

Remembering her story about being the normal person in a family of monsters, he doubted that, but wasn't about to argue with her.

"Okay. Now that we have that settled . . ." He reached out and playfully pulled the sheet down from her shoulders. He hadn't expected to reveal a scar that ran down the left side of her back and curved under her left breast. He sat up. The last time he'd seen a scar like this was at a poolside party, a friend of Liz's who'd been operated on for lung cancer.

Cancer. Liz had *died* of cancer. He felt a chill all the way down to his toes.

Reaching out, he ran an exploratory finger over the slightly raised scar. "What happened here?" he asked.

She stiffened, then rubbed the back of her neck and

laughed in a rueful way. "Okay, you've got me, I've had some angst in my background, but let's not spoil the day, okay?"

He could tell by her voice that she had switched off emotionally again.

"Okay." He didn't have much choice but to agree, she was already heading for the bathroom.

Sighing, Connor followed her.

A half hour later, they were in his home office, Rosemary Barrett's laptop open in front of them.

It was probably no more than fifteen minutes before they had a breakthrough, and it was a major breakthrough.

Diana had gone checking on Windows Explorer and discovered that though there was no AOL icon on the desktop, Rosemary had subscribed to America Online as well as the local Internet service provider.

"We need Rosemary's password to get into AOL," she pointed out as the familiar logo appeared on the computer screen. "Most people use something simple, something personal."

They tried Melissa, Dmitri, Rosemary, Rose, Mary. Then Connor telephoned Melissa.

"Mama's middle name was Anne," she told him after she'd asked a lot of questions and he'd avoided the answers.

Anne didn't work. Annie did.

Diana clicked on Read, then New Mail, Old Mail, Sent Mail, Filing Cabinet. All were empty.

"I guess she didn't use AOL," Connor murmured.

"Why pay for it then?" Diana asked.

She clicked on Sign Off to see if there were any other screen names. Annie was listed there, too. So was Barrett.

"Okay, if she used Annie as a password to get into Rosemary, maybe she used Rosemary to get into Annie," Diana muttered.

She was wrong.

She thought for a while. "What did she call her cat, do you know?"

"It's an orange cat," Connor said.

"Marmalade," Diana guessed. "Every orange cat I ever knew about was called Marmalade."

She typed it in. "Nope, that's not it."

Connor tried to remember. "She gave me a whole lecture once on why male orange cats outnumber female cats three to one, which led to a lot of discussion of X and Y chromosomes, which she called gender chromosomes." He grinned. "Most people call them sex chromosomes, but not our Rosemary. Anyway, her cat was a female. She was pleased about that."

He paused. "Ginger. She called it Ginger."

"Bull's-eye," Diana said.

This time Filing Cabinet contained a long string of E-mails, dating back to the start of the year. All from the same person. Someone called Bertie.

"Annie and Bertie. Sounds too cute to be innocent," Diana said.

The E-mails were so hot they could have set the laptop on fire. Full of "my darling" and "my beloved" and sexual references that left no doubt Annie and Bertie had been getting it on for some time.

"Sheesh!" Diana exclaimed after reading a particularly detailed description of a lovemaking episode.

"I feel like a voyeur," Connor said.

"Me, too." She glanced at him sideways. "I haven't been this shocked since I found the underwear."

"What underwear?"

"I tried to tell you about it before, but you shut me up. While I was in the Barrett house, I sort of poked around

Rosemary's bedroom, and I found this amazing underwear that looked as if it came out of Victoria's Secret."

"It was just lying around?"

"Sure." The tip of her tongue appeared between her teeth. "It was lying around in Rosemary's dressing table drawer."

His eyebrows climbed.

"As I told you earlier, sometimes the end justifies the means."

"Uh-huh. So tell me about the underwear."

She did.

The thongs surprised him, too. *"Rosemary?"*

"Ms. Proper herself."

"A red garter belt?"

"Hard to imagine, I know."

"If I had thought about it, and believe me, I never did, I would have thought jockeys."

"She had those, too. Nice pristine white ones. For her real life. Unless the thong life was what she considered the real life."

Connor nodded. "So I guess the extremely important question of the hour is—who is Bertie?"

"Well, to start with, Bertie's probably not his real name. Annie wasn't Rosemary's." She thought for a few seconds. "On the other hand, Annie was *part* of Rosemary's real name. She wasn't a particularly imaginative woman. Maybe Bertie wasn't an imaginative man—apart from sexually anyway. What we need to do is examine everyone who had a connection with Rosemary, then see if we can fit the name Bertie in there anywhere."

"She was involved with a lot of people in the various groups she belonged to. Church and the arts groups and friends of the library, city council, the hospital. She was even involved in hospice at one time, that's where she was when she was so rude to Liz."

"What did she do?"

"Told her she must accept God's will. Liz wasn't one to 'go gentle into that good night.' "

"I would hope not. You know the rest of that? Well of course you do—you're Irish, poetry's in your genes."

Connor smiled. " 'Old age should burn and rave at close of day; / Rage, rage against the dying of the light.' " He paused before going on. "Liz had vowed to fight the cancer tooth and claw, and that's what she did. She told Rosemary that she didn't believe it was God's intention that she should get sick. She said people were always too ready to blame God for everything that happened to them. Her God wasn't all that punitive, she said."

"And Rosemary came back with . . . ?"

"She called Liz a heretic. Liz was in the last stages of cancer then. She died a month later. I never forgave Rosemary."

"Our Rosemary was a real sweetheart, wasn't she? It's going to be difficult to decide who did kill her. Seems as if a lot of people had a motive or two lying around waiting for an opportunity."

"I didn't kill her, Flash," Connor said solemnly.

"I didn't think you did," Diana said. She was every bit as serious. "I'd like you to believe that I didn't either."

"I do believe that."

She smiled. "Good, then we don't have to worry anymore about what Rosemary had, or thought she had, on me, right?"

Niftily done, Connor thought. However, as he was still feeling the satisfied buzz brought on by their lovemaking, and was definitely hoping for more, he wasn't going to argue with her. Not now, at least.

Chapter 16

CONNOR TOOK THE evening newspaper to bed with him. It was the first time since Liz's death that he hadn't read it while eating his dinner. He had no regrets about not reading it earlier this evening.

He felt happy, he realized, and immediately wondered if he should even read the newspaper, which was usually a depressing thing to do.

No new wars had broken out, he was pleased to see. The various war stories that had been revived for Armed Forces Day had concluded in the Sunday edition. The Dow was fairly stable. One story disturbed him greatly—a story that was not exactly common, but seemed to be turning up far too often: a border crossing turned deadly. A truck found abandoned in a California rest area had contained the bodies of twenty-three people. Eighteen were Mexicans, five from South America. All had died from lack of air in the unventilated truck.

Connor remembered reading a similar story about people found in a sealed truck in Dover, England, another one in Texas.

These particular poor people had been brought in from Baja California. No doubt they had paid someone to bring them into the U.S., probably with the promise of work, food, housing. Desperate people, taken advantage of in the worst possible way. Authorities suspected an organization known to operate out of Brazil and El Salvador, an organization that smuggled in immigrants along with drugs. If the immigrants were caught, well, the drugs were obviously theirs.

Connor knew that many U.S. citizens were against any kind of immigrants, legal or illegal, seeing them at best as job-stealers, and at worst as potential terrorists. Many wanted to impose Draconian measures to keep immigrants out. They forgot that *their* ancestors had come to this country hoping for a better life, as his parents had come when they couldn't find work in Ireland. Most immigrants, according to all reports he'd read, were hardworking, honest, and honorable people.

Turning the page, he came to the Letters to the Editor. Otto Schmidt, the feisty old guy who had punched him in the eye at the photo show, had written at length about his petition to ban future "evil" photographs from being shown in Quinn Center, *"Our* Community Center, the beating heart of our town, which should be a pure heart, catering to the pure in heart."

Didn't matter where you were, there was someone against something.

At the end of his letter, Otto reiterated his invitation for one and all to come by and sign his petition.

The letter seemed like a good excuse to talk to Diana. About to reach for the phone—it wasn't all that late—Connor changed his mind. The letter also seemed like a good excuse to go *see* Diana.

* * *

HE WAS EARLY for his 7:30 A.M. walk with Sarah the next morning, so he stopped off at Photomania, hoping Diana might be up. He was disappointed to see by the discreet sign in the window that he was an hour and a half ahead of opening time. Diana was probably still asleep. The street was almost deserted, only a couple of cars and a handful of pedestrians in sight. Diana's big red get-away van was in the parking lot. Just beyond the whimsical sign that said, Otter Crossing, an otter was humping along the waterfront, tail dragging and bouncing. Connor laughed.

Realizing the tide was out, he walked around the side of the building on the off chance that Diana might be taking an early morning jog like the otter.

His spirits lifted like bubbles in a champagne flute when he saw her on her own little beach, wearing black sweats, her hair pinned up in a knot, practicing her Tai Chi. The early sunlight painted her shadow on the wet sand. He watched with pleasure as her slow and graceful movements flowed seamlessly from one position to another, hands and arms now outstretched, now pulled back, now lowered, her body turning from the hips, left to right to left again, feet sometimes following, sometimes staying put as she shifted her weight forward and back.

And then she did the whole thing over again, only faster. Much faster. A blur of motion that ended with Diana in a position he'd seen on television—the yoga warrior pose—her body stretched taut as an archer's bow, her arms forming the arrow.

His breath exploded out of him. "Whoa!" he exclaimed.

"How long have you been standing there?" she asked, coming out of the pose.

"Long enough to be reminded of Muhammad Ali."

She smiled her magical smile. "I'm the greatest?"

He shook his head. "Floats like a butterfly, stings like a bee."

She laughed, and he walked across the sand and kissed her.

"You're out early," she said, not quite returning the kiss.

He backed off a little. "Look who's talking. I saw your get-away van in the parking lot." He paused. "Interesting name, that."

She gave him a wry smile this time. "It was the name of the van that first appealed to me. I've spent a lot of effort getting away. From Edensong, from Larry, from—well, whatever."

She'd broken off abruptly, and the kiss had been tepid. Would he have to storm the castle all over again? He'd better play it cool, see if maybe the armed guards would go off duty. He didn't want to push his luck. She might want to get away from him.

"Believe it or not, I walk with Sarah Hathaway most mornings. I'm due to meet her in fifteen minutes, but I wanted to talk something over with you first."

She glanced at her watch, then indicated a large driftwood log up close to her property. "The Thanksgiving Day storm left me a sofa."

"You're lucky it didn't blow your house down."

"You keep hearkening back to those wolves, don't you?"

He laughed, but then seized the opening. "I was thinking last night about where people come from."

Surprise raised her eyebrows. "Me, too, now there's a coincidence—" She shook her head. "No, it's not, you read that horrible story in the *Journal*, too. How anyone can be so inhumane is beyond me. Two of my grandparents emigrated to this country. I read a story like that, I think of them. It wasn't easy for my maternal grandmother, but nothing like that."

"Is Gordon your maiden name?"

"It was my father's name, yes. I never did change it."

"It sounds English."

"Scottish, actually. His father was a schoolteacher."

He frowned, and she laughed. "Yes, I know. The black hair, the almost-black eyes, the olive skin. My maternal grandmother was Spanish—Carmela Navarro—obviously that's where my genes came from. Though I'm a thrifty woman, so no doubt there's a little of Scotland mixed in there. Both Carmela and my Scottish grandfather married Americans after they got here. *Their* ancestors were immigrants a few generations before."

"Whatever the percentage, it's a great mixture," Connor said.

She smiled warmly, and he felt immeasurably better. She'd even given him more information. Maybe he'd imagined the earlier distance.

Remembering his excuse for coming, he trotted it out. "I think we'd better have an Arts Alliance board meeting."

Diana groaned. "I'd hoped we could avoid one for a while. I'm still stressed from that damn photo show and all of its traumatic events." She groaned again when he didn't respond. "Okay, okay. I read Otto's letter to the editor, too. I agree that something has to be done. We need to decide on a policy. I don't think we'll have a problem with the bulk of Arts Alliance members, it's a pretty liberal group, apart from a couple of the board members. Al, for one. We should maybe ask for a board meeting for tomorrow or Wednesday, give ourselves time to go talk to Otto and see if we can cut him off at the pass."

"Sounds good to me. I'll call Al and make the suggestion. We probably need to confirm him as president anyway."

"Oh God, Big Al's going to be president?"

"He didn't get much of a chance to do anything while Rosemary was in charge. He might turn out okay, Flash. Let's give him a chance."

"Please. Don't go long-suffering on me. Al's hopeless; you know that. A Rosemary clone in trousers. Without her gift for organization."

She twisted on the log and stared off toward the west where the still snow-capped Olympics were showing clearly. It always amazed Connor that though the mountains weren't all that high, they were extremely rugged.

"You want to go see Otto with me later?" she asked, turning back. "I have an hour or so free."

"I work all day on Tuesdays, remember?"

"So you do." There was a smile in her voice. He wished he could spend the whole day sitting on this driftwood log in the sunshine with her by his side. "I'm not working this evening," he said pointedly.

"I'll give you a call after I see Otto," she said.

"Not on your life," he said. "We're supposed to be in this together."

She smiled wryly. "Even when I was—when I worked with other people, they'd complain that I was too used to being a loner. I can't seem to get used to consulting someone else. Something needs to be done, I want to go do it."

"Well, you and I are partners now. Ham and eggs, biscuits and gravy, bread and butter."

"Let me guess. You haven't had breakfast?"

He laughed, leaned over, and kissed her cheek. "I'm going to pick something up at Java Jenny's after my walk with Sarah. Want to meet me there?"

She shook her head. "There's a *Nash Bridges* rerun on at eight A.M. I'm going to have breakfast while I watch it. USA puts the reruns on so infrequently anymore and at such odd hours, I have to adjust my schedule to suit. I can never remember to record it."

He laughed. "I guess I'm no competition for Don Johnson."

"You're okay," she said.

Encouraged, he proposed an alternative. "I have a two hour lunch break. Noon to two P.M. How about then?"

"Can do." She paused. "I actually scoped out Otto's address in the phone book. He lives on Balsam. Is that a tree or a flower?"

"It's the common name for the Pacific silver fir."

"Why?"

"Well, the Pacific silver fir, like other true firs, develops protruding blisters which contain Canadian balsam."

"So what does anyone do with the balsam?"

"The only use I know about is a commercial one. It's used as a mounting material for microscope slides."

"You are so knowledgeable! Queasy dillers, balsam . . ."

There was a teasing note in her voice that he was glad to hear. It seemed to promise a little hope.

"A regular fount, that's me," he agreed.

"Hmmm." She giggled, obviously providing a salacious meaning to his comment. He laughed, too, then headed off toward the police station and his meeting with Sarah.

BUT AFTER ALL, he had to call at 11:30 and postpone his date with Diana until 12:30, when one of his regular patients called to say she'd sprained her ankle while jogging in Bromley Park and she could be in his clinic in half an hour.

He didn't actually speak to Diana, she was busy with a customer. Higby took the message. "Tell her not to go anywhere without me," Connor said.

Higby delivered the message without comment but with a face alight with interest.

"Uh-huh," Diana said.

It was difficult for her to discipline herself to wait. She certainly didn't do it patiently. Higby's expression took on more and more curiosity as she paced back and forth in the studio, picking things up, laying them down.

But finally, Connor drove up. He was obviously pleased that she'd waited. "How was Nash?" he asked.

She made a face. "He was okay, but it was the episode where Evan got shot. I don't care for that one." She grinned. "I don't suppose Evan did either. Must be awful for actors when they see in the script that they're about to be wounded. Make them wonder if they are going to be out of work. But I think Evan recovers from this one. It's hard to remember; they show the reruns in any old order they wish. I've no idea why they do that—gets confusing."

Connor risked a quick kiss on her cheek, and she smiled at him.

Otto Schmidt's house had a small porch in front, with rails around it and a couple of benches to sit on. Otto didn't answer his doorbell. Diana tried the doorknob. The door was locked.

"Flash!" Connor chided.

She made a face at him.

"What's up?" Otto asked from behind them, making them both jump.

Thankful that Otto hadn't caught her walking into his house, Diana gave him more of a smile than she might have under other circumstances, which made his eyes squinch almost closed. His face resembled those doll faces carved from apples, she thought. His gray beard had been trimmed since she saw him last.

"I suppose you both read my letter to the editor?" he said in a challenging way, then smiled thinly. "Did you want to sign my petition?"

"We didn't come about your petition," Diana said, hoping to make him more relaxed, receptive to questions.

"So what do you want?"

Apparently, he wasn't going to open up his house to them. Diana sat down on the end of one of the benches to show she was planning on staying a while. Connor sat on the other end and patted the space in between them. Otto sat.

So okay, maybe this partnership thing worked sometimes, Diana thought.

"Melissa Ludlow asked us to investigate her mother's death," Connor said.

"What's Rosemary's death got to do with either of you?"

"Well, we did find her body. And Melissa seemed to think we could help."

Otto turned to glare at Diana. "Never thought you thought much of Rosemary."

"I thought she was awesome." That was true. She had been in awe of the woman's energy and power.

Otto seemed appeased. "She was amazin', wasn't she? She'll be sorely missed." His face was alight with something that was a little more than affection.

"I think you were fond of her," Connor said.

Otto shook his head fairly forcefully. "Fond sounds too personal. I wouldn't have dared be fond. No way. No way."

He'd loved her, Diana thought. Which would seem to rule him out as a suspect.

Unless he'd approached Rosemary and had been refused. If she knew anything at all about Rosemary, it was that she had not usually refused people politely.

"I'm damn mad at whoever killed her," Otto said.

"You have any ideas about who it might be?" Connor asked.

Otto leaned back against the shiplap siding while he considered. "Well, I was sure shocked by Dmitri at the memorial service."

Diana nodded. "We all were."

"But I don't think Dmitri would have shot her. Can't imagine him handlin' a gun. Too complicated, way he is now. A hunk of wood—an ax maybe—that would be more his speed."

Maybe Otto *had* thought about killing Rosemary. Why else would he come up with those specific suggestions?

"You know anyone who might have a gun?" Diana asked.

Otto disappeared inside his own head for a while, his expression totally blank. Evidently that indicated he was thinking. "Well," he said after a fairly long silence, "if you two are serious about lookin' into this thing, you might go visit Bud Knight. He's done some huntin'."

"Rosemary wasn't shot with a rifle," Connor said.

"He could own other guns."

Diana frowned. "His name sounds vaguely familiar, but I can't quite place him."

"He makes a career out of writin' letters to the editor," Otto said.

Well, Otto would notice that, being both newspapers' primary self-elected correspondent. Diana remembered the name now. Many of Bud Knight's letters had been vitriolic complaints about Rosemary Barrett.

She'd even met him once. He was a handsome man. Middle-aged, but bearing up well. Maybe *he* was a discarded lover.

Bud.

"What's his real first name?" she asked, hoping for something that could be shortened to Bertie.

Otto shrugged. "Everyone calls him Bud. Them as talks to him."

"People don't talk to him?"

"People who admired Rosemary don't."

"You know where Bud Knight lives?" Connor asked, standing up and glancing at his watch.

Otto shrugged. "Guess he's probably in the book."

His helpfulness was evidently at an end.

"So do you wanna sign my petition?" he asked.

"Otto, those photographs were beautiful and artistic representations of the human body," Connor said. "There's nothing shameful about the human body."

"Is when it's nekkid," he said, his face flushing. "Rosemary wanted those pictures out. Hadn't been for this woman here"—he pointed a gnarled finger at Diana— "the rest of the committee woulda gone along with her. Disgustin', I call it."

Connor and Diana glanced at each other and stood up, in full agreement that arguing with Otto would be a waste of time.

"You sure you don't wanna sign my petition?" he called after them as they walked back to Connor's Jeep at the side of the street. Giggling dementedly, he unlocked his front door and disappeared inside.

Connor drove to Rainbow Park, pulled into the almost empty lot, and called 4-1-1 on his cell phone to ask for a number for Bud Knight. Unfortunately, his subsequent call went unanswered. "The drugstore," Diana suggested.

His expression was blank.

"Public telephone. Phone book. Address."

"Brilliant," he said, turning on the ignition.

Bud Knight's residence was a fair-size house. Well

cared for, but painted chartreuse, a color that appeared beyond artificial next to the surrounding trees.

Nobody answered the bell. Diana was constitutionally unable to resist trying a doorknob, it seemed. This front door was not locked.

No chiding from Connor this time. He was evidently getting the hang of this investigation thing.

A stereo was blasting Alice in Chains in the living room, immediately beyond the door. There was a state-of-the-art computer system on the far side of the room, including a flat-panel monitor that Diana immediately coveted, and speakers like futuristic metal sculptures.

About to step inside—to call out, she assured herself—Diana heard a shower running. Connor heard it at the same time. "Not a good time to visit," he murmured.

Hurriedly, Diana scrawled a note on her business card, asking Bud to call, then dropped it on the doormat as if she'd pushed it through a crack in the door.

"I have to get back to the clinic," Connor said as he dropped her off at Photomania. "Let me know if Bud calls; we'll work out a time to come back."

Diana nodded.

A short time later she answered the phone at Photomania while Higby was getting a trio of matronly ladies—sisters—in position for a portrait.

"How are you this fine afternoon?" a male voice asked.

She was instantly furious. She'd installed a telezapper, signed up for "Do not call." One thing she couldn't do was install Caller ID. Not much use at a business address.

She hung up.

Almost immediately the phone rang again. "Ms. Diana?" the same voice said. "Didn't you intend that I call? I thought maybe you wanted me to pose for you?" He laughed. "You did leave me your card."

Bud Knight. His sleaziness was her own fault for leaving her business card on the doormat. "I want to talk to you about something else entirely," she said crisply.

"No photograph? No full monty?"

"No photograph of any kind."

"Darn. Well, this won't do, Ms. Diana. I don't trust phones. Never know who's listening in."

Another paranoid resident of Port Findlay.

"You're welcome to come back to my house," he added. "I'm out of the shower now, and you've got me real curious."

No way was she going to do that alone. It took her all of five seconds to decide she had to strike while the contact was hot, however. *Sorry, Connor.*

"How about Java Jenny's in one hour," she suggested, and he agreed, though with obvious reluctance.

He was there ahead of her and made a big show of clattering his chair back and pulling one out for her next to his. She sat opposite him instead, and he immediately sat down and leaned forward across the small round table. "What can I do for you?" he asked.

He was a good-looking man, if you went for slicked-down hair, well-proportioned features, smooth skin, and tailoring that was a little too close a fit. He was a salesman, she remembered. The local automobile showroom.

"What's your real first name?" she asked as Jenny served up their lattes.

He smiled. "I get that a lot from the ladies. I was christened Bud, believe it or not. My old man always said he named me for his favorite beer—guess it was a good thing he didn't care for Hefeweizen."

Diana had expected Bud to be a nickname, had hoped his real name might be downsized to Bertie. Gilbert, Herbert, Albert. Now there was a thought. Big Al. Surely not . . .

Of course there was a good chance Bud wasn't telling the truth about his name. She'd check up on him later.

"I've been asked to investigate Rosemary Barrett's death," she told him.

He leaned back, eyes hooded, face suddenly as smooth as a sleeping baby's. "You didn't tell me you were a cop. Card said photographer."

"I'm not a cop. Rosemary's daughter Melissa asked me to see what I could find out."

His eyes crinkled in a practiced way that was obviously meant to be charming. "You aim to be the Jessica Fletcher of Port Findlay, huh?"

"Nothing that formal. I'm asking around as a favor to Melissa."

"I'm your numero uno suspect?"

She looked at him directly. "No. I've already eliminated a few others. You're probably number four or five."

He laughed. "I'm glad to hear it. I thought everyone else in town was part of the general Rosemary Barrett lovefest."

"Judging by your letters to the newspapers, you weren't."

"Well, I didn't hate her enough to knock her off, if that's what you're getting at. My letters were intended to shake, rattle, and rile her from time to time. I got terminally tired of her being in charge of every damn thing, always showing up in a profile story in the newspapers, citizen of the year, queen of clubs, queen of hearts."

"Not the queen of your heart, I gather."

"Better believe it. Wasn't it the queen of hearts who was forever yelling, 'Off with their heads!' Doesn't that describe our Rosemary to you?"

She was surprised he'd read *Alice in Wonderland*. But he was right, the description fitted Rosemary Barrett.

"So you didn't exactly love her, but you had no real grievance against her?"

"A ton of grievance, but nothing to inspire violence, I assure you. Besides which, on that particular Thursday morning I was in Seattle at the annual automobile show, along with my two partners and several hundred potential witnesses." He smiled a winning "I can sell you this BMW before you can tell what hit you" kind of smile.

Finishing her coffee, Diana thanked him for his time, excused herself, and returned to Photomania, where she discovered that Big Al Rutherford had called an Arts Alliance board meeting for 7:30, which, following her afternoon appointments, gave her enough time for a tossed salad and a piece of chicken left over from a couple of nights before, plus a brief conversation with Lena Green before the rest of the board members arrived at Port Findlay's library's meeting room.

Swearing her to secrecy, she told her about Rosemary's E-mails to "Bertie," without revealing the exact contents, or how she'd come by the information.

Lena nodded in a knowing way. "I thought she must have a lover."

Diana was terribly tempted to ask if Higby's bit of gossip about Lena herself was true but reluctantly decided it wasn't germane to the present issue.

"Connor thinks we ought to tell Chief Hathaway about Bertie," she said instead.

"Not a good idea," Lena said immediately.

"My thought exactly. But what makes you say so?"

Lena hesitated, then sighed. "The chief is religious, which is not a bad thing in my opinion, you understand, but she's also narrow-minded, which *is* a bad thing. She divorced her own husband when she suspected he had an affair. She doesn't believe married people should stray even in their thoughts."

She grinned. "Like Jimmy Carter, remember, saying he had lusted in his heart."

"How do you know all that?" Diana asked.

"It was in all the newspapers."

"Not the thing about Jimmy—*President*—Carter! How do you know all that about Sarah Hathaway?"

Lena's usually smooth brow furrowed. "I've no idea." She shrugged. "Someone said. You know how it is in this town. People talk."

There were sounds in the corridor outside, heralding the arrival of other board members. Connor was about the sixth arrival. He was wearing his sexy black shirt again. His face lit up with a smile when he saw her, and she felt her face warm up a smile of its own while her pulse revved way above its normal seventy-six. No doubt about it, she was getting hooked.

That thought gave rise to a set of warnings that traveled through her brain as though they were printed on ticker tape.

ATTENTION! This is a man who talks to his dead wife in the cemetery. This is a man who lives in a house that could have been modeled on the Starship Enterprise. *This is a man who ADORED his wife.*

She took her seat at the long table, avoiding Connor's gaze.

"Does anybody ever call you Bertie?" she asked Al while they waited for the rest of the board members to stop chatting and get seated.

His fleshy face went completely blank. "Why would anybody want to do that?"

"Well, Albert—Bert—it's a natural . . ."

"My name isn't Albert, Diana, it's Alojzy—pronounced A*loy*zeu. It's Polish."

"Rutherford doesn't sound Polish," Diana said.

"My mother was Polish. Not my father. Alojzy is not so easy for people to say, so I go by Al." He showed his large, nicotine-stained teeth in a feral smile. "You can call me Big Al."

"Mmm," Diana said.

The meeting began. Big Al was elected president by a landslide. Nobody else wanted to follow in Rosemary's efficient and imperial footsteps, so there wasn't much choice. Higby agreed to serve as vice-president. Names were suggested for a new board member.

The agenda listed several items for discussion. A change in the date for the fall crafts fair, a new location for the art show, various other upcoming events including speakers for monthly meetings. First to be decided was the matter of setting a policy for entries in future photography shows. "We should examine this issue the way Rosemary would," Al said.

"No, we shouldn't," Diana and Connor said at the same moment.

"Let me amend that," Big Al said. "We must take *all* opinions into consideration."

Connor gave Diana a smug smile, which she interpreted as a reminder that he'd suggested giving Al a chance to show what he was made of.

Al proceeded to outline Rosemary's position on nude photographs, which allowed no compromises. Then he gave each of the board members a chance to state their views. Higby was in agreement with Diana and Connor: "Freedom of expression is essential to any artist."

Lena abstained, which evidently surprised Al. "Come

on, Lena," he said. "If you want to stick by Rosemary's position, say so. You've already told us you signed Otto's petition."

This was news to Diana, and she gazed at Lena in shock.

Lena squirmed uncomfortably. "Well, Otto asked me to, and he's, well, he's a friend."

Diana experienced a sudden amazing insight. "Otto?" she murmured to Higby, who was sitting next to her.

Higby smiled broadly.

Otto Schmidt was Lena's lover?

Diana's brain flashed an image of tough, scrawny Otto with his carved apple face and gray beard, his shaggy gray hair. She stared at Lena, flushed and pretty and plump, and wondered how she could possibly . . .

Lena was smiling wryly.

Otto? Diana mouthed.

Lena leaned forward. "I don't look at his face," she murmured.

Diana tried to hold on to her laughter until she was about to choke and had to let it go. A second later, Lena joined in.

"What's so funny?" Connor asked.

"Girl talk," Diana said.

Al banged his newly acquired gavel on the table.

Otto. Diana still couldn't quite believe—but then she remembered an early boyfriend or two she'd made the mistake of getting involved with because she was lonely, or feeling unloved and unwanted.

"Okay," Lena said, sobering abruptly. "Forget the petition. I thought those nude photos were beautiful."

Diana mimicked applause.

Bertha Miller, a tall, thin, solemn woman with iron-gray hair, who never had much to say at board meetings or any other time, murmured that she also liked the photos in question. The rest followed along.

The board members gazed at Big Al. "Me, too," he said, then added loyally for the benefit of Lena's minutes, "though I certainly appreciate Rosemary's position on the matter."

He then presented an obviously well-thought-out policy statement against any refusal of entries without full consent of the board, which Lena dutifully wrote down, Bertha moved and Higby seconded and everyone passed unanimously.

There would be repercussions from some Arts Alliance members, Diana felt sure, but she felt better about Al Rutherford being in charge. Who knew, maybe sometime she'd even bring herself to call him Big Al.

"Do people call you Bertie?" she asked Bertha Miller as the meeting broke up a half hour later.

"Over my dead body," the woman said, then shot a terrified glance all around as though afraid a stray murderer might be listening in.

Diana caught Connor's eye and realized he'd overheard. He twitched an eyebrow at her.

"Sorry," she murmured.

Bertha grunted.

"Does anyone know what Bud Knight had against Rosemary?" Diana asked the room at large.

"Well, for heaven's sake, Diana, everybody knows that," Lena said.

"I don't," Connor said.

"Me neither," Diana said.

Lena hunched her shoulders in apology. "I'm sorry. We're all so fond of you both we forget you are relatively new in town."

She smiled sweetly at Diana. "A few years ago, Rosemary beat Bud out for director of the Clean Water Project and for president of the historical society. She also ran against him for city council. He was the incumbent. She won. Somebody had been calling people at three o'clock in the morning, telling them to be sure to vote for Bud and to send money to support his campaign. Annoyed the hell out of them, as you can imagine. Bud was convinced it was Rosemary doing it."

"You sure it wasn't?" Diana asked.

"Of course. Rosemary would never stoop to such tactics."

Diana wasn't at all sure of that but restrained herself from arguing. What was the point?

"Bud told me he didn't have any feelings that would lead to violence against her," she said instead.

"You talked to him?" She hadn't realized Connor was standing next to her.

"Um. Yes." Might as well get the confession over with.

"I see." His smile was suddenly cool around the edges. "Did our partnership get dissolved when I wasn't paying attention?"

Uh-oh.

"Bud called me back," she told him. "He was ready to meet me right away. I didn't think I should put him off."

His expression held a certain amount of suspicion. Was her nose getting longer?

"He agreed to meet me in an hour," she amended. "Sleazy kind of guy."

"All the more reason I should have been with you."

"I played it safe, met him at Java Jenny's. I figured you'd still be working." She abandoned subterfuge in favor of truth. "Patience isn't one of my noticeable attributes."

She hated apologizing for her actions when she thought they'd been necessary. His face seemed . . . set.

He sighed, then put his hand to her elbow and eased her out of the room.

"Are we going to have a fight about this?" Diana asked.

"I'd rather make love than war," Connor said.

"Sounds like a hippie slogan."

"The hippies got some things right."

She laughed. Their eyes met. "Your place or mine?" she asked.

"Which would you prefer?"

She thought of the photo of Liz smiling serenely on his dresser. "Mine."

"I THINK IT'S time to talk to Sarah," Connor said as they were dressing after their shared shower.

Sitting on the side of the sleigh bed she'd found in one of Port Findlay's antique stores on the day after her arrival, Diana paused with her T-shirt in her hand. "I'd rather not do that."

Connor was squatting, tying his shoelaces. He had a great sense of balance. "Why not?"

"She'll wonder why I'm involved."

"You're involved because I asked for your help."

"But she'll still . . . I'd rather not go to her yet, Connor."

He stood up. "Okay. What next then?"

She glanced at the old schoolhouse clock on her bedroom wall. "Nine-thirty already? Too late to do much now. How about tomorrow evening we go back in that damn laptop again? We were so amazed by the letters to and from Bertie, we didn't go any further. But Dmitri said Rosemary put stuff in her computer about *people*, so she could *get* them. Maybe there's something in there about her adversarial relationship with Bud Knight. I also want to poke around and ask around, to see if I can find out if the guy's name is really Bud and not Bertie."

"With all the fights they had, you really think he could be Rosemary's Bertie?"

"Stranger things have happened when people want to cover up an affair."

His face showed doubt, then it brightened. "Tomorrow after work at my house then? I'll cook Italian. Pesto fettuccine."

He glanced at her clock. "It's not really all that late, Flash. What do you say we rustle up a glass of wine, sit and talk a while?"

She glanced behind her at the rumpled bed. "Fine with me. Though we should possibly have a change of venue. I'm not sure we could manage to sit and talk right here."

He nodded. "It's a wonderful bed." He regarded her searchingly. "I'm taken by the anomalies in your character. You are very much a woman of today—independent—"

"Bossy?"

"That, too. Yet you prefer old movies, TV shows, still like film in this digital age. You own an antique bed—"

"The mattress is new," she pointed out. "I appreciate old things, but not at the expense of comfort."

A glint appeared in his blue, blue eyes. "Hanging out here could possibly lead to other activities, all the same."

She felt a knot of interest form in a certain area of her jeans.

His suggestive smile told her he was experiencing a knot of his own.

"What happened to the flesh being weak?" she asked.

"Some things improve with practice."

She laughed. "One of the warm-up exercises I do before Tai Chi is called the prayer wheel. As you shift your weight from one leg to the other, you place your hands palm facing palm in front of you, shoulder width apart, and lift them up and around in a circle as though you were holding the rim of a wheel and turning it toward yourself. As you do so, you can feel the energy between your hands. Another exercise involves holding an imaginary ball. Again with hands facing each other, you can feel energy between them."

He was interested, but obviously puzzled.

"Sometimes that same kind of energy happens between two people," she continued.

"Energy. Used to be pheromones."

"Admit it, energy's better."

His grin was salacious.

"I'll get the wine and bring it in here then," Diana said. She tossed her T-shirt onto the chair at the side of the bed. "I guess I won't be needing that."

Connor grinned. Without a word, he sat down on the edge of the bed and began untying his shoelaces.

Diana laughed. She liked this man a lot, she thought.

Chapter 17

"THE ONLY DIRECTORIES left are listed under the Barrett screen name. Recipes, Menus, and Supplies," Diana said.

It was the following day, soon after quitting time for both of them. They were in Connor's office at his clinic, at Diana's suggestion. They would be more likely to stick to business there, she'd suspected. An adjustment table was hardly an inviting venue for lovemaking. Connor would cook their Italian dinner later.

So far their renewed search of Rosemary's laptop hadn't turned up new information, except for the fact that she listed (under Appearance) everything she wore for each occasion she attended, which Diana supposed was to prevent her from wearing the same outfits to the same places too many times. The woman had obviously been anal.

Diana opened up the Recipes directory, mostly for something to do while they tried to come up with some other place to check.

"Recipes One and Recipes Two," she muttered. "Is that like meals for the A list and meals for the B list?"

"I doubt Rosemary would cook for the B list."

"Good point."

Recipes One was full of elaborate meals Diana would never dream of attempting to prepare.

Recipes Two was full of surprises.

The directory held a long list of files, all named for residents of Port Findlay. No Bertie, Diana noted.

"We were going to check on Bud Knight," Connor reminded her.

Rosemary had hired a detective to do just that, they discovered. The detective had reported on a few questionable financial deals Bud had made here and there, a suggestion that he might not be revealing all to the IRS, a couple of married Port Findlay women he'd had affairs with. Eve Bertram was one of them. "People are amazing," Diana commented.

"You suppose Rosemary threatened Bud with exposure?" she asked.

Connor nodded at the screen. "Did you notice the date?"

The reports had been filed five years previously, which didn't necessarily exonerate Bud but made it seem unlikely that if he'd found out about Rosemary's snooping, he'd take his revenge that much later. There was nothing in the file to indicate he'd known about the investigation. Nothing in the brief file on Eve Bertram either. An upstanding citizen, married many years.

Nothing to indicate she might have become Bertie.

"You think Rosemary's lover might be female?" Connor exclaimed.

"Does that shock you?"

"It surprises me. . . ." He seemed embarrassed. "Rosemary came on to me from time to time."

"Some women play both sides of the court."

He grunted something noncommittal. "Eve *Bertram?*" he queried.

"I wouldn't exclude her on the basis of appearances. Who'd ever suspect her of having a fling with Bud Knight?"

"True. Is there anything there on Dmitri?"

"He doesn't show up in the *B*s or *D*s."

Glancing down the list of names, Diana had noticed Connor's last name and her own. She sighed. "I'm not sure I want to spy on all these people the way Rosemary did."

"Me neither," Connor agreed. "I'd like to see what she said about me, though."

"According to Dmitri she said you were an honest man."

"Open the file, Flash," he said. "I have nothing to hide."

The file revealed that Rosemary had hired the same investigator to look into Connor's business practices and past life in Seattle, plus Liz's life before her marriage. Connor's mouth tightened as he read. "Damn busybody," he muttered. "Why the hell would she be interested in Liz's college years?"

"She was digging for dirt, obviously. Just as obviously, she didn't find any."

"Squeaky Clean," either Rosemary or the detective had written at the end of the notes on the Callahans.

Connor still had his teeth clenched.

Diana stared at her own name on the list. She felt, rather than saw, Connor glance at her face then back at the laptop's screen.

"Tell you what, Flash," he said in the most casual voice imaginable. "We've been having a little problem with the pump in our fish tank lately. How about I go check up on it while you look at whatever you want to look at?"

They exchanged a glance. "You are the most amazing man I have ever known," Diana said.

Connor leaned forward and kissed her cheek, then stood up. At the office door he hesitated. Without turning around, he said, "If you were to delete anything, I probably wouldn't even notice."

He closed the door behind him without waiting for a response.

Diana took a deep breath, let it out, then double-clicked her own name.

It was all there, evidently uncovered by the same extremely thorough detective. Rosemary must have had him on a retainer. The report included a complete description of *Gordon & Jeffers Investigations.* Nothing shameful to be uncovered there. "Everything apparently aboveboard," he'd written.

Apparently? Diana queried—and imagined Rosemary doing the same.

A few minutes later she came upon her doctor's name, the hospital address, details of the surgery to remove Stockman's bullet.

The detective hadn't uncovered anything about Sam Stockman except for his name and the fact that he was black. But he'd found out who Diana's parents were and where they were now. Six months ago, someone among the Edensong faithful had been struck by lightning during an outdoor service conducted by Diana's father. The elderly woman had been struck down while sitting in a metal bistro chair. Diana hadn't heard anything about that, but then she hadn't spoken with her parents since she left San Francisco.

She scanned the next few paragraphs until she found the name of the victim. A name she vaguely remembered. Her father was quoted as saying the drama of the death was obviously a sign from above that Edensong was among the chosen. He always had believed God was watching him approvingly at all times. Who else could possibly be of more interest to God?

Diana felt sick. Rosemary Barrett had read all this, had known about Diana's peculiar background, had smiled her tight little smile at Diana, all the time knowing . . .

The detective had made inquiries at several insurance companies Diana and Brad had done work for. He had evidently not talked to Brad himself. There was no other mention of her partner. And Brad would have told her if the detective had questioned him, which the detective might have guessed.

The detective *had* talked to a couple of her neighbors. That's where he'd first heard about her being shot. The shooting had been reported in the San Francisco papers; the full text of the articles was reprinted here.

The detective had then talked to the police department about her, had been told of their interest in her because of Sam Stockman's disappearance immediately after the shooting. Sam Stockman had not been seen again, Diana's nemesis, Sergeant Morrison, had told the detective.

"WHY NOT!" Someone—probably Rosemary—had typed at that point.

Morrison had asked Rosemary's detective where Diana was living now and what she was doing. The detective had told him.

Great!

Diana sat back, staring at the brightly lit screen. She'd been furious when she found out Morrison had leaked the whole story to the newspapers. And then he'd talked to Rosemary's detective.

Diana had always thought it was odd that Sam Stockman had disappeared after he'd been questioned and released. The police had found no evidence against him—no gun, no witnesses.

Had someone—Morrison again?—suggested it would be a good idea for Stockman to disappear, in case a witness *did* show up?

Had Stockman gone into hiding, resenting her for surviving the shooting, for accusing him?

Had she *not* been paranoid in the wake of the intruder's visit after all?

Was it possible that Sam Stockman had shown up in Port Findlay, learned that she was going to be opening up the community center, and mistaken Rosemary for Diana? He'd only seen Diana at a distance, after all.

Had Sam Stockman killed Rosemary Barrett, thinking she was Diana Gordon?

She read the rest of the file, then closed it and stared at her name for a long moment. After clicking on File Options, she held the cursor steady on Delete for a long moment, then shook her head and clicked away from the options.

A minute or so later, while she was still staring at the screen, her thoughts tumbling, Connor opened the door.

She glanced at him, at the concerned expression on his face, and stood up. "I want you to read this," she said.

"There's no need, Diana."

"I want you to," she repeated.

His gaze examined her face.

"I'll go visit the fish," she said.

He appeared in front of her a long fifteen minutes later.

She was feeling much less harried by then, having been soothed by the back-and-forth swimming of the fish, the swaying of the tall green plants, the bubbling sound of the aquarium pump—which she noted seemed to be working fine.

"I think I'll get a goldfish," she said as she stood up.

"Messy creatures, goldfish," he said.

His expression was solemn, and her heartbeat speeded up. But then he put his arms around her and pulled her in close against his body. "I was almost relieved to find out you'd been shot," he confessed, his breath stirring her hair. "When I saw that scar, I was afraid you'd had lung cancer and there was a chance I'd . . ."

He hesitated. He was thinking about his late wife, Diana felt sure.

"Not much chance of the bullet coming back, I suppose," Diana said. "Were you shocked to find out I'd been a PI?"

"Astonished. Though I'd wondered a couple of times how you'd acquired your knowledge of police work. I guess you weren't as addicted to *Nash Bridges* as you made out."

"Oh, that part was true," she said with a grin, then sobered. "I expect you figured out it was because of getting shot I moved up here. I'd had a few close calls before. I decided I didn't want to live like that anymore."

He nodded. "I can understand that. What I haven't figured out yet is how you reinvented yourself as a professional photographer."

"Oh, that part was easy. As I told you, I'd always been interested in photography. All that I told you about my ex-husband is also true. He did teach me a whole lot and he did leave his photography stuff behind when we separated. I used photography a lot as a PI. I often did work for insurance companies, investigating fraud of the many various kinds lowlifes can come up with. It can be dangerous work. I remember reading about Guy Richie, Madonna's husband, filming some kind of reality show in England. The cameraman was catching people doing illegal acts, which was mostly what Gordon & Jeffers was all about. A man stabbed the cameraman with a screwdriver."

Connor winced.

"The man who shot me was running for a cable car when he was supposed to be unable to walk. He was a musician who'd fallen off a stage. He'd been drinking, lost his balance. It was obviously his own fault, but he blamed the company that owned the concert hall and filed a claim. Just as obviously, he saw me photographing him and shot me. I've never carried a gun. I don't believe anyone should unless they are prepared to shoot to kill, and I couldn't ever imagine doing that."

He held her away from him and examined her face. "We have no way of knowing who Rosemary might have told about you. The detective gave away your address, or at least that you were in Port Findlay. It wouldn't have been difficult for anyone to find out exactly where you live."

Diana nodded. "I think the killer *and* my intruder could be Sam Stockman. Stockman is a big guy. The intruder seemed big, and he had big hands. The man who broke into my studio was apparently going through photographs that were labeled San Francisco. I don't have the Stockman photos, but he wouldn't know that. He might even have come to the studio intending to kill me." She put her hand to her throat, which was still tender. "He certainly gave it a try."

She remembered something. "I asked my former partner, Brad, to burn me a CD of the photos I took of Stockman when he was running for that cable car. The package didn't arrive yet. If it doesn't get here tomorrow, I'll call and remind him. He's a dear man, but he gets a bit absent-minded from time to time."

Connor frowned.

"Brad was strictly my business partner," she assured him. "He's happily married to his wife Yvonne and a doting father to his two boys."

He smiled. "For some reason, that was suddenly important to me." He gazed at her searchingly. "I think we should study those photographs thoroughly."

"I agree, but while we're waiting for them to get here, we need to deliver Rosemary's laptop to Chief Hathaway."

His gaze searched her face again. "You've changed your mind? You mean to turn it over as is?"

"Exactly as is. I hate the thought of what Sarah might make of me having been a PI and getting myself shot, but I wouldn't feel right about taking out the file that dealt with me. That directory is full of possible evidence. I've no desire to dig into the secret lives of everyone Rosemary checked up on. But the records might reveal something to Sarah."

She hesitated. "If the chief had *asked* me to get the laptop, she'd have needed a search warrant because then I'd be acting as her agent and we'd have this—relationship. But as Rosemary's daughter gave it to us, and the cops in no way solicited the information, it should be okay to give it to the chief. I'm a bit concerned about the tie to Dmitri. If Sarah really suspects him . . . He's Rosemary's husband. If he were to lay claim to the laptop . . ."

She shrugged. "It's important for Sarah to see the computer. *She* can worry about the way it came to her."

"Melissa won't be happy."

She laughed shortly. "I don't think anything would make Melissa happy. The truth has to come out about her mother's murder, one way or another. And you did warn her that if we found anything significant, we'd have to tell the chief."

She touched his face, and he dropped his arms away from her. "I still think we should keep checking on anything we can think of with regard to Rosemary, but at the same time, if you're game, we can expand our investigation to find out if I was the intended victim."

"Try and keep me out!" He hesitated. "Are we going to tell Sarah we suspect the killer made a mistake?"

She nodded. "I may not care a whole lot for Sarah's attitude or her politics, but I'd like to have her on my side if push comes to shove."

She laughed. "But for tonight, I'd as soon forget the whole thing and find out what your plans are for dinner. I'm getting hungry."

"Me, too." He grinned at her. "I do have plans, yes. I was supposed to have plans for dinner?"

"You were going to make pesto fettuccine."

"So I was." His eyes glinted with pure mischief. "Takes a while though. Couldn't we grab a quick sandwich and find something else to do?"

Chapter 18

"SO DO YOU know any more about Ms. Gordon than you did before?" Sarah asked without any lead-in at all.

She and Connor were walking under lowering skies through Bromley Park's rhododendron garden. All of the rhodies were in full bloom, Connor noticed. He had planted some of the same kind behind their house—scarlet with black throats, extremely dramatic. "Like dance hall girls wearing black underwear," Liz had said.

"I've come to know Diana quite well," he said evasively, thinking of the previous evening that had lasted well into the night, trying not to smile.

"I was thinking of her past."

"What I do know is private."

"So did she tell you she used to be a private investigator?"

"She brought the laptop in already?"

Sarah stopped walking, so he did, too, then saw by her face that she was puzzled, verging on angry.

"What laptop?" she demanded.

Uh-oh!

Connor talked fast. "Melissa Ludlow asked Diana and me to poke around in Rosemary's laptop to see if there was anything on there to indicate who killed her. We wanted Melissa to bring it to you, but she was afraid you were too set on convicting Dmitri. We found some stuff you need to know about, nothing to do with Dmitri. So Diana's bringing the laptop in. She'll meet us at the police station after our walk. I told her I'd prepare you for our meeting."

Sarah was frowning ferociously, not moving, even though a few drops of rain had fallen, and by the look of the sky they were in for many more.

"I know we should have brought it to you right away, but we didn't know if you could use it as evidence if it was done that way. Whether you'd need a warrant or not. Diana didn't think you could ask for it if you heard about it. So we thought we ought to at least take a look. We haven't changed a thing."

"But you've tainted any possible evidence by having the laptop in your possession."

"I guess we didn't think of that. We didn't really expect to find anything, Sarah. This was Rosemary, remember? Rosemary the saint."

"What *did* you find?"

She'd started walking again. Was that a good sign? Or was it that she didn't want to get wet?

"Better you see for yourself. It gets complicated." He paused, glanced at her sideways, and decided her lips weren't as tightly compressed as before. "How did you find out Diana was a PI?"

"I'm a police chief, Connor. I was a detective for a long time. I did what a detective does. I made inquiries."

"In San Francisco?"

"You *do* know her better than you did." She glanced at him sideways. "After she was shot, she gave up her PI work. Supposedly. So what's she doing investigating a murder in my town?"

"I brought her into this investigation on Melissa's behalf, Sarah. I was nervous about being around Melissa without company."

She regarded him with what he hoped was amusement. It was sometimes difficult to tell with Sarah. "Fancied you, did she? Melissa?"

"It would seem so. I think maybe she misses having a father who is—"

"Father? Ha! You underestimate your inherent sexiness, my friend."

He glanced nervously at her, and she laughed. "Don't worry, Connor, I like having you for a friend, but you don't light any of my fires. I have my own *private* life."

"Good for you," he said, trying hard to suppress the question of *Who?*

"Well, I guess I'm glad to see you taking an interest in another woman," she said. "Was a time I was afraid you'd buried yourself along with Liz."

"I did do that, at least emotionally, for a while. But I'm coming out of it."

"With Diana's help?"

"You could say that."

He tried to read her expression, but couldn't. "Just because Diana was a PI doesn't mean—"

"A thing. I know. But we'll let her tell me about it, okay? That is, if she really is waiting for us at the police station."

"She is," he said with absolute conviction.

And she was. Enjoying a latte, courtesy of Adrian Lawrence, who was hovering much too close to her, Connor thought. Adrian Lawrence was a body builder. He'd competed for the Mr. Northwest title during his senior year in college. He was also several years younger than forty.

Connor chided himself for suddenly showing a possessive streak, but he was pleased when Sarah said, "Thank you, Officer Lawrence," in a firm voice, and Adrian took the hint.

Diana described their joint investigation with remarkable clarity, he thought. She didn't leave anything out.

Sarah had a remarkable ability of her own: she could listen without interrupting, or even showing any particular expression. She did blink when Diana got to the part about Bud Knight being in the shower and coming on to her over the phone, but that was about it.

Sarah already knew a little bit about Bud, she told them. "And by the way, his name really is Bud," she added. "I checked on a couple of his deals and discovered they were legal by a hair. In the course of that inquiry I found out Bud wasn't a nickname."

She pursed her mouth. "I've been in police work long enough to think nothing could surprise me, but I'm surprised to the depth of my soul about Rosemary snooping into everybody's life. As for her having a lover, I'd have sworn she was the most devoted wife, mother . . . I'm certainly going to be tracking down this Bertie, whoever he might be. Seems our most likely suspect."

"There's another wrinkle in the case," Diana said. "Something that has to do with me and my previous life."

Sarah regarded her with interest. "Good thing I found out you used to be a private investigator, or I'd be worried you were into reincarnation."

For Sarah, that was an unusual venture into humor. Connor smiled at her, then realized Diana was staring at him, her dark eyes narrowed.

"Connor didn't rat on you," Sarah said, saving his skin.

"I did a little poking around and ended up talking to a Detective Sergeant Will Morrison in your last location's police department."

"Lovely," Diana said. "I'm sure he gave you an earful."

"He did. Suppose you tell me your version."

Again Diana summed up clearly and concisely.

"Sergeant Morrison told me about Stockman disappearing," Sarah said when Diana was through. "Morrison seems to have it in for you. What did you do to him?"

"I accused him of leaking my name and occupation to the press when he picked up Sam Stockman. Made him mad. Morrison, I mean. But I don't know who else could have known I was following Stockman when he shot me. I guess you probably know that Stockman managed to get rid of the gun somewhere before the police caught up with him. And nobody saw anything, of course. Morrison retaliated by accusing me of being responsible for Stockman's disappearance, even though I was barely half conscious in the hospital when he was released for lack of evidence."

"Didn't *anybody* see he had a gun?"

"Only my partner. And that was from some distance away."

Sarah leaned her chair back, steepled her fingers under her chin, and regarded the ceiling for so long that Connor stole a surreptitious glance at his watch. Nine-fifteen A.M., and he needed to shower and change and grab some cereal. He had an appointment at ten A.M. at one of the local businesses to give exercise instructions and go over needed ergonomic changes.

Eventually, Sarah straightened up and fixed her gaze on Diana as if she were trying to see the inside of her brain. "So. This wrinkle you mentioned. As I recall, you were late arriving at Quinn Center, the day Rosemary was killed. Reason being you were supposed to arrive earlier to open up, but Rosemary made you hand over the keys and said she'd do it herself."

There was a flash of admiration in Diana's eyes as she nodded.

"So, considering that you and Rosemary share a similar build and coloring, you're thinking maybe you were the one who was supposed to be the victim? In which case you're thinking your friend Stockman may have reappeared?"

"I may be paranoid."

Sarah gazed down at the closed laptop for a moment, then glanced up at Diana. "Someone once sent me a greeting card, said something like, 'You're not being paranoid, they really are out to get you.' "

"Sounds like a threat," Connor said.

"I thought so, too."

"Are you saying you agree that Flash—Diana—might have been the intended victim?" Connor ventured.

"You had a break-in a few days ago, right?" Sarah said to Diana.

"Sunday, yes. The guy spilled a box of photographs. Some I'd taken in San Francisco."

"Which is where you were shot."

"Yes."

They gazed at each other for a long moment. Connor got the impression that while they might not yet be ready to form a friendship, they had somehow gained respect for each other during the telling of Diana's story.

"On the other hand," Sarah said, "it sure seems as if our Rosemary had a few enemies. Maybe that lover you uncovered turned sour. Bertie could have known about the change of plan that morning. Maybe Annie and Bertie had arranged a tryst. It's probably a good idea to look in both directions. I have no problem doing that. Someone once said my name should have been Janus, like the god of gates and doorways, always depicted with two faces gazing in opposite directions." She laughed shortly. "Maybe he meant I was two-faced."

She stood up. Evidently the interview was over. Connor couldn't read her expression, but she at least smiled at Diana as Diana dropped her coffee container in the trash can and got to her feet. "I'll let you know if I hear of anything pointing in your direction," Sarah said.

"Thanks." Diana hesitated, then held out her hand. Sarah took it and shook it.

"I'm still mostly inclined to think Rosemary was the one the killer meant to kill," Sarah said.

Diana nodded. "You're probably right. It's just—I'm not much of a believer in coincidence. And the break-in made me wonder."

"Well, coincidence sometimes happens, but I'm with you on that one. I'll be turning over any rocks I find lying around."

"Me, too," Diana said.

"I picked up the Stockman CD from my post office box this morning," she murmured to Connor as they walked out. "Could we look at the photos at my place after work?"

"It's Thursday, I'll be through by noon." He glanced at his watch. "I'll have to hustle to get home and clean up and drive to my ten o'clock appointment. It's not at the clinic."

"I have to work until two o'clock. Let's get together at two-fifteen, okay? Higby is leaving at two to drive to Seattle, so that would work out well. I don't want him wondering what we're up to."

Connor nodded, then jogged off through the now steady drizzle in the direction of the Jeep, which he'd parked as usual at the side of the police station.

Chapter 19

RAIN WAS DRUMMING on the windows of Diana's little office, thunder grumbling in the distance. In the bay, waves were rolling high, breaking on the beach white with foam.

"We seem to spend a lot of our time gazing at computer screens," Connor said.

Diana laughed as she booted up her computer. "Well, at least my computer has a bigger screen than Rosemary's, and we have pictures instead of words. I'm hopeful we'll see something Brad missed. The software I use now is really good. Brad couldn't enlarge details as much as I can without the picture dissolving into pixels."

She brought up the photographs on the compact disk as thumbnails first, then clicked on each one to enlarge it to fit the screen. Stockman—a large black man—leaving his apartment on crutches, Stockman getting into his car, sliding the crutches into the backseat. Stockman driving into Chinatown, parking in a garage.

"He doesn't resemble anyone I've seen around Port Findlay," Connor commented.

"It should start to get interesting about now," Diana murmured, sitting forward.

The next picture showed Stockman getting out of his car, followed by three quick shots of him glancing left, right, behind, then one of him *walking* away. Sans crutches.

"Caught red-footed," Connor said.

"Yes indeed," Diana said, enlarging one picture after another of Stockman walking through Chinatown, zooming in once in a while. Stockman's hands were empty, but she pointed out a bulge in his jacket's right pocket. "Could be a wallet, could be something else."

In the next picture it was obvious that Stockman was running to catch up with the cable car that had shown up beside him in the previous photo. Diana had been running along behind him, not too far back. There was a row of shops on the right hand side of the photo, people walking on the sidewalk, a couple of men standing outside one of the shops, apparently talking, others going into and out of other stores.

In the next photo there was a glint of something in Stockman's right hand. Diana's breath caught in her throat. Stockman was on board the cable car and had turned around to face in her direction.

She zoomed in on that picture, 400, 500, 600 percent, enlarging as far as she could without blurring the image, her heart beating in time with the rain on the windows.

Stockman was holding onto the cable car's handrail with his left hand. Diana wasn't breathing at all now.

"There's definitely something in his right hand," she said excitedly. She zoomed in closer and clicked on the directional arrows until Stockman's right hand filled the center of the screen.

"Oh my God!" she exclaimed.

Connor squinted at the screen. "That's not a gun."

Diana was almost in tears. "It's a cell phone," she said.

The next picture showed the surface of the street. Obviously her finger had pressed the button as she fell.

Connor was still staring at the screen. "But if he didn't have a gun, then who . . ."

"Who shot me?" she finished for him.

She closed the file and shut down the computer, then slumped over the keyboard, her head bent. Connor put his arm around her shoulders.

It took a few seconds, but then she straightened. "The police officers were right all along," she said, more to herself than to Connor. "Brad was wrong, I was wrong. Will Morrison was right. Stockman never did have a gun."

She stared at Connor, her eyes glazed over. "I saw a program on TV once, I don't remember where or when, but it was about some kind of experiment designed to test racist leanings. People were shown photos of men holding something in their hands, flashed on the screen one at a time in fairly quick succession, a black man, a white man, two more black men, another white man and so on. The students swore that each of the black men was holding a gun. But one had a camera, one had a flashlight. The conclusion drawn was that the viewers had *expectations* that the black men would be holding a gun."

Her eyes cleared. "I swear, Connor, I've never had a racist thought in my life. Yet I was sure Stockman had a gun in his hand."

"You were following Stockman because he was defrauding an insurance company," Connor pointed out.

"While you were following him, right after he hopped on that cable car, you saw something in his hand that looked like a gun. As you turned away, you were shot in the back. Your assumption that the shooter was Stockman was a natural one."

"But just now, looking at the photos—"

"You hoped to see a gun, because you wanted to know for sure what happened."

Her smile was a little weary around the edges again. She leaned toward him and put her head down on his shoulder. He continued to hold her. The rain continued to fall.

"Let's examine this more objectively," Connor suggested after a while. "Disregarding this whole Rosemary thing. Stockman *did* get on that cable car. He *did* look your way. You were taking photographs that were going to prove he'd defrauded an insurance company. He looked your way, and you got shot. Chances are pretty good that it was Stockman who shot you. You thought that all along until you saw the cell phone. Maybe the second after you took the photo, he dropped the cell phone and pulled out a gun. By the time the police caught up with him, he'd gotten rid of the gun."

"He didn't even have gunshot residue on either hand."

"He'd taken a shower. His mama taught him to scrub good. Don't interrupt, I'm on a roll here."

She laughed, feeling immeasurably better.

"The only other possibility is that some other enemy of yours was watching you while you were watching Stockman, and he or she took a shot at you. Which is a bit of a stretch, but possible, so let's examine that theory."

He paused, thinking. "Who else is there who might have had some kind of grudge against you?"

"Well, there'd be plenty to choose from, but I doubt any of them had anything to gain by knocking me off. Revenge is a good motive, I suppose. But most of the cases I've been involved in, the people had enough sense to know getting revenge on me for exposing whatever crime they were involved in would get them in deeper trouble."

"What about the gang you said were on the photos that were in the box your intruder got into?"

"Those guys were livid," she admitted, "but I turned them in several months before I was shot. They were out on bail almost immediately. You'd think they would have had other opportunities to take me out before that particular day and time."

"Your ex-husband?"

"Larry? Larry would never use a gun. First thing he asked me when we met was if I carried a gun. He was deathly afraid of guns, wouldn't have had anything to do with me if I'd been armed."

"You said you had to get a restraining order on him."

"He stalked me. But that was all he did. Turned up everywhere I went. Stared at me. Whether I was alone or with friends. Made my friends nervous, but he never did anything. He couldn't accept that I didn't want to stay married to him. But then eventually he met another woman and married her. I told you that, didn't I?"

He nodded. "It might not be a bad idea to check up on him all the same."

"Okay, if you insist, but . . ."

"I'm not going to insist on you doing anything you don't want to do, ever. I'd feel better if he was eliminated from the list of suspects."

She smiled at him. "You are a nice guy, Connor Callahan."

"Damn. Is that anything like saying I have a nice personality?"

"Possibly. But you're also tall, fair, and handsome." She paused, then added, "And extremely sexy."

"That's better," he said, and kissed her.

"I guess nothing's really changed," she said after a while, noting with some amusement that her voice sounded softer than before, sultry even, heavy with suggestion. "It probably *was* Stockman who shot me. As he's still missing, there's not much I can do about him. The intruder could have been someone prowling around, who saw my back door was open."

She sighed. "I guess we're back to Rosemary again. Thanks for not saying I'm crazy."

"Crazy can be sexy, too," he said.

She smiled at him, feeling a lot perkier. Then they both stood up and held on to each other.

"We should probably go talk to Melissa," Diana said after a while.

"You sure know how to turn a man off."

She put her hands on his rear and pulled him close, wiggling her hips.

"Then again, you sure know how to turn a man on again." He hesitated. "It's really raining hard now," he pointed out. "Probably unnecessarily hazardous to drive in conditions like these. Hasn't rained in a few days—the roads will be greasy. There'll be skid marks all over town."

Diana smiled. He kissed her again and gazed at her inquiringly. "I don't suppose Higby happens to have a nice little French boudoir tucked away in the prop room?"

"Sorry, no, but there is an exercise mat in there somewhere."

They had evidently decided, without even talking about it, that Melissa could wait until later.

MUCH LATER, AS it turned out. It was going on 7 P.M. before Connor called Melissa, 7:30 before they were standing on her doorstep in what had become a light drizzle, being greeted by a scowling Wayne Ludlow.

According to Lena Green, Wayne had been a linebacker in his high school days. Unfortunately, muscles have a way of deteriorating when they aren't used enough. Although Wayne was gainfully employed as an auto mechanic, which surely demanded a certain amount of manual labor, it was clear that he spent a little too much of his spare time as a couch potato. He even had the TV remote in one hand. Pretty soon, Connor thought, babies would be born with a remote control growing out of one arm and a cell phone out of the other.

"Missy's in the kitchen," Wayne said.

That was evidently enough social intercourse for Wayne. As Connor and Diana entered the kitchen, he went beyond them to what appeared to be a family room. Diana could see an adolescent boy and girl sprawled on the floor in front of a theater-size TV screen. The big tabby cat lay between them, on its back, paws folded on its chest. It needed only a lily stem. Diana wasn't sure it didn't qualify for one, but as she stared at it, it rolled over onto its side, stretched out its neck, and stared back.

"Hey," Melissa said. She was pouring coffee into four mugs, one of which she took in to Wayne before returning to serve Connor and Diana at the dining table.

"Have you got anything yet?" she asked, as they all sat down.

"Not a whole lot," Connor said, then added, as they'd rehearsed, "We had to turn your mother's laptop over to Chief Hathaway. You'll remember I said it might be necessary."

Melissa's face turned bright red, and the always-ready tears filled her eyes. "But then she'll know, everyone will know . . ."

"I'm sure she'll be discreet," Diana said.

Melissa buried her face in her hands for a few seconds, then shook herself and glanced from Connor to Diana. "I suppose that means that *you* know."

They had rehearsed several ways of talking about the delicate subject, and had rejected all of them in favor of a fairly direct question. "Did *you* know your mother had a special friend?" Diana asked.

Melissa burst into tears.

Wayne turned up the volume on the TV set. To protect the children? Or to indicate total indifference?

Connor stood up and brought a box of tissues from the kitchen counter and put it in front of Melissa. She employed several, then sniffed a few times and took a big gulp of the coffee, which was strong enough to corrode an iron bar.

Diana got up and opened the refrigerator, took out a jug of milk, and added a good slug to her cup. Connor smiled at her gratefully and did the same.

"I suspected she was a . . . an adulteress," Melissa said.

Diana loathed the *ess* suffix. Author, poet, waiter, actor, did not need feminization. Adulteress sounded rather quaint and old-fashioned, like a woman in a poke bonnet with a scarlet letter *A* embroidered on her bodice. The way Melissa had said the word left no doubt in Diana's mind that in her daughter's opinion, Rosemary had sinned and should probably be stoned in the marketplace.

"What made you think your mother was having an affair?" Connor asked.

"I found a whole bunch of fancy underwear in her bureau, one day when I was over visiting. Easter. The kids and I and Mama had been coloring and decorating eggs, and I got some purple dye on my blouse. Mama took my blouse to spray it with some spot remover, and I went into her bedroom and poked around in her drawers for a T-shirt or something, and I came across these lacy panties and camisoles and things. There was even a thong there. And a black lace teddy."

She started sobbing again.

Connor and Diana drank some more of the dreadful coffee.

"I brought a pair of the panties out and showed it to her, and she said it was none of my business, but as long as I'd snooped, I might as well know she was having an affair. She said my dad hadn't been able to, well, perform, I guess was the word she used. So she'd found someone else to love."

"Did she say who?" Diana asked.

"No. She wouldn't tell me. She said again it was none of my business. We had a big fight. I called her something." She grimaced, reached for a tissue, and blew her nose loudly. "I called her a whore. My own mother. I was so shocked!"

Suddenly opening her eyes wide, she looked from Connor to Diana and back again. "Are you saying that's who killed her? The man she had an affair with?"

"We don't *know* who killed her," Connor said soothingly.

"We still don't know who, or why," Diana added.

"Do you know anyone named Bert?" Connor asked.

"That's his name?"

"We don't know his name. It's possible it's Bert, or Albert, Herbert, Gilbert . . ."

"The only person I know who even comes close is Eve Bertram. She was one of Mom's best friends. But she'd hardly be . . . What are you suggesting?"

"Nothing at all, nothing," Connor said, backpedaling rapidly.

"This is why I gave you the laptop," Melissa said, misery personified.

"What is?" Diana asked, softening her voice.

"My mother having an affair. I thought maybe you'd find something in the laptop that would show it was her lover who killed her. Books I read, TV shows, it's sometimes the lover. Maybe they had a fight. Maybe Mama broke up with him when she saw how upset I was. Maybe it was all my fault."

Diana guessed that Melissa was one of those people who would seek to blame herself, at least in front of other people, for all the woes of the world.

"We don't know any more than we did before," she said. "The name Bert happened to come up, and we didn't know who it might be."

"Oh. Okay." She seemed satisfied, though Diana thought her own comment had been lame.

"LENA SAID SHE and Eve Bertram and Rosemary had a lunchtime board meeting a couple of days before Rosemary was shot," Diana said. She and Connor were back in his Jeep Cherokee, outside Melissa's house, trying to decide where to go next.

Diana became aware that someone was watching them from the family room window. Wayne, peering between the slats of the blinds that had been closed to keep light off the TV screen.

Chapter 20

IT WAS TOO late to go to Lena's shop, so Connor suggested that they meet after work the next day, maybe have dinner at Findlay's Landing, then continue what he was now calling their "quest."

He made Diana promise she wouldn't question Lena without him being there, and she agreed reluctantly, not sure she'd be able to keep the promise. But Wednesday brought a lot of unexpected walk-in custom, and she didn't have a chance to run next door as she was itching to do. She felt quite virtuous about holding herself back when Connor drove up beside the studio.

She always felt guilty going into Lena's yarn shop. She'd enthusiastically bought a huge bag full of yarn when she first moved in next door to Lena, which she'd planned on using as soon as she learned to knit! She hadn't opened it since.

The Woolly Bear was a seductive shop, its shelves divided into triangular sections full of colorful and interesting materials for knitting, needlework, crocheting, weaving, and spinning. There was even a certain kind of cotton yarn with which to knit towels. People actually did that!

Bright knitting and crocheting patterns filled two wall racks, and posters of models wearing various garments hung here and there.

Lena insisted on serving Connor and Diana tea at her workroom table, where she often gave knitting and crocheting lessons. She even provided cookies.

Connor led the conversation around to Eve Bertram.

Lena shook her head. "No, nobody ever called her Bertie. I can't imagine her putting up with it." Her gaze nailed Connor right between the eyes. "You're surely not thinking Eve was the person Rosemary was involved with?" She laughed heartily. "You have some imagination, you two. Rosemary a lesbian? And Eve Bertram? No way, as the kids say. Not that Eve's terribly heterosexual, mind you. Asexual would be the word. Never has a good word to say about sex. Doesn't even say the word. Calls it 'it.' " She giggled.

Thinking of the note in Rosemary's files that revealed Eve had been one of Bud Knight's conquests, Diana didn't dare look at Connor.

About to pour another cup of tea all around, Lena stiffened. "You're not thinking Eve killed Rosemary! She was in the hospital having her gallbladder removed the day Rosemary was killed. Even if she hadn't been, that's the most ridiculous thing . . ."

She gave Diana a sideways glance. "Besides, Eve has a husband."

"Well, that wouldn't necessarily stop her from . . ." She realized what Lena meant. "You think Rosemary might have been having an affair with Eve's husband?"

"It's more likely than Rosemary and Eve," Lena said, her expression mischievous.

"I don't think I've ever met Eve's husband," Diana said.

Connor shook his head slowly. "I'm not sure I've even seen him."

"Sure you have, he works at the Oceana Gallery, next door," Lena said.

Two minutes later, Connor was asking one of the gallery clerks if Mr. Bertram was on the premises. "Sure," she said. "We're going to be closing in half an hour though," she warned, then gestured at a good-looking balding man of about sixty who was sitting in a wheelchair, framing a poster on a table at the side of the store.

No wonder Lena had looked so mischievous! Diana had seen the man in the wheelchair many times before. So had Connor, judging by the rueful expression on his face. "I've only known him as Frank," he said quietly as they approached the man. "I had no idea he was married to Eve. What an odd couple. He's always so cheerful, and she's so dour."

Diana nodded agreement. "How are you doing, Frank?" she asked.

"Great," Frank said. He paused in his labors to smile brightly up at them. "Doc Callahan, I haven't seen you in a hell of a long time. I guess you've got all the pictures your clinic walls can handle."

Connor nodded and smiled, and Frank wheeled himself out from behind the table and shook hands with him, then with Diana.

"I heard Eve was sick," Diana said. "Is she okay now?"

"Recovering nicely. They took her gallbladder out, said she'd be better off without it. I hope they're right." His smile shifted into a frown. "She's real upset over Rosemary Barrett's death though. Depressed." He glanced from Connor to Diana. "I understand you found her—Rosemary—must have been a hell of a shock."

"It was," Connor said. "I'm sorry to hear Eve's so upset."

"Yeah, she adored that woman. I don't know why, but there it was. Personally, I thought she was over the top. Rosemary. Dabbled in too many things. Had to be important, center of attention, queen bee."

"That must have created a problem between you and your wife," Diana said.

"Nah. I never had the heart to tell Eve I disliked her best friend. I managed to avoid Rosemary as much as possible." He glanced up at Diana. "Eve and I have a good marriage." He patted the wheelchair's arm. "She's taken great care of me since I came home with this. It may sound funny to say it, but I think we've gotten along better since I got wounded."

Diana found herself remembering Lena's comment about Eve being asexual.

"What happened?" Connor asked. "I don't think I've ever heard."

"Vietnam," Frank said. "Land mine. Prefer not to talk about it." He sighed. "Thought of shooting myself at the time, but I got over it, got used to it."

"You have a gun?" Diana asked, seizing the moment.

"Not anymore. I used to have a rifle. Used to go duck hunting year after year. Moses Lake, east of the Cascades. Liked getting out in the fresh air, getting the exercise."

"I expect the ducks did, too," Diana said.

Frank Bertram regarded her with narrowed eyes for a second or two, then shrugged. "Like I said, I thought about ending it all, pretend I was cleaning the rifle maybe—a tragic accident—I could see the headlines. But instead I got rid of the rifle. Didn't see how I'd be hunting again. I don't own a handgun either."

He glanced from Diana to Connor. "Was there something you wanted?"

Connor answered for both of them. "No, we're browsing. You've got some great local art here. I like the Indian piece you're framing, is that a whale?"

"It is indeed," Frank said. "It's a north coast art–style orca. Almost looks like a wolf, doesn't it?"

As they discussed the traditional elements of Indian design, Diana wandered off to justify Connor's "browsing" comment.

She had visited the gallery many times but had not noticed previously that some of Joshua Patton's Mount Saint Helens photographs were displayed in one alcove, along with autographed copies of his coffee-table book, which was large enough to form a coffee table by itself. Diana hauled one up onto the top of a glass case that displayed rainbow-colored Christmas ornaments made from Mount Saint Helens ash, then leafed through its pages. Fallen trees, stripped of branches and leaves, lay all over the hills like acres of giant toothpicks. Dense gushers of smoke and ash billowed skyward. Steam rolled above a literally boiling river next to houses half-buried in mud. Visions of hell.

Patton was a tremendous photographer, Diana was forced to admit. And obviously courageous. Arrogant with it, yes, but perhaps he deserved to be, though personally she preferred celebrities who managed to remain humble. He had certainly earned his celebrity status with these amazing photographs, however, and she regretted dismissing him as a pompous ass.

Most of the photographs had been taken immediately after the eruption. He must have been right up near the summit when the volcano blew, in spite of all the warnings that had been issued. According to the book's introduction, he had kept taking photographs even after his shoes disintegrated and his feet were badly burned.

It crossed her mind to wonder if Joshua Patton had a middle name. A middle name with a *B* in it. But then she remembered he'd said he'd never actually met Rosemary. He'd offered his services, he'd said.

He hadn't appeared to recognize Rosemary when the four of them came across her body.

Moving on to the next alcove, she thumbed through an amazing variety of note cards, and came across some that particularly appealed to her. The style of artwork was familiar, she realized. Turning the pack over, she searched for and found the artist's signature. Ashley B. Robinson. She had decided to buy the note cards before the middle initial made an impact.

Ashley B. Robinson, she remembered, had been the first to fling herself on Rosemary's body. She'd thought it a strange reaction at the time. It still seemed so.

Melissa had done the same thing. But she was Rosemary's daughter. Ashley was—what?

She could hardly wait to show the pack to Connor. First she showed it to Frank Bertram. "Ashley Robinson was one of the judges at our photography show. I love her work. You know what the middle *B* stands for?"

He shook his head.

Connor did the same when she showed him the pack after she'd paid for it and they were back in his Jeep. "You're going to go crazy tracking down all the *B*s around."

She grinned, then remembered suddenly that Ashley's bio had accompanied the brochure the Arts Alliance had put out for the show. They had planned on eating at Findlay's Landing, but stopped by Photomania first so she could check the brochure.

"Beatrice," she said triumphantly, showing him the page. "Ashley Beatrice Robinson."

"You're trying to get Bertie from Beatrice?" he asked.

"It's not that much of a stretch. And remember how distraught she was when we discovered Rosemary's body."

"Dead bodies disturb most people," he pointed out.

"All the same, most people don't go around throwing themselves on top of a corpse. . . ." She stared at the pack of note cards as if it might provide an answer.

Connor laughed at her, and she blew him a raspberry, which ended up in some mild tussling, which of course ended up with something more than tussling. Somewhere along the way, Diana told him she was going to visit Ashley Beatrice Robinson in Seattle. "But," she added, "if she does turn out to be Bertie, she might have a problem talking in front of you about her relationship with Rosemary."

Connor thanked her for at least letting him know her plans this time. He agreed so easily to her going alone, she was sure he thought her journey wasn't worth the effort.

But still, as they ate their pub dinner, she kept remembering details of Ashley's extreme reaction to Rosemary's death.

And tomorrow was Saturday. A good day to make a call on someone.

ASHLEY LIVED IN a penthouse apartment in an upscale and contemporary condominium building that might have been unloaded all in one piece from a tall thin box.

Diana had to call up to be buzzed in. Fortunately, Ashley was home. When the elevator stopped, Diana exited into a beautiful rooftop garden, with entrances to four

apartments. Ashley's was the one with the stunning view of
Elliott Bay, with Bainbridge Island in the distance. Seattle's real estate having skyrocketed in recent years, Diana
thought it was highly probable that Ashley had either inherited or married money. Or maybe she'd won the state
lottery. She was a terrific photographer, but all the
same . . .

Ashley didn't seem to mind that Diana had dropped in.
Not that she was all that excited about her visit. Actually,
she seemed apathetic.

She had just now returned from an opening at SAM—
Seattle Art Museum—she said. Diana was glad to hear it;
she'd have hated to think Ashley actually hung around at
home in her tight little leather skirt. At least this time her
blouse covered her navel, even if it was practically see-
through and had flowing, flared sleeves.

Ashley had slipped her shoes off, Diana noticed. A pair
with impossibly high stiletto heels lay on their sides in the
entryway.

Diana took her sneakers off, too, as soon as she saw the
white fuzzy carpeting ahead. She was wearing boring old
blue jeans and a white cotton shirt herself, but she felt perfectly comfortable with the contrast. What she didn't feel
comfortable with was the fact that she needed to go to the
bathroom. Why was it, she wondered, that in the television
detective shows she watched, whether the sleuth was an
amateur or a professional, nobody ever suffered from this
embarrassing urgency?

The bathroom, as might have been expected, was large,
beautifully tiled, and furnished with marble counters and
ornately framed mirrors. The faucets appeared to be gold
plated. After washing her hands, taking care not to splash,
Diana helped herself to a tissue from a beautifully carved
walnut box that looked familiar. She stared at it for several

seconds before remembering to blow her nose and dispose of the tissue in an elegant receptacle on the floor next to the vanity. She hoped that was what it was for.

When she emerged, Ashley provided her with a glass of mineral water and settled Diana onto a couch that was surprisingly comfortable.

"I'm sorry to arrive unannounced," Diana said.

Ashley shrugged. "I'm glad you came," she said as she seated herself in a purple chair opposite. The chair matched her eyelashes, Diana noted.

She didn't *look* glad. She appeared pale and exhausted, as if she hadn't been sleeping well. Diana doubted she'd been eating well either. She'd been model thin a little over two weeks ago; she appeared half-starved now.

"This is a beautiful building," Diana said in an attempt to put her at ease.

Ashley smiled and nodded. "My father designed it," she said. "Otherwise I couldn't afford to live here," she added with disarming candor.

Diana mulled that over for a few seconds before a light-bulb popped up in her memory. Robinson was a common name, but Ashley's father had to be Miles Robinson, one of the most famous architects in the country.

While Diana was considering how to start a conversation that would lead to an opening, Ashley forestalled her. "I guess they haven't . . . I mean . . . I've watched the newspapers and television news, and I never did see anything about the police catching whoever killed . . ."

"Rosemary."

"Yes." She wasn't making eye contact.

"So many people had been through the main hall the day before, it made it almost impossible for the crime scene investigators to single out much in the way of physical evidence. And nobody seems to have seen whoever it was who entered Quinn Center between Rosemary arriving and the four of us getting there."

"Well, it's awful that someone could get away with killing someone so—in such a horrible way. Awful, awful. It was a terrible thing to happen. And she was—I mean, she seemed as if . . . she must have been beautiful." Her voice trembled.

"She was very attractive, yes," Diana said.

Ashley's eyes were moist, Diana noticed. She was evidently a sensitive young woman. Though certainly, it would take a hardened heart not to have been affected by the sight of someone who'd been shot to death.

"Did you know Rosemary at all?" she asked as casually as she could manage.

Ashley blanched, her mascara and lip gloss glowing jewel bright in contrast. The hand holding her crystal water glass trembled, and she set the glass down with great care on a side table. "Oh. Gosh. No. Of course I didn't. I didn't, *don't,* know *anyone* in Port Findlay. She . . . Rosemary . . . Mrs. Barrett . . . called me up out of the blue, said she admired my books, wanted me to help judge the Port Findlay Photography Show. I'd never been to Port Findlay, but I'd heard it was pretty, thought it would be fun to go there."

She was suddenly gazing at Diana questioningly.

"I had to come see you," Diana said. "I felt bad that we didn't have a chance to talk after the—afterward. Chief Hathaway took you in right after letting Connor and me go, and we left without even remembering we'd promised to take you and Joshua Patton to lunch. We were so unnerved—"

"Oh, I quite understood," Ashley said, apparently relieved, now that she knew why Diana had come. What had she thought? "I was totally unnerved myself. I couldn't even drive back to Seattle. I had to call my mom and dad to come and get me, so one of them could drive my car home. I was in absolute shock."

"We should have thought of driving you home," Diana said, genuinely annoyed with herself for her lack of thoughtfulness.

"No. It was okay. It was best my parents came. I couldn't think, couldn't talk . . . I'd never . . . ever . . . and I couldn't face coming back to Port Findlay. I'm terribly sorry that I didn't come to the reception or the show. I did get your message of course, but I couldn't . . . I had such terrible nightmares about . . . my father said he'd . . ." She swallowed hard, then lifted her chin. A little of her color came back. "It was kind of you to come. But really, there was no need, I mean, I did understand. . . ."

"Well," Diana said, "I knew how upset you were, even trying to revive her and so on, so I should have—"

"Oh, but I've had CPR training, you see. That's why. I took a course in it at a school not far from here. I have a certificate." Her color had returned, especially high around her cheekbones. "I had a problem with the mouth-to-mouth resuscitation practice—an allergy to the disinfectant they wiped the mouth of the dummy with. The instructor told me not to worry, if I ever had to do it in real life, chances were the person wouldn't have been disinfected."

Her lips were trembling. She seemed on the edge of falling apart.

Diana leaned forward, wanting to comfort her, but at the same time wanting to get at whatever truth there might be. "I actually had a second reason for coming. Melissa Ludlow asked me, well, me and Connor Callahan, Dr. Callahan, you remember, he was my cochair of the photography show?"

Ashley nodded, calmer now. "I remember him, of course. He was nice, kind, when I . . ."

She wasn't finishing too many sentences.

"So anyway, Melissa asked Connor and me to check into . . . Did you ever meet Melissa?"

It was a shot in the dark. Diana didn't really expect anything to come of it, hadn't really expected anything to come of this visit, but Ashley was becoming increasingly nervous, and the question came into Diana's mind and popped out without her thinking about it.

"No, no, of course not. I told you, I didn't even know her mother."

She was an intelligent young woman; she realized immediately what she had said. Her eyes widened. She tried to cover up at once. "I didn't know anyone at all in Port Findlay, I told you that." She sat forward. "Really, Ms. Gordon, if there's nothing else . . ."

"But you did know Melissa Ludlow was Rosemary's daughter, didn't you, Ashley?" Diana said gently. "You're Bertie, aren't you?"

"Oh God!"

She sat back in her chair, hands over her eyes, tears flowing from beneath them.

Diana got up and went into the bathroom and retrieved a handful of tissues from the beautifully carved walnut box. Such a distinctive box. The last time she'd seen one like it was on Rosemary Barrett's dressing table. Exactly like it, she thought.

Ashley made use of the tissues, while Diana went to the refrigerator in the kitchen and brought out a fresh bottle of mineral water. After filling Ashley's glass and her own, she sat down again.

It took a while for Ashley to recover. Diana felt sorry for her but wasn't quite ready to sympathize.

"How did you know?" Ashley whispered finally.

"When Melissa asked Connor and me for help, she gave us Rosemary's laptop. There were letters."

Agony showed on her face. "Then you know everything."

Diana nodded.

"Oh God!" She closed her eyes.

Oddly enough, she suddenly seemed more relaxed than she'd been since Diana's arrival. Secrets had a way of being a huge burden, Diana knew from her own experience. Being found out could often bring great relief. Police officers had told her there was often great internal pressure on people who had committed a crime to confess to it. They played on that sometimes, telling the person they'd feel better if they cleared the air, told the truth, everything would be better then. Which probably explained why criminals often confessed to their crimes, when if they'd continued to deny everything they might not have been convicted. There was always that question of a reasonable doubt.

Diana waited until the young woman opened her eyes. "Where did you and Rosemary meet?" she asked.

Ashley took in a deep, deep breath. "She wrote me a fan letter," she said, with a ghost of a reminiscent smile. "She'd come across one of my books of photography in the state library. She said she really admired my work and would love to take me to lunch and discuss it. Then when we met—we had dinner, actually, at the Four Seasons Olympic—she told me that when she saw my photograph in the back of the book, she'd felt she had to meet me. We talked and talked. I had never felt so . . . understood."

Diana waited.

"We became . . . close. I hadn't known." She waved one hand in a stilted sort of gesture. "It took Rosemary to tell me, and it explained everything. All my life I'd felt knotted up inside. I'd never quite fitted in, you see, never dated. That's probably why I took up photography, it was something I could do alone. I had always been alone."

Nothing more seemed to be forthcoming, and Diana was reluctant to probe any further into the relationship between Rosemary and Ashley—Annie and Bertie.

"Did you quarrel?" she asked finally.

Ashley appeared shocked. "Never. We never had a cross word. She was my friend, my mentor. She came over on the ferry every Tuesday. Right from the beginning it was as if we'd been meant to—"

She broke off, then crossed herself as fervently as she had when they'd come across Rosemary's body. "Oh God, no, you can't mean, you surely don't think I'd ever have done anything to harm her? I loved her. No, no, no, not in a million years."

Pulling herself together with an obvious effort, she looked Diana right in the eye and said with great dignity, "I did not kill Rosemary. I don't know who did. I wish I did. I'm not sure I could kill anyone, but I think if I knew who killed Rosemary, I might be tempted."

Diana believed her. Remembering that Ashley had flung herself on Rosemary's body in an effort to resuscitate her confirmed her belief.

"You arrived in Port Findlay the night before you and Joshua Patton were to judge the photo show. Did you see Rosemary then?"

Ashley nodded. "I called her when I arrived, and she came to the hotel." She hesitated. "The main reason she asked me to judge the show was so I could see Port Findlay. I'd been curious about the place where she lived. She drove me around on a tour. She'd always felt it was too dangerous for me to visit her there—for her reputation—

but there was the excuse that I was one of the judges, and she was the president of the Arts Alliance."

Diana remembered Sarah saying she might have seen Ashley before. It seemed possible she'd spotted her during that tour.

"It was a magical time," Ashley said with a sigh.

"Did she spend the night with you?"

"No. I wanted her to, but she couldn't risk it, not in her own town. We had dinner—quite openly—and then she left. I didn't see her again until—" She broke off, but this time didn't break down.

"What happens now?" she asked. "I suppose you have to tell someone."

"I think it would be better if you told Chief Hathaway yourself," Diana said.

"No. I can't. I couldn't. She'd tell the newspapers. My parents . . ."

"They don't know?"

She shook her head.

"I'm sorry," Diana said. "But you'll have to tell, you can't *not* tell. Even if I didn't, and you know I have to, sooner or later Chief Hathaway would figure it out."

"She'll think I'm—"

"No, she won't."

Actually, Sarah probably would.

"Your sexual preferences have nothing to do with what happened to Rosemary," Diana continued. "Do you have any idea—did Rosemary ever say *anything* about anyone in Port Findlay, give any indication that there was someone who didn't like her, hated her enough to—to kill her?"

"Never." Ashley shook her head quite violently from side to side. "Rosemary never actually said, but I definitely got the impression that everyone loved her, respected her, admired her. As I did."

Well, that sounded like Rosemary for sure. She'd never appeared to suffer from unnecessary humility.

"I wondered about Melissa," Ashley said after a brief silence. "Rosemary did say she'd been a problem at times. She'd married someone Rosemary thought was really awful. And then I guess Rosemary's own husband wasn't all there."

"He has Alzheimer's."

"I know. Would that make him violent, do you think?"

"I don't know. But I haven't heard of too many people with Alzheimer's going berserk," Diana said.

Ashley stared at her with haggard eyes. "I've been afraid Melissa or her father might have found out about Rosemary and me and killed her because of it. I was terrified that whoever did it would come after me next."

Lena wasn't the only paranoid woman around. All the same, Diana wouldn't dismiss that kind of motivation out of hand.

"Did Rosemary tell you—" Diana broke off. She'd been about to ask if Rosemary had told Ashley that Melissa had discovered their affair. But if Rosemary hadn't, it wasn't information *she* wanted to be passing on. If possible, she wanted to avoid any trouble with Sarah Hathaway. She was probably going to be in pretty deep as it was.

"Did Rosemary tell you anything about her relationship with her son-in-law?" she asked instead.

Ashley shook her head. "Only that she didn't like him, didn't approve of him. And he was disrespectful."

"Hmm."

Diana tried to decide what to do next. Somehow she had to get Ashley back to Port Findlay and into the police station.

"Knowing Chief Hathaway, I'd say she's not the type to blab anything to the paparazzi. I think if you explain to her that your parents don't know about you and Rosemary, she'll be discreet. In any case, you don't have any choice. You have to tell her the truth. Your best bet would be to be completely up front with her. It's the only way."

Ashley nodded, appearing to be on the verge of collapse.

"Would you like to come back with me?" Diana asked. She was prepared to insist if necessary, but wanted to give the young woman every chance to act of her own free will.

"Yes," Ashley whispered.

Diana felt a huge wave of relief wash over her. She hadn't relished the idea of having to call the local cops to come and pick up Ashley Beatrice Robinson.

This was an enormous step she'd taken. She was lucky it had paid off.

A moment later, she reminded herself that she was still no closer to knowing who had killed Rosemary Barrett.

Chapter 21

"FLASH BROUGHT ASHLEY Beatrice Robinson back to Port Findlay yesterday," Connor told Liz, sitting on the bench next to her grave. "Sarah interviewed her up one side and down the other. Poor girl seemed positively dehydrated when she was through. Diana and I decided there's no way we're telling Melissa who her mother's lover was. Sarah agreed to keep quiet about that aspect unless it becomes absolutely necessary to reveal it. Melissa would go into cardiac arrest to start with, and then she'd probably kill Ashley Beatrice Robinson, which would be a great loss to the art world."

No response from Liz came to his mind at all.

Diana had called him as soon as she and Ashley arrived in Port Findlay. She'd wanted his support at the upcoming meeting she'd arranged by cell phone with the chief.

She hadn't said, "I told you so," though she must have been dying to do so. But what had really impressed him was the great sympathy and delicacy with which she had treated Ashley. There was no indication of triumph that she'd found her out, no trace of smugness when they met with Sarah and Ashley confessed about her relationship with Rosemary.

Diana had been quite adamant with Sarah that she was sure Ashley was innocent of any involvement in Rosemary's death. Sarah had been inclined to agree, though she'd insisted on reserving judgment for now.

Ashley herself was open and heartrending in her grief, which she had been unable to express until now. And she had an alibi of sorts. She'd breakfasted at the hotel that morning, in the tower restaurant, in full view of a room full of tourists and the restaurant staff. She'd been joined around nine A.M. by Joshua Patton, whom she'd met once before when they both spoke at some Seattle gathering. He'd been to the fitness room, he'd said. His hair was wet.

A call to the hotel confirmed that Patton had checked into the fitness area at eight-thirty A.M. Sarah called him, and he confirmed that he'd met with Ashley at nine A.M. or maybe a little earlier. He'd been swimming laps in the hotel pool.

"He wanted to know why we thought that sweet little chick was a suspect," Sarah had reported to Connor on this morning's walk. "Reminded me, like I needed reminding, that Rosemary was shot, and could I really believe pretty little Ashley was capable of such a crime."

She'd rolled her eyes. "I've known a couple of pretty little ladies, butter wouldn't melt, did far worse than that. There was that young woman on one of the islands a few years back—killed her husband and tried to put him through a commercial brush-shredding machine."

Connor decided he'd prefer not to dwell on the image that statement brought to mind. Even Flash, strong woman that she was, had shuddered.

"Sarah didn't find any reason to hold Ashley Robinson," he went on. "Though she did tell her not to think of going anywhere away from home for a while, in case Sarah needed to get in touch with her. Ashley said she didn't want to go anywhere anyway. She was going to work on a new book and dedicate it to Rosemary's memory, she said. She might possibly use images of Port Findlay for this one."

He brought his attention back to Liz's grave. The freesias he'd planted were doing well, filling the air with the scent she had loved and he remembered so well.

"I think I'm feeling pretty strongly about Diana Gordon," he blurted out.

His mind remained stubbornly silent.

"It's not that I wasn't happy with you, you know how content I was," he said. "But then I was needing someone, and Diana came along—and hell, it's not a case of needing so much as wanting. She's such an amazing woman."

There was still no response in his mind.

He supposed he must have some vestiges of guilt-feelings left. Even though he knew without any doubt at all that Liz would have wanted him to find someone else, to be happy—in fact, in the early days of their marriage, they'd discussed such a situation and agreed . . .

But there was still some small, accusing voice—he wasn't sure if it was his own voice, or Liz's—telling him falling for another woman was a betrayal of all he and Liz had meant to each other.

Or maybe that voice that kept murmuring—no, not murmuring, *muttering*, in a surprisingly bad-tempered way—was the remnant of ancestral influences telling him he was supposed to have flung himself into Liz's grave with her. The way, long ago, Hindu widows were expected to immolate themselves on their husbands' funeral pyre in the tradition known as Suttee.

Suddenly impatient with his morbid thoughts, he stood up and turned away from his wife's grave.

It was a wonderfully clear day. Windy and bright. Beyond the downtown buildings, Sunday afternoon sailors kept their boats' sails ballooning as they tacked across the white-capped waters of the bay. The sun shone on the water and on the huge white ferryboat coming into the state ferry dock. He couldn't see the beach, but there would be people down there, walking, jogging, swimming, or wading in the playful edges of the waves.

"Who will see the view," his old friend Sakae had asked.

"Those who are left behind, Sakae," he said aloud. "I can see the view."

He wished he could see a little farther. He wished he could see whatever future was waiting for him out there. He wanted to be happy. He remembered being happy. He wanted life to be good again.

It was an odd sort of way to be thinking in a cemetery. But when the sun was warm on your head and the wind was spreading sweet-smelling air around, it was hard not to be aware of your own heart beating and your own breath filling your lungs.

He suddenly remembered Liz telling him about a magazine tip she'd read that was directed at people who found it difficult to make decisions. "You toss a coin after assigning heads or tails," she'd told him, her eyes sparkling with amusement. "If it comes down heads and you're disappointed, then the tails choice was the right one for you. And vice versa."

Smiling, he realized maybe Liz had spoken to him after all. He took a coin from his pocket—a nickel—threw it up and said, "Heads for Diana."

Catching the coin, he flipped it over onto the back of his left hand and gazed at it. Heads. He was *not* disappointed. He was elated.

Now all he had to do was convince Diana that *he* was the right choice for *her*.

Chapter 22

THEY GATHERED IN the break room at the Port Findlay Police Department—Chief Hathaway, Connor, and Diana. Connor had returned home to find a voice mail asking him to attend this meeting. Evidently Diana had received a similar call.

Sarah was in civvies, a smart navy blue suit with a white blouse. Apparently she'd come straight from church. Diana was wearing a black T-shirt and tan jeans. Except that his shirt was a black polo shirt, Connor was identically dressed, which made them both smile. Sarah served them coffee. She seemed even more serious than usual. After a couple of minutes, young Timothy Valentine—the fresh-faced detective who had been off having his appendix removed—joined them.

"You feeling better?" Connor asked him, more to break the somber silence than anything else.

"Stitches all out, everything feeling more comfortable," Tim said. "I can't go running yet, so I'm having to watch the calories, but all in all, things are good."

"I asked Tim to sit in, so he could hear you tell what transpired the day Rosemary Barrett was shot," Sarah said. "Reading a report is one thing. Hearing it in your actual words might be better. And I think it would be helpful for us all to go through it one more time."

"Shouldn't Joshua Patton and Ashley Robinson be here, too?" Connor asked.

Sarah nodded. "Quite possibly. But I don't trust either of them. I do trust you two."

Diana appeared surprised but pleased.

"How do you want to go about it?" Connor asked.

"With a time line if you can manage it. And as much detail as you can recall." She glanced from him to Diana. "Feel free to interrupt each other. And I may ask questions as we go along. Are we all on the same page?"

"Sure," Connor said. He narrowed his eyes, withdrawing temporarily from his surroundings, thinking, remembering. "It was raining, but I rode my bike down the hill. I met Joshua Patton and Ashley Robinson outside Quinn Center; they'd walked over from the Best Western together."

"Time," Sarah said.

He nodded. "It was five minutes past ten A.M. when I parked my bike. I was expecting to find Diana waiting for us. When she wasn't there, we stayed under the porte cochere until she came and told us—"

"Over to Diana," Sarah interrupted. "Tell us why you weren't there."

"I'd intended getting there around nine-thirty A.M. Connor and I had agreed I'd open up, turn on the lights, and have some coffee ready. He'd arrange to meet the judges there around ten. They'd walk over from the hotel, which was right next door."

She paused to think. "I'd picked up the keys from Rick

Langley the previous morning. But that afternoon, Wednesday afternoon, Rosemary Barrett came by the studio—around four P.M.—and asked, no, *demanded* that I give her the keys to Quinn Center."

"Did she give any reason?" Tim asked.

"She'd decided that as she was president of the Arts Alliance, she should meet and greet the judges. She told me she'd be at Quinn Center at nine A.M., and I should come along at ten."

"But you were late," Sarah said.

"Deliberately," Diana said.

Connor shot her a surprised glance.

"I know I told you I'd gotten off to a slow start, but the truth was I felt Rosemary had treated me like one of the help, and so I staged a minirebellion of eighteen minutes. Unfortunately, that left you all out in the rain, but I had no way of knowing that."

"I couldn't raise Rosemary, so I called Rick Langley to let us in," Connor said. "By the time we got our coats hung up and explained the layout to the judges, it was probably ten-forty when we got around to looking at the photographs."

"Dmitri was at home when you called, you said," Sarah put in.

Connor nodded. "He was at home, yes, but there was nobody home, if you know what I mean. He accused me of being a telemarketer. Seemed to think I was calling in the middle of the night."

"Nobody made coffee?" Tim asked.

Connor and Diana exchanged a glance. "We never checked," Diana said. "We were late getting started, we just went ahead."

"I didn't even think about the coffee," Connor said. "If

we'd gone to the kitchen, we'd have seen Rosemary's body earlier, maybe—"

"No maybes," Sarah said. "If Rosemary was on time— and I know all about her obsessive punctuality—and if she was shot on arrival as we figured and seems most likely, then she was already dead before you arrived at the community center."

"Joshua Patton took Ashley Robinson to the lobby," Diana said. "He said he'd noticed a coffeemaker there. I guess he was going to make coffee. None of us checked the kitchen. You suppose the coffee is important?"

Sarah shrugged.

Tim frowned.

"It was probably the best part of an hour before we got to where Rosemary was lying," Connor went on. "The judges didn't always agree on which photographs deserved the awards."

"Patton was a pain in the . . . neck," Diana said.

"You didn't hear or see anyone in the place before you found the body?" Tim asked.

Diana answered. "Rick Langley went into his office after he let us all in. Connor and the two judges went into the cloakroom to hang their rain gear up."

She hesitated.

"What?" Connor asked.

She frowned. "I don't know. Something went through my mind there about the rain gear. I don't know what it was."

"Ashley had on a see-through raincoat," Connor said.

Diana grinned. "You noticed."

He ignored her. "I was wearing my bicycling jacket. Patton had on a blue something or other."

"A Soggy Trails jacket. That's probably what struck me.

I used to have one. It's well-made. Water repellent rather than waterproof, but it's tightly woven, so it does a good job of keeping you dry. Only problem is that it's a pullover style and it has a hood, so it's not all that easy to get on and off. I gave mine to the thrift store."

"Are we going to keep this fashion commentary going all afternoon?" Sarah asked.

Diana shrugged. "Something about that coat . . . Well, okay, I checked the ladies' room to see if Rosemary was there. We didn't check anywhere else. I hollered when we came into the main hall where the photos were displayed. Nobody answered."

"Everything seemed okay until we came around the end of that last row—Special Effects—and there she was," Connor said. "Rosemary. It was a hell of a shock."

"Ashley screamed," Diana remembered. "God, that must have been so terrible for her." She took a breath. "I froze. Connor called nine-one-one."

"After I checked for a pulse," Connor put in.

Diana nodded. "Then Ashley threw herself down on Rosemary's body." She glanced at Tim. "Rosemary was sprawled on her back. Before we could stop her, Ashley dropped down and started pumping her chest. Next thing I knew, Patton was down there, too, lifting up Rosemary's neck, getting ready to do mouth-to-mouth."

Sarah sighed. "What with all of that and all of the people involved in setting up those stands and hanging the photographs, it was impossible to come up with any usable physical evidence."

"That's what Flash told them," Connor said. "She yelled at them that they were messing up the crime scene."

"Flash?" Tim queried.

"It's a nickname," Diana said.

Tim looked blank.

"You're too young to remember Flash Gordon, the action hero, I guess," Connor said.

"I've heard of him."

"Diana's a photographer."

"I've got it," Tim said.

He sounded as if his feathers were ruffled, Connor thought. He must have felt Connor was impugning his abilities as a detective.

He glanced at Diana. Her eyes appeared glazed, as if she had divorced herself from the whole proceeding. He'd seen her do that before. It meant she was thinking something through. Any minute now she'd come out with some conclusion she'd drawn.

But instead, after a few seconds, she moved her head and shoulders in a minishrug. A moment later, she brought her attention back to the meeting, but she didn't say anything. Sarah and Tim were discussing some point of procedure.

"What?" Connor murmured.

She gave him a surprised glance, then her lips twitched in a partial smile. "Later," she murmured back.

Sarah started her off on remembering again, and between the two of them, she and Connor managed to recall all of the details of that horrible morning. Then Sarah filled Tim in on some of the following events: the fights at the photo show, Milly Schreiber, racist rumors, Dmitri's outburst, Ashley's confession.

It was a lot for anyone to take in, but Tim seemed to absorb it all, and Connor and Diana were released in time for Connor to suggest Findlay's Landing for dinner again.

"Okay," he said, after they'd ordered beer and fish and chips, which Jock advertised—truthfully as far as anyone could judge—as the best outside of the British Isles.

Diana raised an eyebrow at him. "That sounds like your inquisitor type of okay."

"How well you know me."

She took a sip of her beer. "What is it this time? We're through with the werewolves, aren't we?"

"While everyone was talking back at the station, there were a few seconds when you did some pretty hard thinking."

She tilted her head about the same way she had then. "Sounds as if you know me well, too." She hesitated, both hands lightly clasping the cool beer glass. "We were talking about when we discovered Rosemary's body. Something suddenly struck me as odd. It had to do with motivations."

She thought it through again, while Connor waited patiently. "We talked about Ashley throwing herself on top of Rosemary and starting CPR . . ." She paused. "She actually has a certificate! She took a course in school. Anyway, her confession provided a reason for that—she loved Rosemary, wanted to save her life if it was possible."

"Melissa had a similar motive," Connor said.

"Loving Rosemary. Yes. I tend to believe Ashley more than Melissa. Having read Bertie's correspondence with Annie, we *know* she loved Rosemary. Are we as convinced that Melissa did?"

She checked off on her fingers. "Mama was hardly ever home, Mama didn't approve of Wayne."

"Having met Wayne . . ." Connor began.

"We don't approve of him either," Diana agreed with a sigh. "All the same, it was a strike against Rosemary from Melissa's viewpoint."

She took in a breath, let it out, and lifted her beer glass. But before it touched her lips, she set it down again. "Which brings us to Joshua Patton."

"Who also tried to revive Rosemary."

"My point being—was he really intending to, or did he want it to appear that he was going to?"

"Maybe he has a CPR certificate, too, Flash."

"You think?"

Connor shrugged. "So what are you saying? You suspect Patton?"

Diana frowned. "More that I'm trying to eliminate him from suspicion. Not that I've eliminated either Ashley or Melissa, though Melissa may seem the strongest suspect to me because I'm identifying with the rotten mother part."

"Patton said he'd never met Rosemary before," Connor said. "Do we know if that's true? No. But what motive would he have for killing her? She was thrilled to get him as a judge. The only odd thing there, that I recall, is that I got the impression she'd really worked to get him to agree to judge, whereas Patton said he'd *offered* to judge because of the amateur jobs done in most small-town shows."

"If Rosemary was telling the truth, why would he lie? More likely that Rosemary lied, actually. She always made a big deal out of everything she did. If it was already a big deal, she made it even bigger."

Another synapse in Diana's brain activated itself. "Didn't Patton tell that TV guy, the day of the memorial service, that Rosemary had *invited* him to judge?"

"I didn't notice."

"I'm pretty sure that's what he said. So if she did invite him, would she write him or call him? If she wrote, would there be a copy of the letter in her laptop?"

"Too late to find out, now that we've passed it on to Sarah."

Diana sighed. "Well, going back to him throwing himself down beside Rosemary—did he strike you as the good Samaritan type?"

"No."

"Me neither." Diana pursued the thought. "The only other reason I can think of for him getting down there was to muddy up the crime scene, either to protect someone or to give a good reason for the presence of anything he might have shed if he was the killer: hairs, fibers, fingerprints, whatever."

"Same reasoning could apply to the two women."

"True."

Their dinners arrived, and they stopped talking while the waiter dispensed the usual freshly ground pepper, refilled their water glasses, and asked if they wanted more beer. They both refused.

"I guess we need to sleep on it," Diana said finally.

Connor looked hopeful.

"I really meant sleep," she said with a grin. "It's a workday tomorrow."

"So it is." He brightened. "I never did cook Italian for you. How about I pick you up after I'm through working—probably around six-fifteen?"

"I could probably manage that," Diana said.

Chapter 23

PORT ANGELES WAS a little over an hour's drive from Port Findlay, most of it alongside the Strait of Juan de Fuca. Only a ferry ride across the strait was Canada, specifically the city of Victoria on Vancouver Island. Diana meant to take that ferry someday but so far hadn't managed to get around to it. She had driven the road that led from Port Angeles to Hurricane Ridge in the Olympic National Park the previous summer, camped out in her get-away van for a week, and come back with some superb mountain and wildlife photographs. She had a different destination in mind today.

The weather wasn't at its best—a slow but heavy drizzle, as though the solid cloud cover was melting. None of the usual spectacular mountain views were visible. But that didn't matter today. Close to the ferry terminals were some interesting shops, a marine science center, and a gallery that was owned by, and featured the work of, a certain famous photographer.

Connor was probably going to kill her, Diana decided, as she watched for an inconspicuous place to park her conspicuous red get-away van, settling for a spot near the city hall.

It was hardly her fault that the Cummings and Porter families had returned from their joint vacation suffering from Montezuma's revenge and had canceled the photo shoot scheduled for today. By the time they had called, Connor was already at work. It wouldn't have been fair to disturb him and his patients. So went her rationalization.

She wasn't quite sure what she was going to do, or how she was going to do it, but back in the day when she was a licensed investigator, she had often started out with camera in hand, but without a plan in mind, just to see what might develop, so to speak. She'd learned in school about aboriginal people who had taken off on long walkabouts. It had often seemed a good idea to imitate them.

Walking back to the ferry terminal area, she decided a latte might be a good idea, especially as the café with the espresso sign was within viewing distance of the Mountain Man's Gallery, as Joshua Patton's showroom was called.

There wasn't a lot of foot traffic in the area, but cars were already lining up for the next ferry. A young woman in the gallery was flitting around with a feather duster.

Diana wondered what she had expected—that Patton himself would be serving behind the counter?

"What's in the Mountain Man's Gallery?" she asked the young woman who had made her excellent latte. There was nobody else in the café.

"Mountains," the woman said with a wide smile. Teri, her name tag read. She had long brown hair with purple streaks, several earrings decorating each ear. "A ton of pictures of mountains. Joshua Patton likes mountains, even though one of them blew up on him."

Diana acted out a lightbulb turning on. "Joshua Patton? I've heard of him. I guess he's something of a native son around here. Do you know him?"

Teri leaned over her counter in a confiding way. "He's really famous. I wouldn't say I know him, exactly. He comes in sometimes for lunch. Lousy tipper. Hardly ever talks to anyone."

"Is he married?"

"Not as far as I ever heard. Word is he prefers middle-aged married ladies. They are more desperate."

If she'd heard that before learning Bertie's identity, she might have picked Joshua Patton as a leading candidate, Diana thought.

Teri nodded at Diana's small digital camera, which she'd placed on the table. "You planning on sitting at the Mountain Man's feet?"

"No way," Diana said. "I'm merely curious. He's the one who got those great photographs of Mount Saint Helens."

"Before I was born," Teri said. Glancing from left to right as if she were afraid of being overheard, she said softly, "Word is he does drugs."

Diana stared at her.

"I had this boyfriend in high school. Jack. I dropped him when I found out he was a dealer. He ended up getting arrested. I don't know where he is now. But my friend Marky told me Mr. Patton was one of Jack's regular customers. Mr. Patton taught a course out at the school." She giggled. "Photography, not drugs. I didn't take it." She giggled again. "I didn't take drugs either. Still don't. Don't smoke or drink either." She rolled her eyes. "Boring, huh?"

"Intelligent," Diana said.

Teri smiled. "I like your hair," she said. "What dye do you use?"

"I don't. I was born this way."

Teri sighed. "Some people are born lucky."

"What kind of drugs?" Diana asked. "Mr. Patton, I mean? Marijuana?" She tried to think what it was called nowadays. Mary Jane sounded old-fashioned. "Grass? Weed?"

"Hard stuff, Marky said."

She stiffened suddenly, glancing at Diana's camera again. "Hey, are you a reporter? Listen, that was all gossip, okay? Joshua Patton's well thought of in this town. He won a Pulitzer and everything."

"I'm cool," Diana said. "No need for you to worry."

But Teri began suddenly wiping down the counter, and it was obvious she regretted running off at the mouth and wasn't going to do it again.

Leaving the café, Diana wandered around downtown until she found a phone booth and a telephone directory. Patton was listed, which surprised her. His house wasn't too far out of town, and the rain had stopped.

Patton drove out of his driveway as she approached. She doubted he would have come out to check on any pedestrians who might be lurking, but she quickly stepped to the other side of a nearby tree just in case. He was apparently heading for the waterfront. Maybe going out of town. Maybe going to catch a ferry.

She walked quickly in the same direction and saw his Land Rover parked behind his gallery. She mentally debated the wisdom of going into the gallery and pretending surprise at seeing him there. *Such a coincidence,* she could hear herself exclaiming. *I had no idea you had a gallery here!*

She could almost see the sardonic expression that would appear on his face. The same one he'd greeted her with the first time she'd met him.

She frowned. Something about that first meeting was still bugging her.

"Hello!"

The voice was Joshua Patton's. He was in the act of closing the back door of his gallery, awkward because of the large box he was carrying.

Diana was startled, she hadn't noticed the door opening. But at least, she quickly assured herself, the fact that his sudden appearance had made her jump must make her seem innocent of any kind of subversive behavior.

"Mr. *Patton?*" she said, with what she thought was the right amount of disbelief in her voice.

"Ms. Gordon."

She forced a smile. "I'd forgotten you lived in Port Angeles. I'm here for a quick visit. I was thinking of taking the ferry to Victoria, but I decided the weather was—"

Shut up, she told herself fiercely.

"Damp," he agreed.

"I meant to write you," she found herself saying, which provoked the same voice that had told her to shut up to ask, *What about?*

"What about?" he asked.

"With all of the—trauma—I forgot to send you a thank you for judging our photography show. We really were, are, grateful that a photographer of your stature would—"

"A Mrs. Lena Green sent me a card along with a check for my expenses," he said.

And of course, as secretary of the Arts Alliance, it had been Lena's job to do so.

She nodded in what she hoped was a knowing sort of way. "Yes, of course, I knew that, but because of the circumstances, I meant to write and . . ."

And what? the voice in her head asked. *Apologize for the unexpected appearance of a corpse?*

". . . tell you we appreciated your taking up the slack when Ashley Robinson couldn't come to the photography show."

He made a dismissive sort of motion with his right hand. It struck a chord. Yes, he'd made that same motion when she yelled after him and Ashley that they shouldn't leave the building.

Something else nagged at her memory, but she didn't have a chance to think about it.

"I have to put this box down," Patton said.

"Oh, gosh, yes, of course." She started to back away.

"Don't you want to come in and see my gallery?" he said, as he opened the Rover's door and put the package down on the backseat.

Come into my parlor . . .

"Um, no, I, er—as long as it's stopped raining, I might check on the next ferry to Victoria."

He eyed his wristwatch. "It left fifteen minutes ago."

"I'll get in line for the next, then, thanks." She had no idea what she was thanking him for.

He had that same sardonic expression on his face as she turned away. She tried to walk at a regular pace, resisting the urge to run.

Why did she want to run?

Instinct?

Stupidity probably. She could have gone in his gallery. There was a woman in there. It was the middle of the day. The gallery had a huge picture window on one of the main streets.

She clicked the van's electronic key. It was odd, she thought, that Joshua Patton hadn't asked if Rosemary's murderer had been apprehended. He hadn't even mentioned her death.

Probably he'd been as startled to see her as she'd been to see him.

And yet . . .

As she drove back toward Port Findlay, she found herself thinking about her food processor. She wasn't the world's greatest cook, though she could produce a decent meal, a nutritious meal, if not a fancy meal.

But inevitably, she had trouble putting her food processor together. Usually, she discovered she'd put the handle at the back instead of the front—or was it vice versa?—or she'd get that right and move it in the wrong direction for latching. About the time she was all sweaty and cussing and ready to throw the damn thing in the trash, it would suddenly click into place.

There were parts of the events surrounding Rosemary's death that kept roiling around in her brain, stirring up bits and pieces of images. What she needed right now was for something to click into place suddenly, magically. Only thing was, her brain didn't always cooperate any more than her food processor did.

SHE WAS LOOKING at the Stockman photographs when Connor stopped by the studio. Higby had left after spending the day organizing the prop room as she'd kept intending to do. She was grateful to him. He deserved a bonus, she decided. If there was any spare profit at the end of the month, it would be his.

"Ciao," Connor said, making her jump.

She swiveled her office chair around and gazed up at him blankly. "Chow? It's dinner time already?"

"C-i-a-o! *Ciao*. Meaning hello, are you ready for your Italian dinner?"

"Oh. That."

He put a gentle knuckle under her chin and raised it. "Are you okay?" He glanced beyond her. "You're going through the Stockman photos again?"

"I wanted to see if any of the photos would release something that's going on in my head. I can't seem to pull it out. Give me a few minutes, okay?"

"I came by earlier," he said as she turned back to the computer. "Higby said you had a big cancellation so you'd taken the day off."

She nodded. Not relishing a lecture, she didn't want to tell him where she'd been.

"Your front door isn't locked."

"I haven't got around to closing up yet, Connor. I do that when I leave. I have to leave it open for potential customers."

"Uh-huh."

He watched over her shoulder as she opened and enlarged and closed photos, then he pulled over a chair to sit alongside, complaining of getting dizzy because she moved things around so fast.

She brought up the photo that bothered her the most. The one where Stockman was hopping onto the cable car.

For Connor's benefit, she increased the size slowly. And so it was that something caught the edge of her vision, something she'd noticed before but had not paid close attention to.

The people at the side of the street. Two men in particular, standing outside a shop window. The one with his back turned had a blue jacket on. The jacket's hood was neatly folded at the back of his neck.

"That's a Soggy Trails jacket," Diana said. "Joshua Patton wore a Soggy Trails jacket the day Rosemary was killed."

"Are you sure?"

"Did his jacket have a zipper?"

"I don't know."

She sighed. "And I didn't notice. I was so mad at Rosemary when I realized she hadn't informed you of the change in plans, and that she'd made things worse by not turning up, there was a red fog in front of my eyes."

"Wait a minute," Connor exclaimed. "When we went to the cloakroom, he pulled it over his head. And it *was* blue. There must be more than one around though."

Clicking on the tools menu, Diana put a box around the two men and cropped that part of the photograph, then enlarged it as far as she could without blurring it.

"Look at his arm, his right arm." She squinted at that section of the photograph as she zoomed closer. "See how it's bent at the elbow, with the palm out to the side?"

"Okay." Connor was obviously not catching on.

"Patton has a way of doing that. I've seen him do it twice. Once in Quinn Center when he was taking Ashley out for coffee. And again today, when I was telling him—" She broke off. Too late.

"You saw Joshua Patton today? He was here—in Port Findlay?"

She sighed. "I went to Port Angeles."

To her surprise, he was silent. Possibly he was controlling himself. She hoped so.

"Look there," she said hastily, pointing at the computer screen. "His hair's a lot longer, but it's the right color. The jacket's the right kind and the right color. It has darker bands over the seams, see? And the way he's standing. Kind of slouched. That's the way he was when I first saw him, when you guys were waiting for me under the porte cochere at Quinn Center. And then there's the way his arm is—"

"You really think it's Joshua Patton?"

"I'm almost sure of it. I saw those two men standing there before. See how close they are to the cable car where Stockman is? Maybe he knew them. Maybe he yelled at them that I was taking pictures of him."

"So then the one you think is Patton turned around and shot you?"

She slumped over the keyboard. "Sounds ridiculous, doesn't it?"

"Tell me about seeing Patton today."

She sucked in a breath and sat up, still staring at the photograph.

"I was wandering around Port Angeles. I'd thought about going on the ferry to Victoria."

Well, that part was true, she'd just left out the *someday* part.

"And you happened to run into Patton where?"

"At the back of his gallery. He owns a gallery there. The Mountain Man's Gallery. The woman in the café next door said it's full of his own photographs of mountains. She says she thinks he's on drugs."

"Good grief, Diana. Why would she tell you that?"

"This guy he's talking to," Diana said, ignoring Connor's question, still staring at the photograph, "he's sort of familiar, too." She laughed shortly. "Yeah, sure. He's a dead ringer for Robert Redford in *The Way We Were*. Old movie—seventies, I think. I saw it on TCM."

Connor peered at the screen. "That's not Barbra Streisand with him." He sat back. "So what do we have— Joshua Patton in a conspiracy with Sam Stockman and a guy who looks like Robert Redford?"

Diana leaned back, too. "Remember what we were talking about before? *Motivations*. Why Patton would throw himself down on the floor beside Rosemary?"

Connor nodded again. "You thought he might have meant to mess up the crime scene."

"Okay, so for the sake of argument, let's say the guy in this picture . . ."

"The one talking to Robert."

She made a face at him. "Stay with me for a few minutes, okay? Let's say he's Patton."

"Okay. He's Patton."

"Let's think of all the facts we know about him and see if they'll fit my theory."

"Aren't you supposed to go through the facts and then *develop* a theory based on them?"

She rolled her eyes. "We're not in court, Connor."

"Okay," he said. "Go ahead."

"Let's also say that I was supposed to be the woman who was shot that day. Maybe by a guy who was wearing a blue Soggy Trails jacket. The same woman who was shot in San Francisco's Chinatown on the same day this man in the blue Soggy Trails jacket was there."

Obviously about to make some jocular comment, Connor changed his mind and went thoughtful for a few seconds. "Patton gave you a dirty look when he met you."

"Not when he first saw me, not until you told him my name. He was without any expression until then. When you said who I was, he seemed—I don't know—horrified. I almost expected him to say he'd heard all about me, and none of it was good."

"When we found Rosemary, he never did ask who she was."

"If he'd shot her, he knew all along there was a dead woman lying at the back of the hall. He'd have to have guessed who she was, after he met me and we talked about Rosemary taking the keys."

Connor was thinking it through, going along with her now. "He met Ashley for breakfast at nine o'clock. He'd been to the fitness room. He signed in at eight-thirty A.M. He said he'd been swimming. His hair was wet, Ashley said."

"Maybe he didn't swim. Maybe he took a shower?"

"To remove any traces."

"We know he came up with different stories about how he came to be a judge. We know he flung himself down on the floor beside Rosemary. We know he opened the back door for Ashley. If he'd come in that way and he'd shot Rosemary, maybe touched her, it would make sense for him to muddy up the crime scene."

She was silent for a few seconds, then she asked, "Did Patton *know* I was supposed to open up? Did you tell him?"

He thought back. "No. But Rosemary may have done so earlier. She made the arrangements for both judges. Accommodations. She'd have to have informed them that we'd be in charge."

"The notices about the photography show and you and me as cochairs were sent to all the West Coast newspapers," Diana pointed out. "I didn't know beforehand that they went that far afield. People heard about the show in Chicago and Utah. Gardner Malone entered from Oregon. Weren't there some entries from San Francisco?"

"You're thinking Stockman saw one of the press releases, saw where you were living, decided to hire someone to do away with you?"

"It's either that or whoever Rosemary's detective talked to ratted on me."

"Maybe you need to crop that photo again."

"Good thinking." She leaned forward.

"I guess we aren't going to have that Italian dinner?"

"Do you mind?"

"Not at all. I eat too much anyway." His smile moved from his eyes to his mouth. "You get single-minded, don't you?"

"Part of my bloodhound nature, I guess. Once an investigator, always an investigator."

A couple of seconds later she pulled that particular photograph onto the computer screen.

"What do you think?"

"I think it's a big stretch to decide someone's a murderer on the strength of a rain jacket."

"But the way he's standing, the way his legs are. Patton's rather bandy-legged, isn't he?"

"I didn't notice. He limps. I noticed that. He burned his feet on Mount Saint Helens." He was suddenly alert. "What kind of shoes is he wearing?"

Diana scrolled down to the man's feet. "Sneakers."

"Patton was wearing moccasins every time we saw him."

Diana shook her head. "He was wearing sneakers today, and the day of Rosemary's memorial service."

"There's a thing. Why would he come to the memorial service, if he'd killed the wrong woman?"

"To appear innocent," Diana said without hesitation. "I've heard that murderers often do show up at their victims' funerals and such. Detectives watch to see who attends."

"You suppose Sarah was keeping an eye on all of us at Rosemary's service?"

"Wouldn't surprise me. But I don't know why else Patton would turn up. He hadn't known her, he said. He hadn't even met her."

"Maybe he thought it would be a good photo op. It did turn out that way."

"You really want to destroy my theory, don't you?"

He shook his head. "I'm playing devil's advocate." He leaned over and kissed her lightly. She kissed him back, feeling much more relaxed now.

"So what do we do now, Mata Hari?" he asked.

She took some time out to think, then scooted around to

face the computer again. "I'm going to send that cropped picture to Brad, tell him what we've found out, see if Patton's maybe someone known to him. He was in the business way before I was."

"Did you ever check up on your last husband?"

"I'll ask Brad to look into him, too."

Entering her mail program, she wrote a fast note to Brad Jeffers, attached the photograph to the E-mail, and clicked on Send.

"I've asked him to call me on my cell phone," she told Connor. "Which means I can still come to your house for that Italian dinner." She grinned suddenly. "Or we could send out for a pizza? That's Italian."

"Can we eat it upstairs in your apartment?"

"Of course. We can even eat it in my bed. I have a couple of bed trays we could use."

His blue eyes had that certain gleam in them. "You're well-equipped," he said.

"I'll take that as a compliment," she said as she closed down the computer.

Chapter 24

BRAD JEFFERS DIDN'T get back to Diana until the next day, right at noon, while she was examining some photos she'd taken that morning. Higby was about to leave for lunch, hesitated when the phone rang, but went on out when Diana waved him away. "Connor's coming over," she told him. "He's bringing sandwiches. Take a couple of hours if you like. You've been working too hard."

He grinned. "I'll knock before entering."

"What took you so long?" Diana said into the telephone. "I've been sweating bullets."

"It was worth the wait," Brad said.

She stopped breathing. "You recognized him?"

"Not the guy in the blue coat—that *is* a Soggy Trails jacket by the way, I'd recognize it anywhere. My kids love those jackets. So do I. Yvonne doesn't though, said hers messes up her hair when she takes it off. And she doesn't like that one pocket right in the front. Makes her look like a kangaroo, her opinion. She said to say hi, by the way. Oh,

I almost forgot, your ex-husband Larry is out of the picture. Seems he's settled down in matrimonial contentment. Two kids, working a lot of overtime. Hasn't been out of town in years."

"Brad . . ." Diana made it sound like a threat. He'd always teased her along like this. "Pretend I'm Sergeant Friday, okay?"

"You watch too much old TV."

"I didn't get to watch it as a kid, remember? I'm still catching up. It's better than new TV anyway. Gimme the facts."

"I recognized the other guy, the blond guy."

"The one who's the spitting image of a young Robert Redford? You're kidding."

"I kid you not. But Robert wouldn't be flattered by the comparison. Your blond guy is a bad guy, Diana."

"Damn it Brad, who is he?"

"Name's Van Sant. Arnie Van Sant."

"I've never heard of him. Where did *you* run into him?"

"I didn't. I thought there was something familiar about him, so I took the picture in to Will Morrison."

"You're not serious! Damn it, Brad . . ."

"Yeah, I know. Morrison's a chauvinist pig, but he's also a good cop. No wonder I recognized the blond guy, he's on the most wanted list. Don't you ever go to the post office?"

"No. I get mail delivery here, don't need a PO box anymore. Buy stamps on-line. Wanted for what?"

She was going to reach down the telephone cord and strangle him if he didn't come up with some solid information pretty soon.

"Arnie Van Sant. Smuggler extraordinaire. Immigrants, drugs. He may even be funneling money to known terrorists."

"Over what border?"

"You name it, he's crossed it."

"He have anything to do with those recent immigrant cases—a truck that stalled in the Arizona desert, another one abandoned in a California rest area?"

"He's suspected in several of those cases, swears he was totally innocent. In any case, he says he can't be held responsible for the moral ethics of his employees. All he wants is to do his best for poor people—as a service to humanity. Like I told you, he's a real genuine full-throttle villain. He's even believed to be one of the people involved with agro-terrorism."

"What the hell is that?"

"Importation of harmful pests, plant and animal diseases, jolly stuff like that. Intended to mess up American crops and livestock."

"Jeez. Where do people come up with these schemes . . ."

She paused to think for a minute. "Brad, one of those immigrant incidents happened about the time I was shot. You told me about it when I was coming around. Do we have some kind of tie-in here?"

"It's possible. Van Sant had a cast-iron alibi to prove he was in São Paulo at the time. Your photo would put him squarely in San Francisco."

"What does Morrison think?"

"Morrison's all excited. Wants to know if you've run into Van Sant. If you have, you're to call him immediately."

"I haven't. Tell him I haven't, okay? I don't want Morrison thinking I'm associating with master criminals. He knows when that photograph was taken. It's well over a year ago now. It's the other guy I've run into. Joshua Patton. He's a famous photographer—like I told you in my E-mail. Lives in Port Angeles, Washington. At least I think he's the guy in the photograph."

"You think *he's* the guy who shot you?"

"I don't know, Brad. It's possible he's the guy who shot Rosemary Barrett, the woman at the photography show. It's possible, by a long reach, that he meant to shoot me. I'm still trying to gather some proof, some solid evidence. If this guy in the photograph is Patton, and he *is* associated with this Van Sant character . . ."

"Well that doesn't fit Morrison's theory. Morrison says he wouldn't be surprised if Van Sant was reaching for a gun."

"What! Hang on a sec."

She'd copied the cropped photo onto her computer's hard drive. She brought it up and zoomed in on the blond man. He was staring directly at the camera—at *her*—how come she hadn't noticed that before? Because she'd been too busy studying the guy she thought could be Patton. The blond man had one hand underneath the right-hand side of his sport coat. He might have been getting *anything* out of his pocket. A billfold. Car keys. A cell phone like Stockman's.

But she *had* been shot. She kept coming back to that whenever she suspected she was getting too far out. Someone in that street had shot her. If it wasn't Stockman . . .

"Neither Connor nor I noticed that," she muttered.

"Connor?"

"A friend."

"A male friend?"

"Brad!"

"Okay. What do you want me to do?"

"Tell Morrison I don't know anything about the blond guy, but I might know the other guy. Who conceivably would be acquainted with Van Sant. I'll send you an E-mail with his name and address and whatever else I can think of. I'll probably pass these photos on to our local police department, too. The chief is sharp. She might be able to come up with something."

They exchanged a few more words, then hung up.

And at that precise moment, the hairs on the back of Diana's neck, the ones not long enough to get caught up in her ponytail, seemed to shiver.

She swiveled her chair around and slid on it to the door of her little office. Joshua Patton was right outside. Mountain Man himself. He had his blue Soggy Trails jacket on.

Jumping up, she attempted to slam the door closed, but he put his weight into it and held it open.

She tried to bluff. It's always worth a try. "Oh, sorry Mr. Patton, you startled me. I didn't realize it was you. I had an intruder a few days ago and—"

"I know all about that," he said.

Quite often the bluff doesn't stand a snowball's chance in hell of getting anywhere.

She studiously kept her gaze away from the bulge in the front of his Soggy Trails jacket. The one in the kangaroo pocket Yvonne Jeffers hadn't liked. "What can I do for you?"

"I want the photographs. Plus the negatives, the disk, whatever the hell they're on."

"I'm a photographer, Mr. Patton, I have a lot of photographs. You of all people should know that. Could you be more specific?"

He slanted his gaze to the ceiling, indicating he wasn't buying the attitude. Diana seized the chance to glance around the office for a weapon. The office was not much bigger than a cupboard, so it didn't take long. Nothing. No handy rocks, no fire axes—though she did have one in the prop room along with a full set of period fireman gear. Certainly there was no gun around, except the antiques, again in the prop room. No pepper spray. She used to carry pepper spray. Why had she stopped? And of course she never used hair spray, which would also have been useful. Nothing useful at all . . .

Suddenly mindful of what she'd been doing, she glanced

at the computer screen and was relieved to see that the screen saver—one of the best photographs she'd ever taken of Mount Rainier—had popped up to hide the photo of Van Sant and Patton. It seemed fairly likely at the moment that the man with Van Sant was Patton.

"I want your San Francisco photographs," he said.

"Ah, well, gosh, again that's an awful lot of photos. But if you are that interested, I could certainly—"

She started to get to her feet, and he pushed her roughly down.

"What are you doing!"

"Can the ingenue act, Ms. Gordon. You know why I'm here."

"My California pictures weren't digital," she lied. "If I have any prints or negatives around, they'll be in the closet in the studio."

He studied her face, and she dredged up her most innocent expression, the one she used to use when her mother was demanding to know if she'd gone to the movies—a banned recreation.

Patton had finished thinking. He gestured with his head for her to go on out to the studio. She schooled herself to retain a puzzled expression.

She pulled boxes out of the closet, the way he had done—it was pretty obvious now that he had been the intruder—glanced at the labels on them, and put them aside. At the same time, she kept looking, looking, looking for something she could do to distract him, something she could use as a weapon.

When she came to the box he'd thrown aside that night, she held it toward him. He backed up a step, one hand held over the kangaroo pocket, the other hand indicating she should set the box on the antique table. "Take the damn lid off," he ordered.

When she'd done so, he reached across to pick up a handful of pictures, thumbed through them without taking all his attention from her, and dropped them on the floor.

"I want the pictures of Chinatown," he said, and named the street.

"Oh, you're talking about the Stockman photos!" she said with an air of discovery.

He frowned.

"The photos I took of Sam Stockman when he ran for the cable car? I took that whole series of him walking, then running, and the insurance company would have been real happy to have them, but then he shot me, you know."

She tilted her head to one side, still faking an ingenue style. "You're an associate of Sam's? Or are you with the insurance company? I don't have the photos here, I'm afraid, my partner sent them to Hedrick Insurance a year ago. But Stockman had already disappeared."

He seemed completely befuddled, which was the way she wanted him. Waving her back into the office, he gestured her back to her chair. "What the hell are you talking about?"

"Sam Stockman," she said desperately. "He was defrauding Hedrick Insurance. Did he tell you that? He wasn't supposed to be able to walk after he fell off the stage. He played guitar. But then I followed him, and he left his crutches behind and went off hiking through Chinatown. He didn't seem to realize I was hot on his trail with my trusty camera. I photographed him as he hopped on the cable car."

Patton made a strange sound that she finally identified as laughter. "You weren't taking photographs of anyone else?"

She shook her head, still clinging to the pretense. "No, only Stockman. There wasn't anyone else—"

She broke off as he pulled a gun out of his kangaroo pocket. She'd been afraid he might do that. *God, she did not want to get shot again.*

She stared at the gun while her mind raced for a way out. She'd never owned a weapon, but knew enough about guns and the gun culture to know she never wanted to. All the same, she recognized this one as a Glock because Brad had owned one and had insisted on teaching her how to use it at the gun range where he practiced. She'd hated the whole experience.

Brad had liked the Glock, said it could take a lot of abuse and still keep going and didn't have much recoil.

She'd always heard that a gun looked a hell of a lot bigger when it was pointing at you. It was true.

So far, Patton's right index finger was laid harmlessly along the side of the trigger guard, she noted.

She also noted some kind of change in the atmosphere of the studio. A slight whiff of fresh air? Something. Oh God, Connor? Had Connor come in the front door? She would have heard him surely. But still . . . she needed to distract Patton.

"I don't know what's so funny," she said, feigning indignation. "I don't have the Stockman photos here, so gun or no gun, there's not a whole lot—"

"I heard your whole telephone conversation," he said. He wasn't laughing anymore. "I came in the studio at the front, heard you talking, and stood right outside this door, listening. I couldn't hear the other end, but I heard enough to know you have the photographs I'm after. *And* you know a lot more that you are trying to hide, and it isn't going to do you any good at all."

He shook his head slightly. "You were taking photographs of someone *else!* I can't believe it. Arnie's not going to believe it."

Okay, so all innocent pretenses were out. Subterfuge was still on the table though.

"I don't know what you mean," she said. "Why would you want the Stockman photos?"

"It's not important that you should know my reasons. Cut the delay and produce the pictures."

"Well, the copies of the Stockman photos are either in those boxes out in the closet, or else I don't have them. By now, the San Francisco police . . ."

She gestured in the general direction of San Francisco, which was a long way south, and felt her elbow brush the computer mouse that was on the pull-out board next to her desktop computer.

From the corner of her eye she could see it, in glorious living color, enlarged to almost fit the screen: the cropped picture of the two men, one blond, one wearing a blue Soggy Trails anorak, his back turned to the camera.

"Shit," she said.

Patton's thin lips moved in a twisted smile. "You've already sent it?"

Subterfuge was out now, too. "Yesterday. The police recognized Van Sant right away. I guess his photo's on the wall at most post offices. Yours isn't, though. You could probably disappear and they wouldn't know exactly what you look like."

"I suppose you wouldn't tell them?"

"I'd be afraid to."

"Yeah right. I've noticed what a coward you are. I have the bruises to prove it." He glanced at the screen. "Is that on a CD or on the hard drive?"

"CD."

"Eject the disk, then prove to me it isn't on the hard drive."

She did as she was told.

"Are you expecting anyone else here?"

"Gosh yes. My assistant, Higby, and a huge crowd of square dancers coming in for some publicity shots."

There was a big square dance festival going on in town, so she thought that sounded fairly believable. Would it stretch believability if she pretended the police chief was a member of the square dance group?

Probably. Patton had met Sarah.

"Then I think we'll get out of here," he said.

She wasn't going anywhere. She was sure of that. If he was going to shoot her, he'd have to do it right here where he might leave some evidence around to convict him. No way was she getting dumped in the bay.

Thinking hard, she put the CD in its case and took her time trying to snap it closed. A convenient memory had popped up in her mind. Patton had already left the photo show before she and Connor took on Gardner Malone and Otto Schmidt. He had never seen her in action. She'd kneed him, but anyone could have done that.

As Patton reached for the CD with his left hand, she pulled it back. Relying on the slight forward motion of his body, she took hold of his wrist and pulled him off balance, at the same time scooting her chair back and out from under her. But as he started to fall, he brought the gun around so that it was pointing at her. Dropping the CD, he twisted her hand with a move of his own, managing to regain his balance at the same time.

But then he suddenly jerked and let go of her wrist.

"Put the gun down and your hands up, Patton," Connor said from behind him, sounding as though he was channeling John Wayne. She wouldn't have been surprised if he'd called Patton "Pilgrim."

For one tension-filled second, Diana thought Patton was going to go right ahead and shoot her and to hell with the consequences, but then his mouth twisted and he laid the gun down gently on the desk's pull-out board.

But rather than put his hands up, he made a grab for Diana and was obviously about to whirl her around to form a shield in front of him.

There was a flash of movement as Connor raised something up and brought it down on the other man's head. Patton crumpled to the floor, leaving Connor staring down at him, still holding the French dueling pistol he'd evidently picked up on the way in.

"I thought I'd better knock him out before he realized this gun hasn't been loaded in a century or so," Connor said in an apologetic tone.

"It's never been loaded at all," Diana told him. "It's a replica, not the real thing."

The expression on his face showed his dismay.

"How did you know Patton was here? You came in so quietly I barely heard you. Luckily Patton didn't either. I did notice a sudden little breeze."

He nodded. "I opened the door as silently as I could. Closing it quietly was even more of a challenge. Took a minute." He smiled at her and answered her question. "I saw Patton's Land Rover in the parking lot. Don't see too many Land Rovers around. When I was twenty I wanted one."

Diana collapsed against him, completely out of strength.

He put his arms around her. "What did I tell you? Ham and eggs."

"You have to be the ham," she said. "Your voice was pure John Wayne, marinated in testosterone."

"A man's gotta do what a man's gotta do."

Patton stirred a little. Diana took a deep breath. "I'll call nine-one-one."

"Good thinking, Sister," Connor said.

Chapter 25

"WE ARE DOING real good," Sarah said, beaming.

Connor almost expected her to rub her hands together. It was a few weeks later, and Sarah had called another meeting to go over everything that had happened since their last one.

"You're saying the FBI doesn't want Patton?" Diana asked.

"Small potatoes. They want him later, as a witness, but we get to keep him in Washington for a while. People flying up to talk to him, but like I told you, he gave up Van Sant. Him, they are excited about."

"There's a sergeant in San Francisco not too happy about the FBI getting Van Sant," Diana said.

Sarah smiled some more. Connor realized for the first time exactly what was meant by someone being wreathed in smiles.

"Some guys mark off their territory the way dogs do," Sarah said. "The main thing here, seems to me, is to get the bad guys off the streets. Doesn't matter to me who does it. But we surely want to prosecute Joshua Patton for Rosemary Barrett's murder before there's any talk of deals going around."

Diana had stood up and gone to the back window of Sarah's office, which overlooked almost the same view as her little beach, though it was way the other side of the wharf. "I can't believe the time thing didn't occur to me," she said. "I said a couple of times that Rosemary was compulsively punctual, and often early. But it still didn't occur to me she might have gone to open up the community center that early."

"Did she really go over there at eight-fifteen A.M.?" Connor asked.

Diana nodded. "I expect she wanted to make sure everything had been done right. You know nobody could do anything as perfectly as she could."

"Well, she did do a good job of everything," Sarah put in.

"I wasn't being sarcastic," Diana said. "I really meant— nobody could do anything as perfectly as she could."

Adrian Lawrence and Timothy Valentine both laughed. "Should have made her police chief," Tim said, which Connor thought was a stupid but brave thing for him to say.

Fortunately for Tim, Sarah thought the comment was funny.

"So Rosemary was there at eight-fifteen A.M.," Diana went on.

"Patton was already there," Sarah said. "Waiting down the street. Watching."

"For me," Diana put in.

"That's what he thought," Sarah agreed. "So then Rosemary arrived, he followed her in, and shot her—thinking she was you."

She paused. "Evidently Van Sant had picked up Diana's

name from the newspaper story about her getting shot. Nothing was said about Stockman in those reports, of course, because there was no useful evidence to show Stockman was the shooter. Van Sant had *seen* Diana when she took those photographs, so he had a general idea of what she looked like. But she left San Francisco before anyone in his employ could track her down. It wasn't until Rosemary's detective went hunting down Diana's past and heard Van Sant had an interest in her that Van Sant knew where she'd gone. The detective, of course, had seen an opportunity to make some cash."

"Ironic that Rosemary hired that detective and that led to her being killed," Tim said.

Sarah nodded agreement. "So then Van Sant remembered Patton lived in Washington somewhere and gave him the job of dispatching Diana. Patton heard about the photo show and got in touch with Rosemary."

"From which time he was in like Flynn," Connor said.

"Had it made in the shade," Sarah countered. "But then he made his big mistake by shooting Rosemary. He jogged back to the Best Western next door. Nobody seems to have seen him, but then if they had, they'd have thought he was a tourist. He signed in at the fitness room at eight-thirty A.M. Took a good hot shower, scrubbing like mad no doubt, swam a couple of laps, then joined Ashley for breakfast at nine A.M. He showed up right on time at Quinn Center to judge the show. Cool customer for someone who'd killed for the first time. As far as we know. It wasn't until Connor introduced Diana to him that he discovered his mistake."

"There's a hole here," Tim said.

Connor hadn't realized raised eyebrows could look dangerous until Sarah was the one raising them.

Tim leaned forward over the table, his expression earnest. "What I mean is—why Patton? How did Van Sant know him, and why would Patton agree to kill Ms. Gordon?"

"You haven't been paying attention," Sarah said.

Tim blushed.

"Drugs," Sarah said. "Patton confessed all when he gave up Van Sant, remember? He wasn't *buying* drugs from the schoolkid the waitress told Diana about—he was *supplying* them. Patton was badly burned on Mount Saint Helens twenty some years ago. He spent a lot of time in the hospital. Got hooked on morphine. After he was discharged, he managed to connect with a dealer who had ties to an organization in California."

"Van Sant's organization," Diana put in.

Sarah nodded. "Van Sant has a reputation for using anyone he has even the least tangible tie with. Patton seemed useful to Van Sant because he was this famous photographer, could get into almost anywhere. Van Sant started him out with a few little jobs here and there—quid pro quo!"

She glanced at Tim. "That means an equal exchange."

Tim blushed again.

Connor wasn't sure Tim was going to make it far in the Port Findlay Police Department.

"Patton eventually cleaned up his act with the help of methadone," Sarah continued. "But by then he was making out like a bandit working for Van Sant and his gang. Supplying, smuggling. He wasn't sure he could quit, wasn't sure he wanted to quit. They all had code names. Patton's was Phoenix—apt, don't you think? He did rise from the ashes. Seems like he'll get consumed again, one way or another."

"In any case," Sarah continued, "Patton had his own fish to fry. He and Van Sant had just concluded a meeting inside the building in Chinatown when Stockman hopped on that cable car. They were tidying up a few details outside when

Van Sant saw Diana take what he thought were photographs of him. He wasn't supposed to be in the country.
Very much persona non grata."

She glanced at Tim but refrained from translating this
time. "Van Sant reacted according to type," she continued.
"Shooting first without bothering to ask questions."

Diana made a small sound in her throat that indicated
pain to Connor. He reached for her hand under the table
and held it.

Sarah regarded her with sympathy. "When it turned out
Diana was too tough to die, Patton was as concerned as Van
Sant—for his own sake. He didn't know how much of himself had shown up in those photos. He felt he had an inter-
national reputation to protect. Plus he was this big hero.
One phone call from Van Sant, and he was raring to get Diana out of the way. But he killed the wrong woman."

Diana nodded. "So he broke into my studio, hoping to
find the photographs. I interrupted him, and he figured it
was a second chance to take care of me."

"Only he didn't know what a warrior you are," Connor
said, so much pride and fondness in his voice that the others exchanged knowing glances. "He had to come back and
try again. And again you knocked him off balance."

"And you finished him off," Diana added.

"Exactly," Sarah said. She smiled at Tim, showing all
her teeth. "We ever need a replacement chief around here,
Diana Gordon and Connor Callahan should be considered."

Diana and Connor grinned. Tim didn't.

Chapter 26

"YOUR PLACE OR mine?" Connor asked after the meeting had broken up and they were in the police department parking lot.

"Mine," Diana said without hesitation.

Connor nodded agreement, realizing as he walked to his car that now was the time to settle a certain question. Maybe even two.

A short time later, they were seated next to each other on the huge driftwood log on Diana's beach, each with a glass of champagne from a bottle of Dom Perignon that Connor had picked up from the state liquor store across the street. In front of them was a folding type TV tray that held some of Diana's favorite snacks, including an Asian mix of nuts and sesame crackers that she was addicted to.

The sun was low, though not quite ready to set, the breeze off the water fairly warm.

"There's one other little note Sarah didn't cover," Diana

said. "I haven't even bothered to tell her about it yet. It doesn't directly affect the case against Joshua Patton."

She hesitated, and Connor waited patiently, feeling relaxed and comfortable, enjoying the play of sun on water and the view of the Olympic mountains.

Diana laughed, bringing his attention to her. "Sam Stockman showed up," she said.

Connor almost dropped his champagne flute. He set it carefully down on the rickety table. "Here?"

She shook her head. "San Francisco. Brad Jeffers called me. Evidently, when Stockman was released and found out the insurance company was after him, he hightailed it into Canada from eastern Washington somewhere and made his way east to Toronto. Found work in a honky-tonk, playing his guitar with a country western band. I guess nobody asked for his passport."

"So what brought him back?"

She laughed. "Love. He fell in love. Wants to marry the lady. So he came back to settle things with the insurance company and live straight and happily ever after."

While Connor was trying to absorb all of this, she said, "One more thing. I called Ashley Robinson. I thought she should know we had to turn all her love letters over to the police. I assured her Sarah wouldn't reveal their contents to anyone."

He thought of the young, fragile woman and sighed. "How did she take it?"

"She cried. Then she told me Rosemary had a side to her people didn't know about. She was needy, she said. Nobody loved her, they all used her. But Ashley loved her."

She shook her head. "Maybe she was right. But if Rosemary was that lovable, she sure worked hard to conceal it."

Connor put his arm around her. "My mother always says there's nobody as queer as folks."

He took her champagne flute from her and set it down.

"Uh-oh," she said. "This feels ominous."

"Not at all. It's about real estate." He smiled at her puzzled expression. "I'm putting my house up for sale."

She was completely and utterly taken aback. "Connor, why? You love that house. That beautiful garden—you can't give it up."

"Sure I can. I've thought a lot about this, Diana, and I have a confession to make. I never liked that house. It's too . . . open, too modern, too efficient. The garden, yes, that is a work I'm proud of. But if I did it once, I can do it again."

Diana was still staring at him with amazement. "But Liz—your wife . . ."

"I loved Liz. I always loved Liz. That's why I never told her I didn't like the house. She was so thrilled when she found it. She started right in having ideas of how to furnish it to fit its style, how the kitchen would be so perfect for me to cook in. She was *dying,* Flash, how could I dampen her enthusiasm?"

He touched Diana's cheek with his free hand. "I didn't realize how much I disliked the house until I saw how uncomfortable it made you."

"Connor . . ."

"No, let me finish. You never did say you didn't like my house, but you looked shifty every time you were in it. And whenever I gave you a choice, my place or yours, you chose yours."

"I'm sorry, I didn't realize—"

"Diana, I'm trying to tell you, I agree with you. I could appreciate the beauty of the house and its efficiency, and I was happy that Liz was happy with it. But . . . well, it felt more like a stage set to me than a home. So I'm going to sell it and buy a house I can love as much as she loved that

one. I heard that one of the old Victorians is up for sale. It's been used as a B and B, but the owners want to retire to Arizona. I've made an offer on it, Flash. It's been accepted. The house needs a lot of work, but I've never been afraid of work."

"Lena told me you talk to your wife in the graveyard," Diana blurted out.

"Lena talks too much."

"Is it true?"

He took in a deep breath, then let it out. "It used to be. I was lonely, Diana. And I loved Liz tremendously for many many years. It almost destroyed me when she died. But it didn't destroy me. One of the things that helped was pretending to talk things over with her. Talking about what was going on in my life, asking her opinion, 'hearing' her opinion because I knew her so well, I could imagine what she'd say under almost any circumstances."

"Did you tell her about me?"

"Yes."

She glanced at him sideways. "What did she say?"

"She would have said, 'Was I supposed to be surprised?'"

Diana laughed, her head thrown back. He joined in.

"I think I'd have liked Liz," she said.

"I'm sure of it."

She reached for a handful of the nut and cracker mix and started chewing. She was obviously thinking hard.

"Are you going to start working on the Victorian soon?"

"I expect so. Would you like to help me?"

Delight showed on her face. "I'd love to. I love old houses the way I love old movies and old TV shows. Most of my adult life I've been carving out a past as unlike the one I had with my parents as I could find, experiencing, *enjoying* the things I didn't get to do at the time."

He smiled at her. "So then you'd enjoy living with me in my Victorian house? I promise I'll keep you well-adjusted."

She choked on her crackers and he patted her on the back.

"It's not that bad a pun, is it?" he asked. "I use it often—it's a natural."

"It wasn't the pun that did me in," she choked out.

He topped up her champagne glass and handed it to her.

"Bubbles don't really do the job," she said, but another sip seemed to help. "Whoa," she said softly, "that was a huge thing to spring on me."

"I thought it was a good first step. Seemed to me a proposal of marriage might be a bigger shock."

She swallowed a whole gulp of champagne this time. "Connor . . ."

"Which is why I'm not asking you yet," he went on smoothly. "We'll attack this one step at a time, okay?"

Before she could answer, he took the glass from her again and set it down and then pulled her into his arms and kissed her thoroughly until she relaxed, then kissed her some more until she was limp, and still didn't release her.

"Well?" he demanded.

"One step at a time?" she asked.

"Absolutely."

"Then let's go upstairs."

He smiled.

"Having a little celebration, are we?" Higby's voice said from behind them.

They turned around. Higby was standing in the back door of the studio, dressed in shorts, shirt open to the navel, sandals, sunglasses.

Connor sighed. "When are you going to remember to lock your doors?" he said to Diana.

Lena peeked around Higby, her head showing just

above his waistline. "We saw you from my store," she said. "We didn't know for sure if we should disturb you."

"But we did pick up a couple more glasses on the way," Higby said, and held them up.

"Okay," Connor said, holding up the bottle. "This celebration is officially under way. Later," he murmured to Diana.

"For sure," she said with a smile.